The Bloodline

C. S. Feldman

This is a work of fiction. Names, characters, places, and incidents are products of the author's imagination or are used fictitiously and are not to be construed as real. Any resemblance to actual events, locales, or persons, living or dead, is entirely coincidental.

Printed by CreateSpace

ISBN-13: 978-1542716727

ISBN-10: 1542716721

Cover Design by - Steven Novak

Cover Images Eric Vega

DEDICATION

To my family, my friends, and my readers—
thanks for being there and thanks for your support!

C. S. FELDMAN

CONTENTS

Chapter One 1

Chapter Two 7

Chapter Three 15

Chapter Four 23

Chapter Five 31

Chapter Six 41

Chapter Seven 49

Chapter Eight 59

Chapter Nine 65

Chapter Ten 75

Chapter Eleven 81

Chapter Twelve 89

Chapter Thirteen 95

Chapter Fourteen 105

Chapter Fifteen 113

Chapter Sixteen 125

Chapter Seventeen 135

Chapter Eighteen 145

Chapter Nineteen 157

Chapter Twenty 165

Chapter Twenty-One 171

Chapter Twenty-Two 181

Chapter Twenty-Three 187

Chapter Twenty-Four 193

Chapter Twenty-Five 203

Chapter Twenty-Six 211

Chapter Twenty-Seven 217

Chapter Twenty-Eight 223

Chapter Twenty-Nine 231

Chapter Thirty 239

Chapter Thirty-One 245

Chapter Thirty-Two 253

Chapter Thirty-Three 261

Chapter Thirty-Four 267

Chapter Thirty-Five 273

Chapter Thirty-Six 281

Chapter Thirty-Seven 289

Chapter Thirty-Eight 295

Chapter Thirty-Nine 303

Chapter Forty 311

Author's Note 317

About the Author 319

◆ CHAPTER ONE ◆

"YOU DON'T WANT TO be here, do you?"

There was nothing coy about the shrink's question, and Kat answered it just as directly as it had been asked, if more succinctly. "No."

"Then why did you make this appointment?"

Was that meant to be a trick of some kind? Something to elicit a subconscious slip on the part of the unsuspecting patient? "I didn't." Gran had, and this latest doctor, Dr. Latimer, knew that fact perfectly well.

"Ah, yes, but you did keep it, didn't you?"

Only for Gran's sake, but Kat didn't say so. She kept her lips pressed closed instead.

The woman sitting across from her scribbled something down in the notepad that she held on her lap. Brilliant insight already? And after only five minutes. All of Kat's other therapists would have been green with envy.

She resisted the urge to shift in her seat and remained still, suspecting that even the smallest movement on her part would be analyzed and picked apart. Her gaze went where it wanted to, though, taking in the bland cream color of the walls, soft lighting, and the framed still life that hung just a little higher than eye level. That was bland, too. And safe. Or at least she guessed that it was meant to inspire that feeling in the patients who sat here. It did not succeed. Not with Kat, anyway. No shame in that, though; better rooms than this one had failed.

The scratching sound of the pencil, so loud in this quiet room, stopped. "And why do you think your grandmother made this appointment for you?"

It was tempting not to answer. What was the point? But there were still another forty-five minutes to get through, and silence would not make them pass by any faster. "Because she knew I wouldn't," Kat returned finally, knowing that wasn't quite the insightful answer the doctor was trying to get at but in no mood to make things easy for her. She'd agreed to come; she hadn't agreed to cooperate.

"Yes, but why do—"

No help for it. "You should ask her that."

"I did, actually. I just wanted to know what your take on it is."

She was studying Kat in a way that was entirely too familiar. Like she was a lab specimen or a puzzle to be solved. Kat's fingers dug a little deeper into the faux leather upholstery of her chair. Dr. Latimer sat right across from her in another one just like it, with no desk or other barrier between them. Another deliberate choice on the doctor's part? Probably. Maybe other patients welcomed it. "She made the appointment because she's afraid."

"Of what?"

"Of what I might do."

More scribbling. How much had Gran already told her? "Are *you* afraid of what you might do, Katherine?"

The sound of her full name was jarring. "It's Kat."

"Sorry, yes. Kat. Are you afraid, Kat?'

More intrusion into her head. Attempted intrusion, anyway. Kat stared at the other woman and said nothing.

Maybe Dr. Latimer realized that she wasn't going to get anywhere with that particular line of questioning, because after a moment of silence she switched to a new one. Odds were that she'd bring things around to the first topic again eventually, thinking that she was being subtle. "You have a birthday coming up tomorrow. It's a significant one for you, isn't it?"

"Won't have to worry about getting carded anymore, if that's what you mean."

"It's not."

No, of course it wasn't, which was why the palms of Kat's hands were sweating. She released their hold on the chair arms and folded her fingers together in her lap instead.

"I'm referring to the house, the one you grew up in back east. Legally it's yours as of tomorrow, isn't it?"

Kat nodded. Just once.

"How do you feel about that?"

How do you think? She nearly snapped out the words but managed to bite them back just in time. God, she was sick of these kinds of questions. *How do you feel? What do you think? Why do you think that? What do you remember? Shall we poke and prod your mind a little bit more and see what falls out?* So she lifted her shoulders in a barely perceptible shrug instead of answering and pointedly stared at the clock on the wall above the doctor's head.

"Your grandmother says you've been having trouble sleeping recently." A moment later the doctor cocked her head. "You find that funny?"

"What? No." Not even remotely. Just the part about it being recent. She hadn't had a decent night's sleep in years.

"You're smiling."

Was she? Yes, she supposed her lips had curved up slightly at the corners, but there was no real humor in the expression. She let it slip from her face again.

Another long silence. More rustling of notes. But if she hoped Kat would be tempted to fill the silence, the doctor was in for a disappointment. She waited a few more moments, then: "Do you think you're having trouble sleeping because of the house, Kat?"

The frequent use of her name, as if to force some sort of camaraderie on her, grated almost as much as the question. Of course it was because of the house. The past six years' worth of therapist visits and endless medications and worse were all because of the house, and she'd been haunted by far more troubling symptoms than a lack of sleep in that time. But all Kat said was, "Maybe," and tried not to notice how the scent of the potpourri on a nearby bookshelf was cloyingly sweet and growing more so with each passing second.

"Maybe? Considering what happened there, I'd say it's more than a maybe, wouldn't you?" The woman leaned forward and fixed Kat with a look that was probably meant to be sympathetic and induce her to spill her secrets but only ended up making Kat instinctively lean back and away. She'd seen that same look many times before, and on many faces. It was the look that usually came right before a particularly personal and prying question. "Do you remember much about what happened to your mother?"

"No. Nothing." Mercifully. Although she'd been told that she was the one who'd found her. "I was only five."

"What about your father?" The doctor checked her notes. "You were older then, right? I believe—"

"Fifteen." Kat's voice was clipped as she interrupted. She didn't apologize for it. "Yes, I remember." *Because you people won't let me forget.*

"That must have been very traumatic for you. Would you like to talk about that a little more?"

"Not really, no."

"You're angry."

"No." No more than usual anyway.

"You don't think it might be helpful for you to talk about what happened?"

"I don't know—is picking at a scab helpful?" Even Kat could hear the bitterness in her voice.

"If there's something festering underneath it? Maybe."

The potpourri was truly overpowering now. Her head started to ache, and the knot that had formed in her stomach the moment she'd set foot in this place drew tighter.

"Your father," the doctor started.

Kat reached for the chair arms and dug her fingers back into them. And silently pleaded for the clock hands to move faster.

◆◆◆

THE HINGES ON THE doctor's office door were well-oiled; they made no noise when Kat finally opened it to leave. Gran was seated right where Kat had left her with a magazine in her hands—was that the same page she'd started on nearly an hour ago?—but her grey-haired head was turned absently toward the lone window in the room, overlooking the street outside, and she wore an expression on her face that suggested she wasn't really seeing anything on the other side of the glass. No, her thoughts were somewhere else, and Kat could guess where. Or at least on whom they were focused.

She'd insisted on coming along. It was no bother, no trouble at all. There was nowhere else she had to be that afternoon, and company was always nice, wasn't it? Not that her words fooled anybody, of course. Not Kat and not her grandfather certainly. Had she feared Kat would go back on her word and drive right by the place without a witness there to make sure she actually went inside? Probably. To Gran's credit, it wasn't that farfetched a concern.

Guilt pricked at Kat, the same guilt that made her agree to today's visit in the first place. She was not the only one still struggling with certain things. She closed the door behind her with an audible click to announce her presence even as she hid a folded slip of paper inside one closed hand.

Gran started and looked away from the window to see Kat. She closed the magazine. "All done?"

Kat nodded.

"Was it helpful?"

Her forehead settled into familiar creases, and there was such a desperate hopefulness in her voice that Kat lied and said, "Yes," and some of the creases relaxed. A little, anyway.

"Oh, I'm so glad. I have a good feeling about Dr. Latimer, Kat."

There was no reason to disillusion her; it would be unkind more than anything else. But on her way out behind her grandmother, Kat crumpled the prescription for sleeping pills that the doctor had given her and let it fall unseen into a wastebasket as she walked past.

◆ CHAPTER TWO ◆

IT WAS ONLY A birthday.

Only.

Liar, Kat mouthed, and she rolled over to stare up into the darkness of her room. Somewhere in the kitchen was what was left of the cake that Gran had made for her yesterday, barely touched in spite of the fact that Gran was no slouch when it came to baking. No one had been much in the mood for it last night or for any other birthday festivities, although Kat's grandfather had done his best to crack the usual lame jokes and pretend that nothing was out of the ordinary.

But it was impossible to miss the fact that Gran had chosen to put only one candle on the cake instead of the twenty-one that should have been there, as if by doing so she could somehow change which birthday it was. To please her, Kat had said nothing about it, and she suspected her grandfather did the same thing for the same reason. But the solemn little excuse for a party ended early anyway, and Kat had finally chosen to slip off on her own to town to spare them all more uncomfortable silences. Well, to spare her grandparents, at least; uncomfortable silences seemed to follow Kat wherever she went.

Only a birthday...

She rubbed one hand over her tired eyes. Dawn must not be far off now, because the darkness had begun to fade to the murky grey that meant the sunrise was only minutes away. She glanced at her bedside clock. So much for sleeping. Her thoughts flickered to the crumpled up prescription slip she'd tossed into the trash the other day, but only for a moment. No more pills. She'd already had enough to last her a lifetime, and where had it gotten it her? As screwed up as ever, and, at best, living in a haze. Maybe the haze was preferable to the alternative. Maybe it wasn't.

Her eyes turned back to the ceiling.

The faded but serene angel that was painted on it grew more visible as the greyness of predawn lightened the room even more. It was a lovely if wispy sort of thing. Gran had painted it up there years ago when Kat's mother was just a child and was nervous about bumps in the night and monsters under the bed. Something to comfort her and remind her that she was being watched over, was the way Gran told it, although her smile was sad when she did. No wonder. Apparently even angels had their limits, or at least this one did.

But maybe that wasn't being fair. It had kept watch over Kat for the past six years, after all, and those six had been better than the ones that came before them. Well, the ones she could remember anyway. Or rather, the parts of them she could remember. Some parts still had holes, and she'd been told by more than one shrink before Latimer that they likely always would, at least until her brain was ready to deal with them. Some days those holes in her memory were a relief. Other days they were not. Lately, it was more the latter.

Especially with it being her birthday, and this birthday in particular with everything that came along with it. No surprise that it would start old memories swirling. Even now as she stared up at the painted angel, another angel's face seemed to pop into her head from out of nowhere, this one carved out of cold stone and wet from rain. It was gone from her mind again just as quickly as it had appeared, leaving her to wonder as she so often did whether it was an actual memory or the work of her imagination. Or possibly something worse.

Crackpot.

Crazy girl...

She threw back her covers and sat up, forcing her thoughts to something—anything—else that might drown out that inner voice. Run. That's what she would do. Go for a run. Clear her head in the fresh, salty air. To that end, she traded her nightshirt for a t-shirt and shorts before picking up her running shoes in one hand and tiptoeing out into the hall.

Careful to avoid the floorboards that creaked, she paused outside her grandparents' bedroom and listened. Nothing. Just the occasional whistling breath that served as her grandfather's snore. Satisfied that they were still asleep, Kat crept onward over the smooth oaken floor and into the kitchen, where she unlocked the back door and stepped out onto the porch of the weathered beachfront cottage.

A black lab that was sleeping on a pile of blankets lifted a muzzle that was almost entirely white with age to greet her and thumped his tail. His eternal optimism was nothing short of a marvel, because in all these years, she'd done little more than ignore him. Not because he was a bad dog or even a nuisance, because he wasn't. But he was an unwelcome reminder of another bundle of fur, smaller and softer and long gone. And when his cold, wet nose touched her hand as she slipped on her shoes to tie them, she couldn't help but flinch back.

He seemed not to notice her reaction or at least to be offended by it. Instead, he stretched his arthritic limbs and followed her off of the porch amiably as he so often and inexplicably did, and when Kat broke into a jog on the sand, he trotted behind her in his usual place.

The air was cool this time of day, even early in the summer as it was now; it woke her up as thoroughly as she'd hoped. The running warmed her quickly, though, even before the rising sun could get its chance, and it wasn't long until she was sweating. Her side began to ache, but she sped up instead of slowing down as if speed alone could clear her head. She needed a clear head. There would be decisions to make soon, big decisions involving lots of paperwork and things she'd managed to avoid thinking about for years. Mostly, anyway. Like the fact that the house was hers now, whether she wanted it or not.

She stumbled over an uneven patch of sand, catching herself just in time to prevent a fall and muttering a curse beneath her breath. Stupid. She was being stupid. It was just a house, she told herself, resuming her run along this deserted stretch at an even brisker pace than before until she was panting for breath. Stone and wood, no more and no less. To believe anything else was to give in to foolish childhood fears that she should have outgrown by now. And it was a house that her father at least had loved, even if she had not. But when an image of grey stone and cool grandeur started forming in her head, she thrust it from her mind out of habit.

A bark that was full of reproach made her draw up short and turn to see the lab galumphing after her, too stiff to run any faster. "Sorry, Pete," she acknowledged, waiting for him. He seemed to accept her apology, because a moment later he wagged his tail and trotted off to play in the waves that lapped at the shore nearby.

Kat sank down onto a piece of driftwood to watch him and make sure that he didn't get himself into trouble by wading in too deep. She'd run farther today than she'd intended to already. Any farther and she'd likely wind up having to carry Pete home. Not a good plan.

She picked up a handful of sand and let it trickle out between her fingers. Well, they could rest a while. She wasn't in any hurry to get back home anyway and see the anxious looks her grandparents exchanged when they thought she wasn't looking. She wasn't the only one who had lost a lot to that house.

That house...

It had a name, one that she shared. Delancey Manor. She mouthed the words without actually saying them aloud, and somehow they still managed to leave a sour taste in her mouth. Her gut tightened. She'd been told before by more than one well-meaning person that it wasn't rational to let the place continue to have such a hold over her, and of course it wasn't rational. Rational had nothing to do with it. Which was probably what scared her grandparents most of all. She didn't blame them. It scared her, too.

The manor flickered into her mind's eye again, but this time she stopped herself from forcing it right back out. Just a house, she reminded herself when her hands grew clammy, and if one of them was going to be master over the other, it was going to be her, not it. From now on, at least. She closed her eyes and let the image in.

It was tall, its triple stories towering above even the few trees close to it. A massive structure of carefully shaped stonework. She'd thought it a castle the first time she'd seen it, but she had only been five years old. Any home that large would have seemed grand to her. And elegant. Graceful lines, from its tapering porch to its elongated windows.

Dark windows. And shadows moved in them.

Her eyes flew back open again before she could help it, fixing on the ocean horizon like a lifeline. The sharp sting of a cut made her look down to see that she'd scraped her hand on the roughened edge of a break in the driftwood. Small wonder. Her hands were shaking worse than those of a nervous teenager out on a first date. The only real surprise was that she hadn't scraped them any worse than she already had. She forced them into fists to stop the movement.

Her father was enamored with the house from the first moment he saw it, the three of them standing hand-in-hand and staring up at it in awe after being used to a cramped two-bedroom apartment. But he'd loved it more for the history it represented, a link to his family's heritage. Her mother, though...

Kat wrapped her arms around herself as the breeze off of the ocean picked up, sheltering her fists as much as she could against her body and steadying them further.

Her mother had exclaimed with pleasure over everything when they stepped inside the house that first time; as fuzzy as Kat's memory was about things that had happened so long ago, she could still remember that part clearly. The graceful staircase, the charming antiques hidden beneath old bed sheets that protected them from dust, and, of course, the gardens.

The stab of grief that Kat felt was startling in its intensity considering how long her mother had been gone and how little she could remember about her in the first place. The truth was, she had trouble recalling her face clearly without the aid of a photograph, and if anything, she would have expected memories of her father to weigh on her. Well... the day was young, though.

The breeze died down, and with the sun up past the horizon now and shining on her fully, she shouldn't have been as cold as she was. Getting to her feet, Kat called to the dog still frolicking in the surf. He dipped his muzzle in the water one last time and then trailed behind her as she began jogging toward home.

The position of the sun in the sky by the time they returned to the cottage made it likely that Kat's grandparents were up by now; the scent of bacon in the air confirmed it. Judging by the way Pete bounded up the steps before her—stiff joints and all—he must have smelled it, too. He danced impatiently on his paws until Kat caught up with him, and as soon as she opened the door, he slipped inside. Kat followed.

"Ah," her grandfather greeted her, looking up from where he sat at the table in his faded plaid bathrobe and with the morning paper spread out before him. He adjusted his wire-rimmed spectacles and gave her a once-over. "There's the birthday girl. Can't have done too much barhopping last night if you're vertical and moving at this hour."

His wife shot him a dirty look from where she stood at the stove, scrambling eggs in a pan with a spatula. "Abe!"

"What? She's of an age now, my dear. Shall I remind you of what we did on your twenty-first birthday?"

Gran picked up a nearby piece of toast from off of the chipped Formica counter and tossed it at him with more flair than actual force. He dodged it with an unrepentant grin, and the toast landed on the floor, to the dog's obvious delight.

Taking the plate of food that Gran held out to her, Kat joined her grandfather at the kitchen table. "No bars. Mostly just walked around town a bit."

"With friends?"

Maybe Pete got his sense of optimism from Gran. A lie was no good here; she'd press for details, and Kat wouldn't be able to provide convincing ones. Instead, she mumbled something noncommittal around a mouthful of bacon and refilled her grandfather's glass of orange juice, pretending that she didn't notice the glance he exchanged with his wife.

But Gran wasn't one to give up easily. "You know, I was chatting with Marie Callahan a few days ago, and she said something about a party that her son and his friends were having on their stretch of beach this Saturday. Brad? No, wait—Brian, that's his name. He was in your grade, wasn't he? Anyway, there'll be lots of college kids your age there. She said she was sure you'd be welcome to join them if you want."

That was doubtful. Not that the woman had made the polite offer, but that her son and his friends would be pleased to see Kat there. She'd finished high school with most of them, but none of them were what she would have called friends. Her presence on the beach would only make them uncomfortable, just as it had in high school. And their presence would have the same effect on her. "Some other time."

Gran nodded and turned back to the stove, but her shoulders slumped as she did so. For a few minutes, the only sounds in the kitchen were the clinks of forks against plates and the occasional snuffling of the dog as he waited hopefully for more food to drop on the floor. And then just as Kat's grandfather cleared his throat as if to take another stab at chitchat, the phone rang.

They all froze, all but Pete, who continued searching for dropped scraps. The phone rang again, its sound tinny and harsh in the silence of the room, and Kat's grandfather finally reached for it where it hung on the wall while his wife and Kat watched. "Hello?" he greeted the caller, his face expressionless, and even before he said the name, Kat knew who it was on the other end of the line. "Ah, Grace. We thought we might hear from you before long." A pause, and then, "Kat? Well, let me check." Covering the mouthpiece of the phone, he gave his granddaughter a questioning look.

After a moment, Kat nodded and reached for the phone with more steadiness in her hand than she'd expected. Thank God for small favors. Taking a deep breath, she greeted her stepmother. "Hello, Grace."

◆ CHAPTER THREE ◆

KAT WAS TEN YEARS old when her father returned from honeymooning with his new wife to move her and her two children into the manor with them.

That day was easier to remember than the day she'd actually first met Grace, maybe because Grace on her own was rather easy to forget. She was a pale wisp of a woman, and the stylish and tailored clothes she wore—tasteful as they were—couldn't disguise the fact that she was actually quite plain, a fact that was even more apparent whenever she stood next to her husband. Kat's father had always turned heads even when he hadn't wanted to, like during the first year or two after the death of Kat's mother, Lily. When he finally began to smile again, he turned heads even more. Why he settled on Grace, Kat never quite understood, except that she knew he had a soft spot for things that needed rescuing. After the way her first husband had discarded her and their two children, maybe Grace qualified.

There were few things Kat remembered about that day, other than being pleased to have her father back home again; her grandparents stayed with her while he was away, which was fine, but not the same. They had followed Kat out the front door to greet the new arrivals, their greeting polite but reserved. Small wonder, considering just whose shoes Grace was there to fill.

But a few things did stand out in her memory, even now. The way Grace's eyes followed her new husband around like those of a shy schoolgirl with a desperate crush; the disdain on her teenage son Michael's face when he noticed, although it seemed directed more toward his new stepfather than toward Grace. And the then nine-year-old Alexis sticking out her tongue, of course, when she seemed sure no one but Kat was watching. Michael at least went off to college two months later, and other than a few stiff visits during holidays, he was seldom around after that. Too bad the same couldn't be said about Alexis, and the unwelcome surprises she delighted in leaving for her new stepsister. The rats and mice at least had been dead; the spiders usually were not.

No, the two girls had not become the fast friends their parents hoped they would. Be patient, Kat's father had pleaded with her. Be forgiving. Given the way her own father had all but drop-kicked her out of his life, Alexis was an unhappy child after all.

She wasn't the only one.

Remembering that now, Kat couldn't quite suppress the prickle that went down her spine. She turned her eyes toward the ocean and let the porch swing sway beneath her in a lulling kind of way.

"Thinking things over?" came Gran's voice from the doorway, and a moment later the older woman emerged to sink down onto the swing beside her granddaughter, a steaming cup of coffee in her hand. It was warm out for a drink of that kind today, but old habits clearly died hard. She blew on the coffee, cradling it in hands that were beginning to show the knobbly bends of arthritis.

Kat nodded.

"Well, I suppose it probably is worth a fair bit. You could even pay off your student loans, you know, with a little something left over for a nest egg. Wouldn't that be nice? History buffs would probably go for a place like that. Or... other types of folks." Gran frowned into her coffee, and Kat suspected she was remembering a particularly callous reporter who'd pestered them for gruesome details and an interview after her father's fall. "Grace planning on moving along, or is she after you to be her landlord in an official capacity now?"

"We didn't cover any of that." Not yet. She'd seen no reason to dredge that kind of thing up at this point. A different thought had taken hold instead, a nagging, uncomfortable one pre-empting all others about the house.

"Can't imagine why she'd want to stay in that house anyway. Why she did to begin with is beyond me. Not exactly the homiest place, and after what happened to Jonathan, you'd think she—" She bit her lip then and took a sip of her coffee, casting a sideways look at Kat.

Walking on eggshells again. Poor Gran. Would there ever come a time when she'd no longer feel it was necessary?

"No rush to work out the details yet, I guess," Gran said a moment later, gamely trying again, and she patted her granddaughter's knee. "Sign whatever needs to be signed, and then forget about it for a while. Enjoy the summer first and rest—or wait until next year, even, after you've graduated. Decide what you want to do with it then. I'm sure Grace won't mind putting things off a little longer."

Kat shifted in her seat wordlessly.

Her silence seemed to unnerve Gran, because the older woman turned her head sharply to look at her. Uncanny, the way she so often seemed to have a sense of when she was about to be delivered news she wouldn't like. Or maybe Kat just lacked a decent poker face.

"Gran..."

"What?"

How to tell her? Especially when Kat was struggling so much with it herself. She opened her mouth to try, but her grandmother cut her off before she could, sudden comprehension dawning on her face.

"Oh, Kat, no. *No*."

"I think I have to."

"Nonsense. This is the twenty-first century. If they have paperwork they want you to sign, there's no reason why they can't just fax it all to you or something."

"I'm not talking about the paperwork."

From the look on her face, Gran had been well aware of that fact; she'd just been hoping otherwise. "It's too soon for that sort of thing, though."

"Too soon? It's been six years."

"Six years is nothing. Wait until you're my age, then you'll see. You should wait until, well... until you're..." She trailed off and looked away, her fingers fidgeting with the coffee cup.

"Better?" Kat finished for her, unoffended.

"If you'd just give Dr. Latimer a chance first, honey. Give her a few months and see if things turn around. Couldn't you?"

"Funny. That's exactly what you said about the last one." The last three, actually.

"But—"

Kat shook her head.

"Stubborn girl," her grandmother muttered beneath her breath, and she set her cup down on the porch as if she'd lost her taste for the coffee that was inside it. "All right, have it your way. Just give your grandpa and me a couple of weeks to get someone lined up to cover the shop for us and to look after Petey, and then we can go."

The offer to accompany her ought to have come as a comfort and a relief to Kat, knowing that she wouldn't have to face stepping over the dreaded threshold alone. Instead, the thought of her grandparents being at the house sent a sharp stab of anxiety through her, and it didn't matter that she knew it was irrational—houses couldn't really be unlucky. Her gut lurched anyway. "You're not coming with me."

"Oh, yes, we are! I don't care how old you are now, young lady. I am still your grandmother."

"I don't want either of you anywhere near that place." The words came out more harshly than Kat intended, and she could tell by the expression on Gran's face that the older woman was startled. She couldn't have been completely surprised; she knew Kat's feelings about the house, and she even shared them to some degree. For different reasons, though. She had only ever visited the house, never lived in it. There was a difference. "Sorry," she said after a moment, softening her tone.

Her grandmother was silent. Not, Kat suspected, because she had been offended, but because she worried what Kat's outburst meant about her state of mind.

"I'm not going to try to hurt myself again, Gran, I promise," Kat added, looking the other woman in the eye to show that she meant it but knowing words could only do so much to reassure. And if her grandmother had known the full truth about what had happened before, she would have been even less reassured. "I'm better now. You know that."

"I know you're better when you're *here*," her grandmother said tersely, and although it was hardly a direct reference to what had happened six years ago, it was far less tiptoeing around the subject than she usually did.

"Am I?"

"That's a fine thing to say to me! Of course you are." But Gran looked away as she said it.

Who did she think she was kidding? Not herself, surely, because she whispered so often to her husband behind closed doors about her fears, and not Kat because Kat heard them; the walls in the cottage were thin. Gran was worried that Kat spent so much time alone, worried that yet another roommate had requested a switch in the dorms, worried that Kat wasn't sleeping. Worried that another bottle of pills might find its way into Kat's hands, or maybe something less civilized this time… "I won't be away long, Gran."

"I don't see why you have to go at all."

"I just… I need to see it again."

"Why?"

To see how crazy I really am, was the first thing Kat thought, but all she said was, "You remember what Dr. Mattise said. I have to put the past to bed before I can get on with my future."

Gran's jaw tightened. "You hated Dr. Matisse."

"Doesn't mean he was wrong."

The fact that Gran didn't argue probably meant that she agreed, but her expression suggested that she wasn't happy about it.

"I won't be gone long," Kat repeated. And she wouldn't. All she needed was a week—two at the most, surely. Just long enough to prove to herself that the house had no more power over her and that she wasn't running away. Then maybe she could finally sleep again.

After a while, her grandmother nodded. Once. "I suppose," she said, clearing her throat when her voice cracked slightly and attempting what could only be false cheer, "that it would be good for you to meet Emily, at least. Family is family, even if the blood does start to run thin."

Emily. Kat had forgotten about the little girl somehow. Easy enough to do when they'd never laid eyes on each other, but probably inexcusable just the same. Other than one photograph sent when Emily was just a baby and a few lines in a letter from Grace during that first year away from the manor, Kat knew nothing about her young half-sister. What would she be now, six? Or was she still five? Even her birthdate was hazy in Kat's mind. Her father would have been disappointed about that.

Then he should have been more careful, a voice in the back of her head whispered, and its bitterness surprised her.

"You'll call us if you need anything?" her grandmother asked. "Anything at all?"

Kat nodded.

After a moment, Gran added, "Call even if you don't need anything."

It was not a request. That much was clear in the older woman's tone.

Fair enough, Kat thought, and she reached out to wrap her hand around Gran's while they stared out together at the lapping waves and pretended that everything was fine.

◆ CHAPTER FOUR ◆

THE JOLT AS THE plane touched down startled Kat awake, and the bounce of the aircraft was forceful enough to speed her pulse up before she remembered just where she was. Just as well, though. Sometimes rude awakenings were preferable to dreams, especially the kind of dreams that she tended to have. This most recent one was no exception, even if she couldn't remember what it had been about. But maybe that was just as well, too. Whatever it was, it had been enough to leave her palms clammy.

She glanced out through the tiny window on her left to get her bearings and to allow her heart rate to slow back down again. No use, at least for the former. It was too dark to see anything other than another plane taxiing to a gate and a luggage cart making its rounds. It had been morning on the west coast when she'd left; after three layovers and the switch to east coast time, it was closing in on nine o'clock at night now. Had her destination been anywhere else, she would have looked forward to finally tumbling into a bed. Well, in theory.

She hoisted her bags, both carry-on, to the Arrivals exit. A taxicab driver who was perched on the trunk of his car, smoking a cigarette and glancing through a tabloid magazine, saw her approaching and scrambled down to help her before another driver who was parked further down could. A rental car might have been a better choice, something that allowed her the freedom to come and go from the manor as she pleased, but Kat didn't trust herself enough for that. The urge to put the car in reverse and head right back down the driveway at any time might prove to be too irresistible. She hadn't come all this way to turn coward now.

She slid into a backseat that reeked of nicotine as the driver put her bags in the trunk, turning her face toward the open window in the hopes that the cool night air would offset the way she had begun to sweat. She wiped her palms on her jeans and drew a shallow breath.

A flicker of motion made her glance across the double lanes to where something small made quick and furtive movements. A tomcat, batting something tiny between its paws that made a desperate dart for freedom only to be snatched up and batted around some more. But not for long. The cat ended the game and trotted off into the darkness with its prize dangling from its teeth, and it vanished from sight just as the driver pulled the car away from the curb. Nature just doing what nature did, maybe, but it had the effect of making Kat's stomach twist anyway. She rolled the window up and faced forward again.

It took them perhaps ten minutes just to get out of the city, and nothing about the streets and buildings looked familiar. Had it really been built up so much, or had she just never paid much attention on those rare occasions when they'd driven into town as a family? She'd been too young to do more than dream of a learner's permit back then, back before—

The image of her father lying broken on the ground beside the ladder came into her head before she could stop it, and she shoved it back out again with an intake of breath that was audible enough to make the driver glance at her in the mirror. She avoided his curious eyes and looked out the window again.

It wasn't until they'd left the city behind them that she began to finally recognize things. Not many, especially in the dark like this, but a turn in the road here or a gnarled old tree trunk there... Homes became spaced further and further apart the farther that the cabbie drove until what were essentially fields separated them. Older places on acreage. And the crowning jewel in the neighborhood—

Not that it could be seen from the road, but the gates at the end of Delancey Manor's long and curving driveway certainly could. Old iron things whose rusting bars were twisted into deliberate but vague shapes that all but snuck up on them as the cabbie pulled his car to a stop before them.

Kat's shoulders threatened to hunch up past her ears. Realizing it, she forced them back down again. And the house wasn't even in sight yet.

Coward...

The driver rolled down his window to press a button that was meant to open the gates, but nothing happened. Not surprising. That button hadn't worked for years. It had been on her father's ever-growing to-do list, but it was one of the many things he'd never gotten around to fixing. Apparently Grace hadn't either.

"I'll get it," Kat said when the cabbie started to open his door, and she got out before he could reply. The metal of the gates was cool to the touch. Perfectly natural considering the coolness of the night air, but it sent an inexplicable shiver of distaste through her nevertheless. Ignoring it as best she could, she pushed on the iron bars.

The gates didn't budge.

Thinking they must be stuck, she pushed harder, but still nothing happened. Examining them more closely in the light cast by the car's headlights, she realized why: they were locked.

Of course they were. Perfect. Apparently the house wanted her here about as much as she wanted to be here, or at least that was probably true of someone living inside of it. She was fairly certain she could guess who.

"Locked?" the cabbie called from behind her, and she nodded as she walked back to the car. "Weren't they expecting you?"

She nodded again, and he blinked in surprise. "Someone's way of saying hi," she said by way of explanation. It was just Alexis's style. Neither subtle nor particularly clever. And it was unlikely that it had been an innocent oversight. Grace was too careful and too proper for that.

"Oh." He grimaced. "Want to call ahead for someone to let us in?"

It was worth trying, but when Kat pulled out her cell phone, there was no signal, or at least not enough of one to make a difference. Was the house really so remote out here? She would not have thought so. Considering her options, she studied the curve of the driveway as it disappeared into the inky blackness. "I'll just walk from here."

"You sure? Looks like a bit of a hike."

"It's not that long." She remembered that much at least. Besides, there was moonlight enough even with the clouds overhead to see her way without fear of stumbling—and, she was forced to admit to herself, it would allow her to postpone the inevitable arrival a little longer. Pulling some cash from the front pocket of her jeans, Kat handed it to the driver.

Shrugging in an *it's-your-funeral* kind of way, the driver got out to retrieve her bags from the trunk and hand them to her "I'll wait a minute," he said in a friendly way, nodding at his car's lights. "Give you a little something to see by 'til you're around the other side."

"Thanks." She realized belatedly that she ought to have injected a little more warmth into her tone and returned the smile he'd offered. Too late. Typical of her. She turned her attention forward again.

There was no wall or fence on either side of the iron bars, so while they did serve to keep vehicles from trespassing any further, foot traffic was another issue altogether. Silly, really. The only reason these gates remained standing at all when her parents had moved in years ago was because her father had been so taken with them along with everything else about the place. *History*, he used to say to her with his eyes shining, *this place is full of history, Kit Kat.*

Too much history for her liking. But she looped the smaller bag around her body and picked up the larger one—the small suitcase—

before she could overthink things and started down into the ditch on the right side of the driveway. It was deeper than she expected; the grasses growing out of it hid its true depth from the naked eye, especially at this time of night. She stumbled once and nearly turned an ankle before struggling back up around the other side of the wrought iron and getting solid ground beneath her feet once more.

"All right?" the cabbie called out.

Kat nodded and returned his cheerful wave with a curt one of her own, a gesture that felt stiff and unnatural on her; most things that other people seemed to find normal and easy did. Ignoring the flutter of anxiety inside her chest as both the lights and the sound of the taxi's motor receded, she faced forward and resisted the urge to run after it and beg the driver to return her to the airport.

It wasn't the darkness that unnerved her, not really. Not the solitude of her situation either. She'd come to appreciate both in the past few years; they made it easier to avoid curious glances and awkward conversation. Truthfully, part of her wondered if she wouldn't actually sleep much better stretched out right here beside the gates than she would inside the house. Wouldn't Alexis have a field day with that?

She forced her right foot to move, then her left, over and over again. Gravel crunched beneath them, the only sound in this deserted place and seeming all the louder because of it. There were few trees, but there were shrubs aplenty in which animals of smaller size could have hidden themselves; she half expected to hear a twig snap on one side or the other as her presence startled some little nocturnal creature or at least to see the shadowy form of a bat overhead, silhouetted against the stars, but there was nothing. Had wildlife always been so scarce around here? Maybe she'd spent too much time indoors as a child with her nose in a book to know any better.

Her bags weren't heavy, but she slowed anyway as a cloud moved enough from in front of the moon to illuminate a bend in the driveway up ahead. The biggest bend. Once around it, she'd be nearly there, and the house would be in sight. And for one ridiculous moment a little voice inside her head urged her to run, now, before the house could see her and know that she was there; it wasn't too late yet to turn around and go. The strength of that feeling made her actually pause in mid-step.

"Stop it," she said aloud in a voice that sounded hoarse even to her own ears. Then she shifted her suitcase to her other hand and made herself continue around the bend.

The first thing she saw was the light from the house, reaching out into the darkness from the porch and from the ground floor windows like grasping fingers; Grace must be sitting up for her arrival. A few more steps, and then it was the house itself that seemed to be waiting for her.

Kat's fingers clutched convulsively at her suitcase handle.

It rose up high, seeming to blot out some of the stars with its huge shape. Maybe not quite as huge as she'd remembered—she was both older and a little taller now than she was the last time she'd been here—but three stories high was still plenty big enough. Then the moonlight glinted off of something near the top, and Kat realized it was a tiny attic window. Four stories, then. Yes, she remembered now. An attic so crammed full of old things that it hardly counted as livable space, but it did its part in making the house appear that much taller and more imposing. The shape of the manor was boxy and might have looked plain on something smaller, but certainly not in this case. Its drawn-out windows—on the first three floors anyway—and the decorative lines of the eaves gave it a stately look instead. A look most people exclaimed over, and yet here Kat was ready to revisit what little she'd eaten for dinner.

So what do you think?

From out of nowhere, her father's voice echoed in her head, and she struggled to pinpoint the details of the memory.

I think that's a lot of housework, her mother's voice echoed back not unhappily, and Kat pictured both of her parents then, standing on either side of her and staring up at the house they had just inherited. She'd been much smaller at the time, barely five years old, and in her memory they towered above her. They had grinned at each other like happy coconspirators and then taken Kat's hands in theirs before setting foot inside their new home for the first time.

For just a moment both of their faces had crystal clarity in her head, and then the next they were gone. It was like that sometimes, but not with any memories as early as this one; maybe the manor was stirring up buried things already. And in its own way, that was good. Not easy, but good.

It's just a house.

And repeating that thought over and over to herself, Kat started toward the front steps.

◆ CHAPTER FIVE ◆

SHE WAS HERE.

At first Grace thought her eyes were playing tricks on her, that hint of movement she caught through the parlor window. A shadow on the driveway maybe, or perhaps a feral cat darting after some small and unfortunate prey. But, no, there was definitely a figure coming up the driveway, and it was distinctly human. The momentary spark of alarm she felt at the unexpected sight faded as soon as she made out the silhouettes of luggage and realized that it was not some stranger prowling out and about in this remote area after all, just Kat. Then an entirely different kind of tension took hold of her.

It took her a moment to grasp the fact that Jonathan's eldest child was walking instead of riding up in a car, which struck her as odd. Then again, Kat had always been a little... different. But since she was about ten yards away from knocking on the front door, Grace left that thought unexamined and hastened out of the parlor. She caught herself smoothing nonexistent wrinkles from her tailored skirt and stopped the action with an effort. She was still mistress of this house and had every right to act the part, at least for the moment.

Putting a hand to her heart as if to calm its rapid beating, Grace crossed the foyer to put her other hand on the doorknob, and when her pulse seemed steady enough, she drew a deep breath and opened the door to step outside. "Kat."

Her stepdaughter paused at the base of the porch steps and glanced up. Grace's stomach did an odd sort of flip. She'd grown up quite a bit in six years. The young woman in front of her wasn't exactly the spitting image of her mother, but she bore enough of a resemblance to Lily to startle Grace. Thin, uncannily blue eyes, golden hair... A reminder of everything Grace was not and had never been.

"Grace."

The way she said it struck Grace as less of a greeting and more of an accusation somehow, although she was conscious enough of her own insecurities where Jonathan's daughter was concerned to admit that at least some of that might have been her imagination. She floundered for something appropriate to say. "I thought you'd be coming by taxi."

"Gates were locked."

"Locked? Oh, but—" Alexis. Warmth flooded Grace's cheeks. "I—I'm so sorry. Alexis went out with friends tonight, in town. She must have—I mean, on her way out, they must have accidentally..." She trailed off, knowing the words were as flimsy as they sounded and seeing the same thought written across Kat's face. Her flush deepened. "You must be tired," she managed a moment later, falling back on formality. "Won't you come in?"

Was it her imagination, or did Kat draw back ever so slightly at the invitation? The younger woman eyed the house as if she'd sooner walk across a mine field, and when she glanced upwards at the second and third floor windows above her, Grace realized that there were shadows under her eyes that were much too deep to be just a trick of the lighting. Well, it was only natural for the girl to experience a certain amount of trepidation, coming back here for the first time since...

Grace left the thought unfinished, but it was enough to soften her own anxiety with a bit of empathy for Kat's. "Come in," she repeated, stepping aside and holding the door open. "And... welcome back, Kat."

For a moment, Kat didn't budge. Then she started up the steps with obvious reluctance, and Grace thought that maybe they were both careful not to accidentally brush each other as her stepdaughter passed her and stepped over the threshold.

Well, as homecomings went, it could have been better, but it could also have been a lot worse. Grace took a deep breath and followed Kat inside, barely aware of the way the porch light seemed to flicker momentarily before she shut the door behind them.

◆◆◆

A WAVE OF COLD air brushed Kat's face as she stepped inside, startling the breath out of her that she'd been holding and sending an inexplicable wave of nausea through her. But then it had always been cool in this house; she'd just forgotten, that was all. Year-round this place was like that, as she'd been told many old houses were. Whether fireplaces blazed in the winter months or windows were opened to let in warm breezes during the summer, there were always pockets of air that the warmth never seemed to touch. On the plus side, her father had said cheerfully more than once, it meant that they didn't have to bother disturbing the old walls to install modern air-conditioning. Trust him to find the bright side.

Kat's stomach turned over one more time and then finally settled back down once she was through the doorway. She stopped and let her eyes wander over things that seemed both foreign and familiar at the same time as her memory sharpened. The entryway was so wide that it was nearly a room in and of itself, and the glossy dark wooden paneling gleamed as though it had been freshly polished. Maybe it had. Grace might have wanted to make a good impression. She needn't have worried, though. Whatever opinions Kat had of her stepmother, she certainly had never doubted Grace's sense of responsibility.

The main hallway lay directly ahead and ended at a beautifully carved wooden staircase that wound its way up with right-angled twists and turns before finally vanishing out of view. If one stood at its base and looked straight up, it was possible to see a glimpse of the third floor's ceiling and its crown molding. Her mother had exclaimed over that stairway when she'd first seen it.

"I opened up the bedroom at the end of the hall for you since Emily's in your old room. Fresh sheets."

Kat glanced at her stepmother, who seemed to fidget under her gaze. Still the same Grace. Still dressed tastefully if not expensively, still struggling to lose those last ten pounds, although it looked closer to fifteen now. Baby weight that still hung around, Kat thought then, remembering with a slight start that Grace had been heavily pregnant the last time she'd seen her. Her hair was still styled exactly the same, too. Short and close to her face in a cut that had never quite flattered her features the way it probably flattered most others who adopted it. There were a few more strands of grey in it now, though. A few more lines on her face, too. And tension; Kat was not the only one with anxiety issues tonight. She took a stab at good manners. "Thank you."

Neither of them went in for a hug, and neither, Kat was sure, was disappointed about that.

"If you'd prefer more privacy, of course, there's always the third floor rooms, but I didn't think you'd want to go up and down that many flights of stairs while you were here."

"Second floor's fine."

After an awkward pause, Grace added, "I hope you had a pleasant flight?"

"It was all right." Neither of them seemed to know what to say next, and Kat thought Grace looked relieved when she added, "Kind of tired, though. Think I'd like to just turn in."

"Yes, of course. You've had a long day. Why don't you make yourself comfortable upstairs, and we'll get caught up tomorrow? Emily's long since gone to bed, and Alexis will be out late, I'm sure."

Not late enough, but Kat bit those words back. If Grace could make an effort—and she seemed to be trying—so could Kat. "Tomorrow, sure. Thank you, Grace."

"Of course. It's... good to have you back."

All of the appropriately polite responses that came to mind were too transparent and phony for Kat to offer one up without choking on it, so she settled for nodding instead.

"Right, then. I'll just finish tidying up a few things in the kitchen, and then I'll be heading up myself. The bedroom at the end of the hall," Grace repeated as Kat started up the stairs with her bags, and a few moments later the sound of her footsteps on the old hardwood floor signaled her departure from the room.

One of the steps creaked as Kat stepped on it. Fourth from the bottom, she thought with a sudden flash of remembrance. Funny, the things that stuck in a person's head. She hesitated on that particular step, her gaze traveling ahead of her to the shadowed twists and turns of the staircase. Just a house, she reminded herself, and she used her hand on the bannister to drag herself upwards until her reluctant feet finally followed.

When she reached the second floor landing, Kat stopped and stood there with her bags in her hands. She forgot for a moment that she even still held them as she felt a rising tide of anxiety and had to force herself to slow her breathing down again. In for a count of four, hold it, and then back out again for twice that. And repeat. Maybe it was a good thing that she wouldn't be sleeping in her old room if it was this hard just for her to walk down the familiar hallway. Too many vague memories of night terrors.

Her gaze settled on the door to her childhood room—Emily's room now—in spite of her best efforts. Why the sight of it should fill her with such dread, she didn't know, but the hairs on the back of her neck began to rise anyway. Bad dreams, that was all, or at least that was what everyone else had told her for years. Grandparents, shrinks, even her father. Bad dreams and a child's overactive imagination warping her memory. Along with the creaks and shadows of an old house.

Maybe.

The weight of the bags in her hands reminded her that she still hadn't budged. Choking on fear already? Wonderful. And only about ten feet from Alexis's bedroom door, too. Lucky that her stepsister wasn't here to spot her in this condition; she'd go for the jugular. Willing herself forward again, Kat stopped in front of the bedroom Grace had said was made up for her.

It was right next to Alexis's room, unless there'd been a change in the living arrangements that Kat didn't know about. She'd have to remember never to leave the room unlocked when her stepsister was at home. A thorough inspection of the bed before getting into it tonight would probably be a wise idea, too. Alexis seemed a little old now for collecting spiders and dead rats, but maybe the sheer tradition of it would be too much for her to resist. It would be stupid on her part, considering who now officially held the title to the house, but then again, an overabundance of foresightedness had never been one of Alexis's problems.

Setting down her bags long enough to turn the doorknob, Kat let the door swing gently open. She had seen the inside of it before, but not for a very long time; rooms that were seldom used got locked up to save on housekeeping, except for an annual spring cleaning. It was small, but besides the delicately carved four-poster bed, side table with lamp—which Grace had been thoughtful enough to leave turned on for her—and a large bureau, someone had decided at one point to cram a writing desk and chair into it as well. At least they had drawn the line at including a chaise lounge, or else there would barely have been room to stand, let alone walk.

The key Kat had hoped for was in the lock; she pocketed it after locking the door behind her and turned back around. Heavy drapes were tied back from the windows, leaving only filmy things of lace covering them up from view. Crossing the room—it only took about four steps—Kat pulled them aside to see nothing but darkness as the moon went mostly behind a cloud. Even then it sent a little light into the room to help the tiny bedside lamp in its ineffectual struggle to brighten the place, but Kat untied the drapes and let them fall closed; she preferred privacy to light. Not that there should have been anyone outside to see her through the glass this far from other houses, but she'd felt exposed anyway, staring out into the night and unable to tell if something else stared back. Closing the drapes should have helped. Oddly, it didn't.

To distract herself, she opened her bags and stuffed clothes and other things that were packed inside them into the bureau drawers, everything but a nightshirt and her cell phone. She held the latter up. The signal was a little better than before, so she kept her promise and called her grandparents' number. "I'm here," she said as soon as she heard someone pick up. "I made it."

She recognized the sound of breath being let out: Gran. "Oh, good. Everything go okay? No luggage lost or anything?"

"Mine was all carry-on." Which Gran had known but must have forgotten. Worrying had that effect on a person.

"Right. So..." There was a pause, and then her tone turned careful. "You've seen Grace, then?"

"Briefly." Kat eyed the bed but remained standing in spite of how tired she was. Foolish reluctance on her part; she was going to have to get into the thing eventually. Besides, she had no bad memories of this room. This bed was a blank slate, or at least it should have been.

"And Emily?"

"She was asleep."

"Oh, that's right. I forgot about the time difference. Have you..." Gran's voice cut out.

"Hello? Gran?"

"...barely hear... now. I said have..." She cut out again.

Kat glanced at her phone before returning it to her ear. "Signal's too weak. I'll call you again in a couple of days, okay? Gran?"

"Or sooner."

"Or sooner," Kat agreed, hearing the tension in her grandmother's voice.

"Good night, sweet—" Her voice broke off abruptly, and this time it didn't come back. There was only the silence of a dropped call, and after a few seconds of waiting to see if that was indeed the case, Kat turned off the phone and set it on the bedside table. Pulling the door key from her pocket, she set that on the table, too, and then she turned to face the bed.

It looked inviting enough, swathed in what she guessed was an old and handmade quilt composed of mostly green and cream-colored squares. Something made by a Delancey of old maybe, someone long dead and buried, which somehow made it seem a little less inviting than before.

Knock it off, Kat told herself, performing a cursory search to be sure there were no unpleasant surprises left for her by her stepsister, and then she made herself change into her nightshirt and slip beneath the covers before she could manage to talk herself out of it. The sheets were cool at first, having lain undisturbed until now, but not unpleasantly so. They were soft, too, and they wrapped Kat in the kind of crisp, fresh scent that only comes from recently laundered fabric.

See? Not so bad...

And yet she was as stiff as an iron rod as she lay there.

Breathing slowly and steadily, she turned her eyes to the bedside lamp and the soft glow it lent the room, too soft to send shadows scurrying from the farthest corners. As a child, she'd had a nightlight. Not back at the apartment that was the very first home she could remember, but once they'd moved in to the manor. The creaks and groans of the old house had been too much for her and her child's imagination. She wound up spending the first several nights in her parents' room, creeping in on her tiptoes when they were asleep and burrowing between them under the covers until they finally and firmly informed her one morning that she needed to stay put in her own room like a big girl. The nightlight had been their concession to her fear.

And the light did help. At first, anyway. But it soon started sputtering out after everyone had gone to bed, and nothing her father tried seemed to be able to fix it—or the ones he got to replace it. Faulty wiring, he'd finally decided with a sigh and an apologetic pat to Kat's head.

Nights were her least favorite times in the house back then. They always lasted much too long.

But she was not a little girl anymore, and she hadn't been afraid of the dark in a long time. Well, the dark in other places, at least. Ignoring the stiffness of her limbs, Kat reached out and switched off the light.

And lay awake for a very long time.

◆ CHAPTER SIX ◆

SOMEHOW MORNING FINALLY ROLLED around along with the realization that Kat had actually fallen asleep at some point. A sudden flutter of panic at her new surroundings made her jolt upright as if she expected to find something amiss in the room or maybe someone looming over her. No one was, and the room looked just the same as it had when she'd gone to bed last night. Still, she threw the covers off and yanked open the curtains to let in light, just to be sure.

Nothing. Everything was fine. She was overreacting yet again.

But she'd done it, she'd made it through her first night here, and it hadn't been so awful after all. Long, maybe, but not terrible. Nothing had swooped down on her while she slept, which was a ridiculous thought but one that popped into her head anyway. Closing her eyes, Kat slumped back against the window ledge and willed her erratic pulse to slow down, and when it finally felt normal again, she turned and looked out the window.

It overlooked the winding front drive in all its graveled glory. There was nothing much to be seen except for the graveled expanse itself and a few well-trimmed shrubs on either side of it. The work of a gardener, or had Grace managed to do it herself? Gardeners didn't come cheap, and although Kat's father had left behind some funds thanks to a life insurance policy, the estate he'd inherited from his great uncle Thomas came with more house than actual money. Trust

Grace to manage things efficiently, though. Or maybe that was Michael's doing. He worked in finance now, or something like that. Kat couldn't remember now. She ought to have paid closer attention when Grace called before.

Kat's eyes turned to the other window, the one still shrouded by curtains. She didn't need to look out that window to know what she would see. Knowing the layout of the grounds, she could guess. Had it been intentional on Grace's part to put her where she would overlook the pond? No, surely not. Grace was not deliberately cruel. What had happened there happened long before Grace came along anyway. Doubtless when she looked at the water, all she saw was its beauty. No, her decision to make up this room was almost certainly for the exact reason she gave before: it was far more convenient than going up another full flight of stairs.

Still...

Kat turned away and focused on the first thing she could think of to change the direction of her thoughts, namely the unmade bed. Her movements were slow as she made it up again, and she didn't stop smoothing and tucking things on it until she felt more ready and able to face all the things that lay on the other side of the bedroom door.

Steeling herself, she reached for the key she'd left beside her phone on the bedside table.

And found nothing.

Blinking, she drew her hand back and looked again only to see that the key was there after all, but it was on the far side of the phone. Not where she'd put it—was it...? Her lips parted as if she might speak, but no sound came out. It had been the end of a long and tiring day of travel when she'd set the key down, and she'd been a bundle of nerves—maybe she was just remembering wrong, or maybe she'd just nudged the thing out of place in her mad scramble to get out of bed.

Uncertain, she reached out and picked up the key, flinching inwardly at the initial contact as if she expected it to burn her skin. Naturally, it did not. She turned the cold metal over in her hands and tried to remember clearly where she'd set it before. She could have sworn...

Her hand trembled slightly, and the part of her that had urged Kat to make this trip in the first place did its best to thrust her uncertainty from her mind. It was nothing, just a simple mistake. She'd just have to be more alert to what she was doing from now on.

A noise from downstairs made her look up from the key and listen: dishes being stacked, or possibly unstacked and jostled in the process. Someone was eating breakfast. Crossing to the door, Kat put her ear against it and listened more closely. The hallway outside was quiet. Unlocking the door, she peered out but saw no signs of any activity. The doors to all of the bedrooms were closed, so she could only guess as to who was downstairs already. Grace, probably; Alexis was too much of a late riser, or at least she used to be.

The door to the bathroom was open; no time like the present. Grabbing a few of her things, Kat locked her bedroom up behind her—even five minutes with an unlocked door was too many with Alexis around—and took the opportunity to shower. Several minutes later, she'd delayed the inevitable long enough and was as ready as she was ever going to be. It was time to join the rest of the household.

She crept down the stairs on silent feet, not deliberately but out of habit. The murmur of a voice, its words unintelligible, floated up to her from the direction of the kitchen: Grace. Whoever she was speaking to was either mute at the moment or too soft-spoken for Kat to hear her; that ruled out Alexis, then. It must be Emily.

The fourth step from the bottom creaked when Kat's foot landed on it, and Grace's voice broke off mid sentence. A moment later her footsteps echoed on the floor, and she appeared in the foyer just as Kat reached the bottom of the stairs.

"Ah, you're awake," Grace greeted her a little too brightly, dressed just as smartly as yesterday and more formally than most women who spent their time at home. "I trust you slept well?"

Standard pleasantries. No call for truth-telling here; it would only grate on her stepmother. "Fine."

"I'm glad to hear it. Alexis is still in bed—" A quick and disapproving glance at her watch. "—but I'm afraid our appetites got the best of Emily and me. We've already eaten. There's cereal, if you like, and bread or bagels for toasting. Or I could fix you some eggs—"

"I'll manage on my own."

Grace folded her hands in front of her. "Yes, of course."

Sunlight did its best to fight its way past the lacy curtains shrouding the windows on either side of the front door and light up the dark foyer. It partially succeeded. Kat turned in place, taking more in than she had last night when all her focus had gone into simply making it over the threshold. To the best of her recollection, everything looked the same as it had six years ago. Kitchen and library lay further down the hall, she remembered, and the dining room was on the left. But when her gaze landed on the open door of the parlor to her right, something inside it caught her eye in the jarring sort of way that meant something was different even if she couldn't immediately put her finger on what it was. Conscious of the way Grace's wary eyes followed her, Kat went to the doorway to peer more closely. The elegant Victorian furniture that her mother had loved, threadbare but much of it original to the house, was the same, but... "You changed the curtains," she realized aloud after a moment.

She glanced over her shoulder just in time to see a twitch around Grace's eyes. "Well, yes, but the old ones were really getting quite ratty. I did save them, though, if you'd prefer to put them back up."

She had only meant the words as an observation, nothing more. Whatever did or did not hang on the windows or anywhere else for that matter meant little to her. "It's okay, Grace. Do whatever you want to the place, really. It's your home, not mine."

"Yes, well…" Grace's hands brushed at her skirt. "Not legally."

So that was the real reason she was so tense. Not so much because of Kat's presence here as what she worried it might mean. Well, she hadn't come here with plans to evict anybody, but before she could say as much, she caught sight of movement as someone small came up behind Grace.

Emily.

The little girl stared back at Kat, her eyes somber and her dress somehow too neatly pressed to look natural on a child so young. Her long, dark hair was just as tidy, pulled back from her face and held by a clip with nary a strand out of place. Little kids were supposed to look messier than that, was Kat's first thought. Her second one was, *she looks just like him.*

"Emily, darling," said Grace, ushering the child out from behind her, "Come say hello. To your sister." There was only a moment's hesitation before adding that title, but it was enough to make Kat wonder just how much or how little her stepmother had told the girl about their visitor.

Emily obeyed her mother with tentative feet and only stepped forward as far as she seemed to think she had to in order to be polite. Instead of speaking, she only studied Kat warily, and Kat realized then that they were both staring at each other.

"She has his eyes," she murmured after a moment, surprised to realize she had said the words out loud and unprepared to see so much of her father looking back at her from that small face.

"Yes. Yes, she does." Grace's voice was soft.

Now what? It was the only coherent thought that seemed to form in Kat's head, and somehow she felt sure that the little girl was thinking pretty much the same thing. She had no experience with children to speak of. Babysitting jobs might have been commonplace for her peers during their teenage years, but she'd been in no shape to look after anyone during most of hers. And because word had gotten out about her frequent visits to one therapist or another despite her grandparents' best efforts to keep such information under wraps, no one had asked her to. She'd been relieved, really. Human interaction rated rather low on her list of priorities back then. It still did.

She ought to say something now, though; even she knew that. The silence in the entryway was growing almost oppressive, and it was hardly fair to expect a child to be the one to make the first move, especially when that child looked as uneasy about all of this as Kat herself felt. She opened her mouth to say something along the lines of "Hello," when a new voice spoke first.

"Well, well, look who's here. Medicated and under a shrink's care, I hope."

Apparently Alexis was not quite as late a sleeper as she used to be. Kat turned her head to see her stepsister looking down on her—figuratively and literally—from the stairs. And from the corner of her eye, Kat was aware of Emily shrinking back behind her mother.

Alexis descended a few more steps, her hand trailing lightly over the banister in a deliberate sort of way, and stopped where the light was best and—no doubt—most flattering. Trust Alexis to know how to make an entrance. It was hard to believe she was Grace's daughter sometimes. Trim and tasteful had never been enough for her. Even now, as little as there was to her strappy shirt and skirt, it was obvious that they were of designer quality, and the wrist of the hand that remained on the banister sparkled with something that was too brilliant to be cubic zirconium. Those could not have been things Grace would have bought for her, but it was easy enough to guess who had. Alexis's father had always been good at buying gifts even if he was poor at everything else.

She gave Kat a once-over now—her jeans, her t-shirt, her unbound hair—followed by a look that left little doubt that Kat had failed to pass muster. "Good God, you still dress like an old bag lady, don't you? I guess some things never change."

Grace's hand fluttered to her throat. "Alexis!"

Her eldest daughter only smirked in a way that was all too familiar.

But Kat was less polite than she'd been six years ago, less restrained, and it was better for Alexis to realize that sooner than later. "Guess you're right," she said evenly. "I see Daddy's still throwing money at you instead of affection."

Alexis's jaw dropped, and she began to sputter. "Mom!"

Grace's hand fluttered uselessly again. "Girls, please!"

Kat merely stared back at her stepsister, unblinking. Perhaps realizing that her mother wasn't going to be much help in this particular instance, Alexis shot Kat a dark look and stomped the rest of the way down the stairs with less aplomb and more scowling than with which she'd descended the others. She disappeared in the direction of the kitchen, but not before hurling back over her shoulder, "Looney-bin freak!"

Her mother didn't seem to know what to do and just stood there. "I..."

"I'll lay off if she will, Grace." Breakfast would have to wait until Alexis was done in the kitchen, but that was fine by Kat. She had something else she needed to do anyway, something that was six years overdue, and she headed for the front door to do it.

And felt Emily's eyes follow her all the way out.

◆ CHAPTER SEVEN ◆

THE HILL SHE WANTED sloped gently upward beyond the house and the manicured flower gardens; grassy, natural, and from the look of things, mostly left to its own devices. Which was fine, because the grasses and wildflowers that she passed through were generally short enough for her to find footing among them with no problem save for one near slip on a loose rock. The faintest traces of a footpath were all that remained of what someone had cut into the hillside years ago, decades past maybe, and it was all but overgrown now. Small wonder. The place it led to wasn't the kind of place likely to draw frequent visitors.

It drew Kat, though, and she didn't stop until she reached the wrought-iron fence at the top in spite of the fact that an unseasonably cool morning breeze made her wish she'd brought a sweatshirt. The gate in the fence was latched but not locked; the fence mostly served to keep wildlife out. Or maybe to lend extra solemnity to a place that had plenty of its own already. Most graveyards did, and the Delancey family plot was no exception.

The gate was showing signs of rust at its hinges and groaned in protest as she opened it. Maybe Grace's sense of responsibility hadn't extended this far. Then again, maybe it had, because while the farther headstones were showing signs of long neglect beneath brambles and weeds, it was obvious that the nearest ones had received some care. They were well-weeded, and the grass around them was clipped low and neat. Her father's, of course, Kat thought as she approached the nearest one, but she had not expected to see her mother's grave tended to so well, too. Yes, the only one with flowers on it was her father's, but still—not every woman would instruct her gardener to show the same care and respect to the final resting place of her husband's first wife that Grace had. Maybe Kat hadn't given her stepmother enough credit.

She hadn't had a plan before she came to this place, and now that she was standing here, she wondered if she should have brought some flowers of her own, or some photographs or other family mementos. *Some*thing. She wasn't good with sentiment, though. It didn't come naturally to her, not anymore. So she simply stood where she was and read what had been engraved.

Jonathan Andrew Delancey. 1968 - 2010. Beloved husband and father.

The words seemed lacking somehow, and hollow. Appropriate and tasteful—Grace's work, of course—and very traditional, but a completely inadequate summing up of a man's life and his warmth. And his humor. If it had been up to him, he probably would have preferred a limerick for his epitaph than these stiff and formal words.

The corners of Kat's mouth lifted faintly at the thought, and for a moment she could picture him smiling, too, and it was unexpectedly painful. She turned her eyes toward her mother's headstone.

Lily Michelle Delancey. 1969 - 2001. Unable are the loved to die, for love is immortality.

Dickenson, Kat thought, surprising herself. Something she'd learned in an English class, or had her father told her? She couldn't remember now. It had been his choice, though, to put those words there. Less telling about her mother maybe than about his feelings for her, but still more personal than what Grace had chosen.Closing her eyes, Kat summoned up a picture of her mother in her head, and although it was fuzzy around the edges, the smile seemed familiar and real enough. So did the long, blond hair that Kat had inherited from her, if a little darker and wavier than her daughter's. She had loved her mother's hair. Like strands of gold, and so pretty. She used to wrap it around her clumsy little girl fingers when she sat in her mother's lap, trying her best to turn it into braids but mostly just tangling it up instead. God, her mother must have been a patient woman.

The vividness of that unexpected flash of memory made Kat open her eyes. That one was new, and so real that she could almost feel the strands wrapped in her hands, soft and silky. Maybe the house really was stirring things up inside her head already. And that was what she'd come here for, mostly. To remember and accept. And if her palms grew clammy at the prospect, well, maybe that would wear off if she just refused to let her nerves get the best of her. She'd made it this far anyway.

Kat knelt down between the two graves on earth and grass that was slightly damp with morning dew. The cool moisture seeped into the legs of her jeans, but she was only dimly aware of it. After a moment, she stretched out one hand and laid it on top of her father's resting place. His funeral was hazy in her mind, most likely because of what she'd done afterwards with the pills that day—what everyone told her she had done, at least. Mostly what she remembered was waking up in the hospital. Her mother's funeral was even more vague since Kat had been so young at the time. There had been rain that day, she remembered that much, and people placing flowers on top of what Kat now knew was the casket.

No… that wasn't right. It wasn't her mother's funeral she was remembering after all, because now she had a distinct recollection of her mother picking her up and carrying her. Because it was raining, and she didn't want Kat's shoes to get muddy. She'd carried her all the way up the hill and held her throughout most of the service, too.

Whose service, though? Curiosity got the best of her. Straightening and getting up from the ground, Kat brushed damp dirt from the knees of her jeans and studied the gravestones nearest to those of her parents, trying to place what she had pictured in her head a moment ago. Further back, she decided, although not by much because it had to have been the last funeral held in this place before her mother's, and when she read the dates on the headstone that was the most likely candidate, she knew she'd found it.

Thomas William Delancey. b. 1926. .d. 2000.

That was it. No other words. Nothing personal or even poetic. Her father's great-uncle, a distant relation and the one who had left him the house because apparently he'd had no other living relatives left other than Jonathan Delancey. Her father had been solemn at the funeral, but not emotional. No one had, that she could remember. In fact, there hadn't been that many people there at all. Or was she remembering wrong?

In her mind's eye, she saw a handful of people standing on either side of her parents, huddling under umbrellas and grimacing in the rain. The clergyman had finished his speech, and his small audience turned to file back down the hill one by one.

No, that wasn't completely true. One woman had stayed behind to speak to Kat's father. An older woman with grey hair wound so tightly into a bun that it almost hurt to look at it. Strange, the things that stuck out to a child. Kat's mother decided to go ahead to the car with her daughter so they could get out of the miserable weather, and her father had handed Kat the umbrella to hold over them both. The wind had nearly torn it from her small grasp, but she'd held on tightly, not wanting her father to think she was too much of a baby to do as he'd asked.

But he hadn't been watching. His attention had been on the stranger, the woman. Her words were lost in the wind, but whatever they were, they seemed to make her father angry. He'd said something back in reply, scowling, and then turned to follow after his wife and child.

Looking up from the headstone, Kat's gaze settled on a stone cherub carved on top of a much older headstone, its wings spread and its face downturned. With a start, she recognized it. That was the one she'd thought of days ago while lying in her bedroom at her grandparents' cottage. It was dry as a bone now, of course, but the streaks of rain she'd imagined on its face must have been from Thomas's funeral; both of her parents had been buried on days that were dry. Grey, but dry.

There was something very peaceful about the silence and stillness of this place, but Kat felt a sudden urge to be anywhere else. She was not the superstitious type. It was just…

Never mind what it was. It didn't matter anyway. Turning, she left the same way she had come.

Her walk back down the hill was slow and deliberate, her eyes on the house. She could take the long way around and go in by way of the driveway and the front door, but that would be taking the coward's way out. She hadn't come all this way to do that. So instead she forced herself to head straight for the manicured gardens. And the pond.

The gardens were nothing like the simple flowerbeds common to her grandparents' neck of the woods. These had levels and layers and carefully designed patterns through which to walk on pathways of gravel, and if they could have benefited from a little weeding, they were still in impressive shape for landscaping that had been here for perhaps over a century. Parts of it, anyway. The figurines placed here and there had been her mother's additions—she had loved these gardens—but the carved stone benches had been here long before that. And beyond those…

The pond had been terribly neglected by the time her father inherited the place, and even though her memory wasn't sharp enough to remind Kat exactly how the sludge inside smelled the first time she saw it, she remembered thinking that it had been foul. It was manmade with a perfect circle shape and raised edges that brought the lip just slightly higher than ground level, the bulk of the whole thing sunken a foot or two into the earth. It was smaller than the average backyard swimming pool but far fancier with its sculpted design. No fountain in the middle, but once her father had it cleaned out properly and refilled, lily pads and other water plants were just as pretty in their own way. In retrospect, it would have been better if he'd simply drained it and left it alone, but its beauty was disarming. One didn't look at it and think of it as a drowning hazard. For a child maybe, but not for a grown woman.

Kat drew closer to the water's edge, closer than she felt comfortable doing, truthfully, and made herself look into it. Her reflection stared back at her, its features tense. The water was clear and clean, the stone bottom visible; Grace had let nothing fall by the wayside. The plants in it were flourishing, too. No fish, though. Fish never seemed to last long in the pond, and after what happened to Kat's mother, her father had seemed to prefer to leave the pond alone. Another man might have had it destroyed or at least filled in, but Jonathan Delancey was not one to be vindictive. Accidents happened, he'd said with red-rimmed and shadowed eyes, and besides, Lily had loved it too much for him to ever erase its existence altogether.

Staring at it now, Kat half-expected some vague memory to surface of her mother floating face down, the way she'd been told she'd found her. Nothing did, and she couldn't pretend that she wasn't relieved. She had plenty of the past to confront as it was without that particular missing piece. But when she felt the tension rising in her body, she forced herself to stay by the pool a minute longer until the feeling passed. There. Surely that was enough being brave for one morning. Taking a deep breath, she turned away.

And froze as a tiny sound caught her ear. It wasn't much of a sound, and in and of itself it was rather innocuous, like the sound that the splash of one finger might make when it broke the surface of the water in a bathtub or while swimming. But a sound like that didn't belong here in this place, and that was what jarred her.

Turning back, Kat saw the last echoes of a tiny ripple on the water, all the way out in the center of the pond. The wind, she told herself. Nothing but the wind. And yet she felt a long buried flutter of familiar anxiety, particularly when she realized that the plants around the pool were utterly still. There was no breeze.

A bug landing on the water. Or maybe a fish that Grace had installed in the pool after all in spite of the fact that Kat still couldn't see any signs of life. She averted her eyes before she could be absolutely certain there were no fins to be seen, because the alternative meant that her senses might very well be playing tricks on her the way they used to, and of all the things about returning to Delancey Manor that unnerved her, that possibility was the most unnerving of all.

She stepped back from the edge of the water. Not again. Not now, when she had been doing so much better for so long—

That was when the scent of lavender hit her.

It was the only thing she actually did remember about the day she lost her mother. No sights or even sounds, just that scent. All the many different flowers in bloom, and yet the only one she smelled back then was the lavender, overwhelming all the others. And she smelled it again now, just as potent as it had been back then. Only there was no lavender growing around the pond.

And suddenly Kat found herself on her knees and dry-heaving. Her fingers dug into the graveled ground as if for purchase, and she dug them in even deeper as the world around her threatened to spin.

Deep breaths. In for four, hold it, and out again slowly. And again, she told herself, willing her control back. Bit by bit, she regained it, until she was able to get to her feet again without getting dizzy. It was her own fault. She'd pushed it too much for the first day back. It would have been better to save the pond for tomorrow, but what was done was done.

The floral odor was gone now, vanishing as suddenly as it had come like any hallucination would do, olfactory or otherwise. Just a little slip, Kat thought, hoping it was true. Not enough to make her come completely undone. She would be fine, because she had to be.

Giving the pond a wider berth than before, she made her way to where the edge of the garden met the back lawn and started across with the intention of going in through the back door of the house. She halted, though, when she saw Emily sitting on the back porch steps and watching her.

"Hi," the girl said, giving Kat an appraising sort of look. She twisted a blade of grass between her small fingers and began to tear off little bits of it.

Had she seen Kat's collapse by the pond? Hopefully not. It was not the sort of thing she cared for anyone to witness, and it would hardly be pleasant for a child to watch, either. But Emily didn't seem concerned, and the ornamental grasses and shrubs had likely shielded the pond from her view. "Hi," Kat returned finally, uncomfortable and growing more so with each passing second.

"I like your hair."

The comment, so apparently random, caught Kat off guard and left her floundering for an intelligent response. She settled for the simplest one. "Thanks."

By now nothing big enough to tear remained of the piece of grass, so Emily plucked a new one and began the process over again, seemingly absorbed in it. It struck Kat as being a ruse, though, to cover for something else. Nervousness, maybe? Kat had been known to make plenty of grown men and women nervous or uncomfortable in her time; why should children be any different? But somehow it seemed less like nerves and more like shy fascination in this case. "Are you going to live here now?" Emily asked abruptly, her hair falling forward and hiding part of her face from view.

God, no, Kat thought, flinching inwardly, but she managed a more tempered, "No. No, I'm not."

"Oh." Emily's shoulders slumped.

Kat blinked. Was that disappointment?

The girl gave up on the grass and looked up, and again Kat found the resemblance to her father—*their* father—striking. "Why?"

"Why what?" Kat asked, startled.

"Why aren't you going to live here? Mom said it's your house now."

Lovely. Now she suppose she had small children thinking she was an evil landlord about to start the eviction process. What other ideas had Grace put into her head? Or maybe it had been Alexis; Kat hadn't missed the way Emily had shrunk away from her earlier. "It is, but I'm really just here for a visit. That's all."

"You don't like this place."

It was a remarkably astute observation considering that it was made by one so young, and by someone who had known Kat for less than five minutes. Maybe she'd been more obvious than she realized, or maybe the girl *had* witnessed Kat nearly losing her lunch a minute ago. Then again, maybe Kat was just too inexperienced with young kids to know any better. In any case, the conversation wasn't getting any more comfortable, and she wondered what was the best way to make a graceful exit away from a five—or was it six?—year old. "I just…" Just what? She could hardly be completely honest with her. Even she knew that.

Emily waited.

Apparently there would be no putting her off. "I never really felt like this place was home," Kat said finally, hoping it would be enough to satisfy the little girl.

From her reaction, it was hard to tell. But she nodded in a way that seemed much too knowing for someone so young. "Me neither. Wish we could move."

She said it so fervently that it gave Kat pause. She wasn't used to someone else sharing her distaste for the house; everyone else seemed to think it was a lovely place, if drafty at times and not without a few old-house quirks. "You do?"

The girl nodded.

"Why?"

Glancing down at the ground again, Emily shuffled her feet as if reluctant to answer. "I don't like this house," she said finally, so quiet that Kat had to strain to hear her.

"Why not?"

Her little sister didn't answer. Swallowing her discomfort, Kat stepped forward and squatted down in front of her to get at eye level. "Emily?" she persisted. "Why not?"

Emily wrapped her arms around herself almost like a hug, and then shrugged. "Doesn't matter. Nobody ever listens to a kid."

There was a kind of resignation in the way she said the words that was painfully familiar to Kat. Suddenly she was five years old again, terrified to sleep alone as the house creaked and groaned around her at night. Wishing her parents had never moved them out of their tiny apartment back in Kansas, and wondering why they couldn't seem to understand the dread she felt.

"Yeah," Kat said. "Yeah, I know."

After a moment, she abandoned her squat for the empty space beside her young half-sister on the step, companionable but not too close. And together they sat and stared out at the gardens in silence.

◆ CHAPTER EIGHT ◆

ALEXIS HAD RETREATED TO her room by the time Kat's hunger drove her into the kitchen in search of breakfast. Lunch was more like it, given the lateness of the hour. She ate little but she ate it slowly, reluctant to return to her bedroom. The kitchen somehow felt safer than other areas of the house and always had. Maybe because it was the most modernized room in the house, although why that should make a difference she didn't know. Maybe it wasn't the newer feel to it at all; maybe it was just that in here with the back door only a few feet away she was closer to an exit than she was when she was anywhere else.

When she was done eating and had washed her dishes, she gave her cell phone another try; more likely than not, Gran had slept as poorly as Kat had and would continue to do so until her granddaughter returned. But the signal was still too poor to be of much use. Welcoming the excuse to leave the house again, Kat trekked down the driveway and even a ways down the road before she was able to get anything strong enough to be helpful. Her grandparents' machine picked up when she finally got through, which was something of a relief; had she been there to answer, Gran would have peppered Kat with questions.

"It's Kat. Sorry we got cut off last night. Just wanted to let you know that I'm fine—" A lie, but a well-intentioned one. "—and that I may have trouble using my phone while I'm here, but there's nothing to worry about." There was a landline at the house, of course, but with one of its extensions in her stepsister's room and Alexis's lack of scruples when it came to listening in, she'd have to be truly desperate before she resorted to using it. Trust Alexis to pick up just as Gran was pleading with Kat to start therapy again. "I'll call you again in a few days." She hesitated, then added, "Love you both," before ending the call. It was as close to sentimental as she got and unusual enough for her that now she questioned if she ought to have said it at all. Not because there was anything untrue about it, but because her having said it might make Gran worry more than if she'd said nothing at all.

But what was done was done. If Gran was worried, Gran would call, and landline eavesdroppers be damned. With any luck, Alexis would prefer to spend the day in town with friends again and give Kat a reprieve from her presence.

A girl could hope.

◆◆◆

IN VAIN, APPARENTLY.

Even before she opened the front door, Kat heard the sound of her stepsister's voice on the other side, loud and stringent. The words themselves were muffled, although she was fairly certain she heard her name spat out like an epithet.

She turned the front door knob, loud and deliberate, and Alexis's voice broke off abruptly, replaced by Grace's much softer one, audibly shushing her. To no avail. A moment later, Alexis stalked out of the parlor. "What the hell do I care if she can hear me or not?" she snapped, more at Kat than at Grace, who followed her out and was now wringing her hands together. Her shoulder knocked into Kat as she passed, and there was nothing accidental about it. It was forceful enough to make someone who was unprepared for it stagger.

Kat was not unprepared. She ignored the dark look Alexis shot at her as her stepsister climbed the stairs, ignored her altogether, actually. Instead her eyes went to the small face of Emily, who now peered out from the parlor doorway to watch Alexis's exit with what looked like relief. And it was impossible not to wonder if it was simply because the older girl was so loud or if it was something deeper than that.

"I'm so sorry. She's just... Well, change is very hard for her," Grace said, her cheeks pink.

So was civility, but a sudden flicker of pity for Grace made Kat keep her mouth shut.

The creak of a floorboard made her stepmother turn to see her youngest watching them, and she motioned for Emily to come to her, which the little girl did.

"We've—we've just been practicing our reading, haven't we, dear?"

The girl nodded, her eyes on Kat.

Grace gave her a quick hug that it looked like she needed more than her daughter did. "Emily's already working on her long vowel sounds. She's quite good, really. Her kindergarten teacher was so impressed with her, and Jonathan would have been so proud. Would you like to hear her read? Or are you..." She trailed off as if expecting Kat to beg off with protestations of a busy schedule.

Which was laughable, of course. There was no schedule and nothing to do but pray that the walls didn't close in on her. Even so, Kat's first instinct was to decline and to seek solitude somewhere else. It might have been the mention of her father or maybe the way the child who was studying her now looked so much like him, but for whatever reason, Kat opened her mouth to say no and instead found herself saying, "Okay."

Judging by the expression on her face, Grace was just as surprised by her response as she was. She recovered with admirable speed, though, and patted her youngest on the shoulder. "Won't that be nice? Come, sweetheart, let's go pick out a picture book, shall we? Maybe the one with the little train." Taking Emily by the hand, she led the way back into the parlor.

And, however awkwardly, Kat followed them.

◆◆◆

DINNER WAS CASUAL THAT night. And mostly quiet, too; Grace must have found some way to either cajole or threaten Alexis into upgrading from audible animosity to stony silence. The former was more likely.

They ate in the formal dining room instead of the kitchen even though the length of the table seemed almost absurd for only four people. It did, however, allow Alexis to sit several feet away from the rest of them, which might have been the plan all along. Her eyes met Kat's only once during the meal, and even though the delicate chandelier didn't cast the brightest of light, it was still more than enough to highlight the resentment simmering there.

"Michael will be by with the lawyer in the morning," Grace said amidst the clinking of silverware in what Kat guessed was an attempt to lighten the oppressiveness of the silence on the room. "With some paperwork for you."

"Finally going to get her committed?" came a snide voice from the other end of the table.

So much for stony silence. Kat paid her stepsister's remark no attention, suspecting it would be the best revenge on a spotlight craver like her, and only kept working at cutting her chicken.

Grace, however, shot her eldest daughter a warning look. "The estate lawyer. A Mr. Hargrove. Very pleasant man, and very knowledgeable, too. If you have any questions about the house and... and any plans you may have for it, I'm sure he can answer them for you."

She struck Kat as vaguely nervous. No, not nervous exactly—*uncertain* might have been more accurate. Unsure of her place now, maybe. Living in a kind of limbo while things got sorted out. It had to be odd for her, and more than a little uncomfortable. Had Kat's father thought to update his will after marrying Grace, the house might have gone to her instead. But he had probably not imagined parting with it himself so soon. Unsure of how to respond but feeling that she ought to respond somehow, Kat cleared her throat. "The house looks good, Grace. You've kept it up well."

It was a paltry sort of olive branch, she supposed, and Grace seemed startled to get it. She blinked before recovering. "Oh. Yes, well, I've certainly tried to. Can't get to everything at once, though. Something always seems to need attention around here. Given its age, I suppose that's to be expected, but naturally we've had to prioritize some projects over others, given the constraints on the estate's funds for its upkeep. Please use your fork, Emily, not your fingers."

The little girl complied with her mother's instructions, although she struggled forlornly to loosen a bite of her chicken from the bone with the proper utensil.

"We?" Kat repeated, trying to picture Alexis being helpful in any capacity and failing.

"Michael drives in from town now and then. He looks after us, doesn't he, girls? Anyway, I'm sure he's looking forward to saying hello."

Doubtful. Kat could count on one hand the number of conversations she could remember ever having with him the few times he came to the house for holidays, if the word "conversation" could even be applied to their brief interactions. And if as a little girl of ten she might have initially been in awe of him, seven years older as he was and so brooding, he had paid her so little attention that her fascination with him had soon cooled, and his constant rebuffs of her father's attempts to make friends had only hastened the process. Alexis at least had seemed to appreciate Jonathan Delancey's efforts to connect, and when her own father stood her up repeatedly for birthdays and holidays, it was Kat's who stepped in instead to help dry her tears and salvage the day. With Michael there were no such moments. He made it very clear that he neither missed his own father nor welcomed a substitute.

But let Grace paint it however she liked.

Alexis must have shared Kat's opinion to some degree, because she let out an incredulous snort as she stabbed a green bean with her fork and earned another look from her mother, for all the good that did.

Just another evening at home.

◆ CHAPTER NINE ◆

THE DINNER-THAT-WOULD-not-end finally came to a close somehow with Alexis insisting she had a phone call to make while everyone else cleared the table. No one objected, though; her departure lightened the atmosphere within moments. After dishes were done—the only dishwasher in this house was the kind that came and went on its own two legs; modernization had only gone so far—Grace and Emily retreated to the parlor. Instead of joining them, Kat pleaded jet lag. It was too early for sleeping, but the awkward conversation attempts at dinner had been all that she could handle for one evening. As for tomorrow's meeting... Well, she would worry about getting through that tomorrow.

Night had fallen. The entryway was dark except for one light sconce that hung above the first landing; no sense wasting electricity to light a space people didn't linger in, after all. Kat stood at the base of the stairs and looked up, trying unsuccessfully to pierce the shadows at the top with her eyes.

Just a house...

She put one hand on the smooth banister and fought the urge to turn and flee the other way out through the front door. What was she so afraid of? Shadows? Shadows never bothered her back home. Then again, the shadows at Delancey Manor had always seemed darker to her than most others did.

The sound of a pair of hands clapping in the parlor, delicate and ladylike, caught her attention, and although she knew she was probably just looking for a reason to postpone going upstairs, Kat abandoned the banister to step forward just far enough to be able to catch a glimpse inside the sitting room at what Grace and Emily were doing.

They were reading again, seated beside each other on a sofa whose velvet was worn embarrassingly thin, Emily sounding out the words with Grace prompting her if she got stuck. It was a homey scene, and although it wasn't the kind of one in which Kat belonged now, it used to be. Back when her mother used to curl up under a throw blanket with a cup of tea in one hand and a book in the other.

No, wait—not a book. A crossword puzzle with black and white squares on the pages that Kat could see when she glanced up at them from where she played with her toys on the floor. Sometimes her mother would grumble over a hard clue until her husband would look up from whatever book he was reading and save the day with the correct answer. And her mother would smile at him, and he would smile back and perhaps get up from his chair long enough to put another piece of wood on the fire and to kiss his wife.

It was a lovely image, but it dissipated from Kat's mind as Emily turned her head to look toward the doorway. Instinct or maybe habit made Kat step back out of view before the little girl could spot her. The move brought her close to another door, this one to the library. And since she still didn't feel ready to face the dark stairs yet, she opened the library door instead.

The parlor might have been her mother's favorite room in the manor, but this room had been her father's habitat of choice. Kat's hand found the light and switched it on. Books, books, and more books, everywhere she turned. Dark paneling on the walls combined with the desk and endless bookcases made her think of elite gentleman's clubs; all that was missing was someone smoking a cigar or drinking a glass of port.

The room had been off-limits to her when her father first inherited the home, and she had never been told why exactly. Just that there had been some sort of accident in there, and her father wanted to make sure no more accidents could happen before he allowed her to venture inside. And so the room had been kept locked while her father did something in there with a toolbox until he was satisfied whatever he'd been working on had done the trick. Being only five years old at the time, Kat hadn't been all that interested in the reasons why she couldn't go in; the simple fact that she couldn't enter, though, made her wonder all the more what lay inside. "Like a moth to a flame," her father had observed once, catching her trying to peek through behind him one day as he'd entered. But he hadn't been angry with her. He was never angry, not really.

Once she was allowed inside and had a chance to satisfy her curiosity, the room no longer held as much interest for her as before—especially once she realized that there seemed to be no picture books for children among the vast collection of reading material on the shelves. Oh, one or two of the larger books had photographs of faraway landscapes in them, but nothing to capture the attention of a little girl who was hoping for something more along the lines of Dr. Seuss.

The tremendous globe that sat in one corner intrigued her, though, and seeing it now Kat ventured further into the room to run her fingers over it. She'd spent more than one rainy afternoon playing imaginary explorer in this room as a child, and occasionally she'd even been able to tear her father away from his books for a few minutes to play the game with her. No easy task considering how often he had his nose buried in them. Even when she couldn't get him to join in with her, she often contented herself with curling up on the plush chair nearby and watching him. It was better than playing alone in her room, or being alone anywhere in the house for that matter.

The globe was dusty now; her fingers came away from it grey. Apparently it didn't hold the same interest for Emily as it had for Kat, or perhaps she simply wasn't allowed in here. Kat had seen enough of mother and daughter to guess that Grace kept a close eye on her youngest. Or maybe it was the chill air that kept her out. It had always been colder in this room than in the rest of the downstairs. Well, in some spots anyway. That was one thing her father had never been able to fix, in spite of his best efforts, and so her mother had stuck to the warmth of the parlor while her father merely put on an extra sweater.

The books were less dusty than the globe, although when Kat pulled one from off the shelf and blew on the top, a small cloud resulted that made her turn her head away to avoid breathing it in. She glanced at the title. Small wonder this one hadn't been read recently. Shipping lanes of the eighteenth century didn't exactly make for gripping reading material. Even her father probably hadn't read this one. She put it back where it belonged and tried another whose spine looked vaguely familiar even though there was no title on it to jog her memory. Opening it, she realized why. This one was a private journal, one belonging to one Richard Delancey according to the name inside the cover.

That was why it looked familiar. It had been one of her father's favorites, and he'd showed it to Kat more than once, perhaps hoping she'd develop the same interest that he had in their family's history. His hopes were in vain, though. Barely legible scrawl and faded photographs of people long dead fascinated him a lot more than they had her, and that was still true now. But because it had been a favorite of his, she held onto it instead of putting it back on the shelf.

The air around her had grown quite cool, surprising considering she'd left the door open. If anything, surely it ought to have grown warmer in here since she'd opened the door, but that had always been the way of this room. There were no obvious points of entry for a draft; even if her father hadn't checked the windows thoroughly for one, the heavy drapes which hung from floor to ceiling should have been able to block anything less than a full-scale gale. The current drapes were even heavier than the originals, too, which had to be replaced because of a stain on one of them.

Kat frowned, her memory struggling again. No, not precisely a stain—a scorch mark from something that had nearly burnt right through the material. Her mother had lamented over that fact. A single curtain ruined, and they all had to go then because those drapes had been original to the house and matching ones couldn't be found or recreated. The new ones—new*er* anyway, since they'd hung in their place for well over a decade now—seemed to fit in just fine with the old décor, but the drafts still remained.

The easiest answer to the problem, at least the easiest one at the moment, was for Kat to simply leave. Time to bite the bullet and go upstairs anyway. She started to return the journal to its place on the shelf, then paused and ran her hand over the cover, lightly as if it might break otherwise. Gingerly, she opened it and traced the edges of a sepia-toned photograph that looked too brittle to risk disturbing further. An older man, bearded and grim.

Her father's voice echoed in her head. *See, Kat? That's Richard Delancey. He's the one who built this place. He's your great- great- great, well, something or other. Mine, too.*

Whatever paste had been holding the picture to the page for so many years gave way, and the photo slipped from the book to flutter to the floor. Kat could practically hear her father's horrified gasp, so she picked up the picture with as much care as a collector might handle a Ming vase and closed it up inside the book again for safekeeping. She would bring it with her to her room. It wasn't exactly a memento of her father's, but it was close, considering how often he read it. If she had to be back at Delancey Manor, and if the memories had to come flooding back, at least some of them could be good ones.

Holding the book close to her, Kat switched the light off and closed the door behind her.

◆◆◆

THE SECOND FLOOR LANDING was as dark as ever. At this rate, she was going to have to start carrying a flashlight around with her, just to keep herself from balking like this every time she climbed to this point of the stairs. Shadows, she reminded herself, hating the sheen of perspiration developing on her skin. Only shadows.

And then one of them moved above her.

She gasped and pressed herself against the wall before she recognized the familiar silhouette of her stepsister getting up from where she'd been sitting farther up on one of the third flight's steps. Waiting for her.

"Always were jumpy, weren't you?" came Alexis's voice with an undisguised hint of malice as she paused a step above Kat, whose pulse was thudding loudly in her ears. "Maybe you need to up whatever meds you're on."

Spiteful, vindictive little—

Kat bit back the words she wanted to call her stepsister and settled for giving her a hard and unblinking stare instead.

It seemed to have the desired effect, because Alexis froze in place before being the first to break eye contact. Shifting what Kat realized was a tote bag—no doubt a designer one, too, and expensive—on her arm, Alexis brushed past Kat and started down the stairs, pausing long enough to shoot back, "You know, everyone else may be too gutless to say it to your face, but they're all thinking the same thing. You were a nut job even before you swallowed your little pharmaceutical cocktail and tried to off yourself. You make people's skin crawl just by being in the same room, and nobody wants you here. Why don't you do us all a favor and either go home or find another bottle of pills and finish what you started?"

If she wanted crazy, it wouldn't be hard to give it to her. "Do you lock your door at night when you go to sleep?" Kat took a single step toward the edge of the landing as if she might follow the other young woman down and lowered her voice to barely above a whisper. "You should."

There was enough light trickling upward from the downstairs wall sconce for Kat to see her stepsister's eye twitch. Then Alexis gave her the finger and hurried the rest of the way down the stairs. "Mom," she hollered out loud enough that Grace could have heard her no matter where she was in the house, "I'm staying in town at Tricia's tonight. You guys and the freak show upstairs have fun. Hope she doesn't murder you in your sleep." Then the front door slammed shut, and she and her tote bag were gone.

Letting out the breath she was holding, Kat turned away before Grace's bewildered face could appear at the base of the stairs in search of an explanation.

The lock on her door seemed to have been enough to keep Alexis out, because there were no unpleasant surprises waiting for Kat in her room. It was stuffy, though, perhaps from being shut up so long, so Kat opened one of the windows just a crack to let in some of the cool night air before changing into a nightshirt, early as it was, and sinking onto the bed.

She left the journal from the library on the bedside table, unread. Tomorrow she might look through some of its pages, but not tonight. Tonight she was too restless, too jittery. No thanks to Alexis. Her hand hovered for several moments at the switch of her bedside lamp before she was able to make herself turn it off and plunge the room into darkness.

Not total darkness, though. She'd left the outer curtains open in order to let the air move freely, and the moon was big enough to illuminate vague shapes in the room. Still, she felt a sudden panic at the blackness around her, and for a moment started to reach for the light to turn it back on.

No. She was not a frightened child anymore. She stopped herself just in time and drew her hand back under the sheet. Either she was here to bury her fears or she wasn't; there was no going halfway. So she left the light off and lay in the dark, her eyes wide open and staring at the ceiling above her while a light breeze stirred the gauzy lace of the curtains.

She was still wide awake when she heard the sounds of feet on the stairs and Grace's voice as she reminded her youngest to brush her teeth before going to bed. And suddenly Kat wondered if nighttime was as uneasy a time for the little girl as it had been for her at that age. Night terrors never seemed to be a problem for Alexis, but then she had been nearly ten years old by the time she moved into the house. If any lights ever sputtered out in her room, she never said so, and Alexis was not one to keep any sort of dissatisfaction to herself. But Emily was different.

I don't like this house.

Kat pictured the little girl hunched over on the porch step and hugging herself as she said the words. There was a kind of misery in that posture that she recognized all too well. A helplessness, too. She propped herself up on her elbows and listened to the sounds of the water running in the bathroom as her young half-sister completed her nightly toiletry routine as asked, and it seemed to her that it took longer than it should have. Delaying the inevitable bedtime?

Finally the trickle of faint light under her door that came from the bathroom light further down the hall winked out, and the floorboards creaked ever so faintly as small feet crept over them. A moment later the click of a door handle settling into place signaled Emily's retreat to her room, reluctant or otherwise, and all was quiet.

Still Kat listened, not entirely sure what she expected to hear. The creaks and moans of an old house maybe that sounded somehow like something else, something out of a fireside story or a child's bad dream.

And she felt five years old all over again.

◆◆◆

SOMETHING WOKE HER.

Kat opened her eyes with that vague, unsettled feeling that comes when a person wakes in unfamiliar surroundings, and she blinked her eyes several times in the darkness before she recognized the outlines of the desk and the armoire and remembered where she was. It did not make her feel better.

Because something was off, something that was wrong enough to wake her from sleep. But what it was, she couldn't tell.

Alexis, she thought immediately, almost reflexively, and she threw the sheet off with a flicker of annoyance before going to check her door. But it was still locked, and the key was still right where she'd left it in the lock. There were no creaking floorboards on the other side of her door, either, or sounds of retreating footsteps. And besides, she remembered now, Alexis had gone to stay in town tonight. Her stepsister was not what had awakened her.

The chill in her room might have though. Goosebumps were raised up along her arms, and Kat rubbed them to warm herself. Any stuffiness that had been in the air earlier was gone now, replaced by coolness that was startlingly icy considering that it was summer. Early summer, yes, but still summer.

The curtains on the open window stirred, and Kat crossed the room to close the window up again. It stuck, and she had to use all of her strength to budge it back down where it belonged. But not before one last gust of breeze came through the window, carrying with it a familiar scent. Lavender.

Kat jerked away from the window as if she'd been burned, stumbling backward in the dark until the backs of her legs hit the bed, and she lost her balance and fell more than sat down on it.

"Stop it," she whispered. "It's all in your head. Just stop it." She heard a sound like that of a trapped animal and hated herself when she realized it came from her own throat.

She would not come unglued. She would not. Mind over matter, even a broken mind.

So she forced her attention and her senses to what she knew was real: the smoothness of the wooden bedframe beneath her fingers, the softness of the sheet as she lay back down and pulled it up around her, the sound of her heartbeat in her ears…

And she dug her fingers into her palm to keep herself from reaching for the lamp.

◆ CHAPTER TEN ◆

HE WOULD BE LYING if he said he enjoyed coming out here. Which might be why he never did say so in the first place unless pressed. Not that he had a problem with lying when the situation called for it, but conversations about the manor in general left a sour taste in Michael's mouth, so he generally left the topic happily alone unless it was unavoidable. Today it was unavoidable.

Pulling his Mercedes to a stop in front of the manor, Michael got out and glanced up at the place with a familiar flicker of distaste.

Mr. Hargrove had followed him out from the city and stepped out of his own car now, also a Mercedes although not as new a model as Michael's. His suit was not as new or as expensive as Michael's either, not by half, and it seemed to make the man more deferential. "It really is a magnificent old place, isn't it?" said the stocky white-haired lawyer, casting an admiring glance at the house.

Spoken like someone who wasn't responsible for its upkeep. Michael was the one his mother turned to when problems with the house arose and had been ever since she'd been widowed. Ironic, since the only thing he knew about repairing broken things was how to search the yellow pages for someone who actually knew how to fix them, which was apparently a far cry from the way the sainted Jonathan Delancey had handled things; then again, in Grace's eyes, Jonathan could probably have parted seas if he wanted to. In any account, Michael was now far more intimately familiar with the home's quirks of decay than he would have liked thanks to the reports he received from the numerous repairmen that had to be called in on a semi-regular basis. Loose shutters, leaky pipes, unreliable wiring... He grimaced. Give him modern convenience and sleekness any day, and that opinion had nothing to do with his feelings about the man who'd introduced them to this place. Well, not entirely anyway.

And now Jonathan's daughter was back. She didn't inspire the same sort of bitterness in Michael that her father had. Didn't inspire any feeling, really. Katherine—Kat, he reminded himself belatedly—Delancey was little more than a blip on the radar of his history, a vague presence that he dimly remembered hovering in the background during his few visits to the place.

Except, of course, for one visit.

"Shall we?" suggested Hargrove with a brisk but amiable gesture at the house, interrupting Michael's train of thought.

Right. They were on the clock. Michael led the other man up the porch steps to the front door where he knocked once to announce their arrival but opened the door without waiting for an invitation to enter. As often as he was a visitor out here these days, he didn't really need one.

Before Michael could call out, his mother came bustling down the stairs to greet them, a practiced smile on her face. Not that it was an insincere expression, just automatic and polished. "Thank you so much for making the trip out here today," she told the lawyer while at the same time offering her cheek to Michael to kiss. "I hope it wasn't too much trouble."

"Not at all," the man assured her, his manner as polished as hers. His eyes traveled over the elegant foyer. "Been several years, hasn't it? Looks just as lovely as it did then."

There was no sign of Kat. Michael barely noticed the other two as pleasantries were wrapped up, his attention on the stairs as if he expected to see her come down them at any moment. And for just a moment, he had an all-too vivid flashback to that day six years ago at Jonathan's wake when he'd been sent in search of Kat only to find her on the bathroom floor, an empty pill bottle beside her.

The sound of his name made him tear his gaze away from the stairs. "Sorry?"

"I said, why don't we all go into the parlor? The library's much too drafty, and I think we'll be so much more comfortable in here," his mother said, gesturing toward the sitting room. "Would you like coffee or tea, Mr. Hargrove?"

"Coffee, thank you. Cream, no sugar."

"Certainly. It will just take a minute."

Once the older man was seated in the parlor and out of earshot, Grace lowered her voice and put a hand on her son's arm. "Kat's... running a little late."

Michael frowned, incredulous. "She's not here?"

"Oh, no, she's here. She's just—she's had some trouble sleeping, that's all, and I suspect that last night was particularly rough. The shadows under her eyes..." Grace shook her head. "She'll be down shortly, though. Until then, could you please keep Mr. Hargrove occupied?"

She knew he would, so there wasn't much point in answering beyond a nod. "About Kat..."

Grace looked at him questioningly.

The memory of a young girl lying unconscious intruded once more. "How does she seem?"

His mother hesitated before answering. "I really couldn't say," she admitted finally, one hand playing with the sleeve of the other in a nervous habit he recognized. "But then I couldn't have answered that before... before everything happened, either. She and I have never been close, Michael, you know that. So far she's kept mostly to herself."

"Why is she really here?"

"I beg your pardon?"

"She didn't have to come all this way just for paperwork. So why did she? Is she planning on staying?"

His mother's eyes lit up with sudden alarm. "She hasn't said anything like that, no. You don't really think—no, I can't imagine she plans to do that. She doesn't even like it here."

"She said that?"

"Well, no, but the way she looks at this place and jumps at every sound—she *can't* intend to stay. Can she? After everything that's happened here, I shouldn't think she'd want to."

"No kidding," Michael said with a pointed look at his mother and the urge to shake her.

She noticed and gave him a look of her own. "Please don't start. Not today. I can already feel a headache on the horizon."

It was a familiar excuse, and an old one, but this was not the best time to press. He held his hands up in surrender, and that was when a sound from the direction of the stairs made him look up.

The young woman staring back at him appeared to be assessing him as much as he was assessing her. So this was Kat now. Interesting, what six years could do. There were no more traces of childhood left in her features, although that could have had less to do with the passage of time and more to do with why her childhood had ended so much sooner than most others. He'd seen a picture of her mother once years ago, striking and lovely; Kat looked more like her now than she used to. Knowing his own mother's insecurities about the first Mrs. Jonathan Delancey, Michael immediately felt guilty for noticing. But where Lily's eyes had sparkled with warmth and laughter in her photograph, Kat's were harder and every bit as shadowed as his mother suggested.

"Oh, good, there you are," Grace greeted her, relief visible on her face. "Mr. Hargrove's waiting for us in the parlor, and I was just about to fix some coffee. Would you like some?"

Kat shook her head and descended the rest of the steps, stopping when she was still a few feet away from the two of them.

Had they been true relatives, a hug might have been appropriate for the occasion, or maybe a kiss on the cheek. Even a handshake, although stiff and formal, would have been warmer than simply studying each other this way. But they weren't family, not really, just two people forced into a reluctant proximity because of the choices their parents had made. Choices he had always suspected Kat was about as pleased about as he was, if for different reasons.

So he made no move to close the gap between them and settled instead for a polite greeting. "Kat. You're looking... well."

Her mouth twitched at the corners as if she knew perfectly well that was a lie.

And it was a lie, since up close like this the shadows under her eyes were even more apparent, but she still looked far better than she had the last time he'd seen her. That time she'd been grey and cold to the touch as he picked her up from the bathroom floor and yelled out for someone to call for paramedics. Her eyes had fluttered open once, just once, when he'd shaken her in an effort to get her to wake up, and the look in them had unnerved him more than anything before or since.

Her eyes were guarded now.

"I'll just..." Grace gestured toward the kitchen and excused herself with what looked like relief.

Michael waited until she was gone, but there was no reason to beat about the bush. "Planning to stay long?"

"Just a week or so," Kat returned, and her tone was as cool as the rest of her as her gaze traveled past him and in the direction of the parlor.

He was used to being on the receiving end of many things from women, but cool detachment was not one of them. It made him more blunt than usual. "And what else do you plan?"

That brought her attention back to him. She frowned questioningly.

"You own a house now, Kat. That's no small thing. Surely you must have some idea of what you want to do with it."

"Must I?"

Was that sarcasm? He didn't know her well enough to tell. "No, I suppose you don't. Not from your perspective anyway. But since I have family living here—"

"I have no plans, Michael. Tell Grace she can relax."

"Easier said than done," he muttered out of the corner of his mouth, moving out of the way and gesturing for her to go ahead of him. She did, studying him as she went.

He returned the favor.

◆ CHAPTER ELEVEN ◆

MR. HARGROVE DID MOST of the talking, but it was Michael's eyes on her that Kat was most aware of throughout the meeting in the parlor. It might just have been habit—she suspected he studied lots of women and was probably studied right back by most of them—but she didn't flatter herself. There was nothing of that kind of interest in his glance. It was purely watchful. Wary.

Small wonder. She hadn't meant to be vague in response to his questions about the house, and his concern about living arrangements for his mother and sisters was perfectly understandable and justified. It was only that she hadn't thought past her visit here to consider future possibilities. Facing down childhood fears had seemed like more than enough to fill her plate while she was here.

But now...

She heard her name and forced herself to pay attention to the lawyer's words. He'd come well-prepared and seemed to know his job well; he laid things out quickly and smoothly, and he anticipated questions before they were even asked. By Michael, not by Kat; Kat signed the papers that were put in front of her, but she spoke little. By choice. The few questions that had started swirling in her head were not questions she cared to ask in front of either Michael or Grace.

"And there you have it, Miss Delancey. It's more or less official now," Mr. Hargrove said with admirable joviality considering how unresponsive Kat had been for most of the morning beyond one-word answers. It wasn't that she was trying to be rude; she just wasn't good at chitchat. "Should you have any questions at any time, here's my card. Thank you for the hospitality." This he directed at a smiling Grace, and then he offered his hand to Michael. "A pleasure, Mr. Fairmont. And now if you'll all excuse me, I have another appointment back in town."

Kat slipped the man's card into her pocket. Her budding questions could wait until later. Following him out to his car now would likely only make Grace nervous all over again, and the older woman had only just started to relax now that the meeting was over and all loose ends appeared to be tied up. There might even have been a touch of actual warmth to her smile as she turned it onto Kat.

"Well, good. That's all done with," she said as Michael showed the lawyer out. "Legal business is never very pleasant, is it? But Mr. Hargrove certainly seems nice enough. Are you sure you don't want coffee, Kat?" She began setting cups and saucers on the little tray she'd used to carry them in with in the first place. "A little caffeine to help perk you up a bit?"

Just how sleep-deprived did she look? But she was jittery enough most of the time without a cup of fresh brew, so Kat only shook her head again.

"Some breakfast, then. Or—oh, my—is it really so late? I suppose it's closer to lunch now. You must be starving. There's plenty of sandwich fixings in the fridge, you know. I loaded up on groceries the day before you arrived."

She was babbling as she stacked the dishes so carefully on top of each other. She did that a lot when Kat was around. Or was she like that with most people? Guilt over recent thoughts made Kat try to be conciliatory. She searched blindly for something polite to say and settled for, "Those are very pretty."

Grace paused and blinked at her for a moment before seeming to realize what Kat meant. "Oh, the dishes? Yes, they are, aren't they?"

She turned a delicate teacup over in her hand. "They've always been a favorite of mine, but I so seldom use them. Always afraid they might break, you know? I mean, they're so old, after all. But every once and a while, if we have company—" She stopped abruptly, and her expression became cautious. "Although perhaps you'd prefer if I didn't use them."

"What? Why?"

"Well, they're yours, aren't they? Family heirlooms. Maybe I shouldn't have—" Grace bit her lip.

She'd only meant to make an innocent observation to her stepmother, something casual that might mimic the kind of small talk that came so naturally to others. Why was it always so hard between them? "It's fine, Grace. Use them all you like, really. That's what dishes are for, aren't they?"

"I suppose." Grace's shoulders, which had tensed, relaxed again, and she resumed stacking things on the breakfast tray. "It does seem a pity for things so pretty to be locked away in a cupboard all the time anyway. You know, we ought to take them all out and have a special family dinner, don't you think that would be nice? Something to celebrate your homecoming properly. Jonathan would have liked that."

Probably not as much as Grace seemed to think so, but Kat chose not to express that opinion. She didn't have to. Michael walked back in just in time to hear his mother's pronouncement and responded with a grimace. She had the distinct feeling that his expression had less to do with the idea of dinner than it did with her father, and her gaze when he glanced at her turned a little cooler.

"Tomorrow night," Grace continued, oblivious to them and growing more animated by the second. "You'll come, of course, won't you, Michael?"

"I already have a dinner date tomorrow."

"Well... bring her with you, then, whoever she is. We can set an extra place. How often do we have everybody together like this?"

“I don’t think—”

“Oh, please, darling. It would mean so much to me to have everyone here.”

Michael looked like he’d just tasted a lemon, but he only sighed in what must have been a yes, because Grace patted his cheek before lifting the tray.

And nearly dropped it again when a cry came from upstairs. Emily’s voice.

Michael was the fastest of them to react, first darting a hand out to keep the suddenly wobbling tray from falling from his mother’s hands before bolting towards the doorway. It was enough of a delay, though, that Kat was able to beat him to the stairs even if he was close behind. Even Grace moved with admirable speed to follow, huffing breathlessly by the time she reached the top of the first flight of stairs.

The door to Emily’s room—Kat’s old room—was closed, and for just a moment, the sight of it along with memories of old fears made Kat balk. That slight hesitation resulted in Michael bumping into her, and he moved her aside roughly as he muttered something under his breath that she couldn’t make out. She jumped at the contact, and by the time she recovered, even Grace had overtaken her to hustle through the door that Michael had just opened.

Coward, she thought at herself, ashamed at her behavior, and she made herself enter the room.

She stepped over the threshold in time to see both Grace and Michael kneel down beside the small form of Emily where she lay half-crumpled on the floor beside the corner of her bed, clutching at the back of her head and crying. “Sweetheart, what happened?” Grace asked her, trying to cradle her in her arms and examine her head for signs of injury at the same time. It was impossible to do both successfully, and Michael took over the examination part, brow furrowed in concentration as he did so.

"I—I was just...p-putting my doll b-back," the girl managed between tearful gasps, and Kat followed the direction of her half-sister's gaze to see a crumpled cloth figure slumped between a pair of stuffed animals on a shelf, and below them, a chair that the girl must have stood upon to reach them. And behind the chair, a lone roller skate lying in a precariously-placed proximity to one wooden bedpost. "And—and I s-slipped." She cried out then as Michael's fingers found a tender place on her scalp.

He drew them away and gave her a tiny chuck under the chin. "No bleeding, but there's one hell of a bump forming. Isn't there, kiddo?"

"Oh, honey," said Grace, her eyes lighting on the roller skate, kissing her daughter and chiding her at the same time, "that's why you're supposed to put your skates away when you're not using them, so accidents like this don't happen."

"But I did!" Emily insisted, her eyes wide and her tears still streaming down her pale cheeks.

"Emily—"

"I *did*!"

"Never mind that now," Grace soothed her, paler than usual herself. "Michael will drive us to the doctor now so you can feel all better, won't you, Michael?"

"I think an icepack is probably all she needs," he said, attempting in vain to examine the pupils of the girl's eyes as her mother hugged her tightly to her chest.

"Oh, Michael, please! What if it's a concussion or—or—"

"All right, fine, although at the moment I'm more worried about you accidentally smothering her to death. For the love of God, give her a little room to breathe, Mother. And you breathe, too, would you? She's not dying." Giving Grace an exasperated look, he scooped Emily from her stranglehold and into his own arms. "And please don't pass out halfway down the stairs, because I can't carry you both down at once."

"Gently. *Gently*," his mother pleaded, following him as he led the way out and wringing her hands together as she did so. "Try not to jostle her."

"So no tossing her over my shoulder like a sack of potatoes then?"

"Michael!"

Whatever reply he made to her was too faint for Kat to hear by that time, and she was only dimly aware of the sound of Michael's car starting up a few moments later. Her eyes and her attention were on the skate.

It was such an innocuous sort of thing, just a child's toy lying out in the middle of a child's room. Nothing particularly odd or out of place about it. Even Emily's insistence that she'd put it away wasn't so strange; most children were quick to deny wrongdoing for fear of getting into trouble, weren't they?

Kneeling down, Kat picked up the skate and turned it over in her hands.

Except...

Except that everything else in the room was so tidy and in its place, the sign of habits that by now she was sure Grace had drilled into her youngest, who was clearly far more malleable than Alexis. And because something about this stirred Kat's memory. It wasn't that there had been a steady stream of accidents when she was a child; they weren't so frequent and close together as to raise any red flags. Not for her mother or father anyway. Every child wound up with a few bumps and bruises now and then. It was only natural.

But there had been those times when something had been there that shouldn't have, something left lying out to trip her or something that slipped and fell when Kat knew—she *knew*—she'd put it away properly, or had never even taken it out to begin with. It was a mean house, she used to try to make her father understand, who would ruffle her hair in helpless bewilderment and then usually attempt to distract her with a story or a game. She should have tried harder.

Standing again, Kat put the skate in the bedroom closet where she found its mate and then closed the door again firmly, waiting for several long moments as if daring the house to spit it out again.

It didn't.

Still, she couldn't help but glance back over her shoulder as she left the room, and when she closed the door behind her, she jiggled the knob just to be sure that it had caught correctly and would stay that way.

Something made her turn her head abruptly, something like a flash of movement but that couldn't have been, because there was nothing there. And she realized then that for the first time in a very long time, she was alone in the house.

Her hands began to shake, and it took everything within her not to rush for the stairs in headlong panic.

Don't let it see you're scared, a voice urged inside her head, and it was a ridiculous thing to think, a crazy thing—what was "it," anyway?—but she did her best to swallow back her anxiety anyway and instead made herself take small, slow steps toward the stairs. Deep, even breaths. Eyes focused ahead instead of darting around the way they wanted to.

Don't let it see...

There was something behind her. Surely there was something there? Sneaking up unheard.

Eyes forward. Don't give in. Don't panic.

Reaching the banister, she stretched out a hand to take hold of it and saw that her fingers were trembling even more than before. She wrapped them around the wood to stop the movement. This was all in her head. There was nothing in the house, nothing coming up behind her—

She felt breath on the back of her neck and whipped her head around with a jolt of sudden terror.

Nothing.

There was nothing there. The hall was empty. She was alone after all with her fragile and overactive mind playing tricks on her.

Except that the door to Emily's room was now open.

◆ CHAPTER TWELVE ◆

SOMEHOW KAT MADE IT downstairs and out onto the front porch before her knees gave out on her. She collapsed at the edge of it, fighting the urge to dry heave.

She'd shut the bedroom door. Had *definitely* shut it. Hadn't she? Or was that her mind playing games with her again? Her senses had tricked her before.

No, no, it had been closed. She'd tested it to be sure. She *had*

But had she tested it enough? Maybe it hadn't caught after all, maybe she just wasn't remembering right. Because the alternative...

Hauling herself upright with the aid of one hand on the porch railing, Kat wrenched herself around so she could eye the front door, half-expecting something to follow her out through it and possibly drag her back inside. Her pulse roared in her ears.

A minute passed. Then another. Nothing monstrous appeared, and the only sound was the breeze rustling through branches. Still Kat's heart pounded, and several more minutes went by before she summoned the courage to draw near enough to the door to pull it closed. Then she backed away from it and down the front steps, reluctant to look away even for a moment because a moment might be all it needed. It had always been a mean house, after all.

She didn't stop backing away until she was several yards from the structure, and even then she couldn't bring herself to let her guard down, not right away. But the breeze and the blue sky overhead and the sun shining all eventually worked to pierce the haze of anxiety in her head until the fear that had threatened to choke her on the porch finally eased its grip. And standing here in the open and in the daylight, it was hard to see anything more than just an ordinary manor in front of her, plain and simple. Just a house, and only someone with a disturbed mind could possibly believe anything different.

But she chose to wait outside for the others to return.

◆◆◆

IT WAS A LONG wait. Hunger gnawed at Kat's stomach by the time Michael's car appeared around the bend in the driveway, but the closest she could bring herself to going inside the house was to sit on the bottom-most porch step.

Michael must have interpreted her presence there as anxiety over Emily's condition—and maybe it should have been, she thought with a guilty start—because he spoke even before he was completely out of the car. "She's fine. Just needs an ice pack and some ibuprofen, that's all. And maybe a helmet in the future."

The little girl slid out from the back seat and smiled wanly as if in an attempt to prove Michael's point, once again seeming oddly older than her few years. Grace, however, was still quick to hustle out and around to her from the passenger's seat as if she thought Emily might keel over at any second.

Michael gave her an exasperated look. "You're hovering again."

"I'm being a mother," she returned, scooping Emily up as if she was incapable of walking the short distance to the house.

Kat let them go by her without a word, although her head did turn to follow their progress, and her eyes met Emily's. The little girl stared right back, and Kat would have sworn she turned a touch paler as they entered the house.

"She worries too much," Michael muttered, and either he had forgotten just to whom he was talking or he'd been thinking out loud and forgot she was there at all.

It was easy enough to remind him. Bluntly. "Tragic histories have that effect on people."

He blinked and then averted his gaze as if embarrassed, or at the very least uncomfortable. To his credit, he looked back at her a moment later. "Sorry."

There was no good response to that, at least none that came to mind, so she didn't try to offer one.

If he minded, he didn't show it. Instead he cleared his throat and climbed the steps to disappear inside the house after his mother and Emily.

She would have to follow, of course. Staying out on the porch forever was not an option, and at least the house was less unnerving when there were other people inside it. And she would have to go in sooner rather than later unless she wanted to make them wonder at her behavior. Wonder more than usual, at least. And wondering might lead to questions, questions that she couldn't answer without appearing odder to them than she already did. Not that she cared much what kind of opinion any of them held of her, but oddness had a way of inviting others to poke and prod and delve more deeply than she cared for.

So finally, after another long minute and a deep breath, Kat forced herself to get up and go through the front door.

Voices came from the direction of the kitchen. Michael and Grace. Their words were too faint to make out, and Kat's feet carried her forward instinctively to bring her closer. Before she got close enough to hear anything properly, she passed the open door to the parlor, and movement out of the corner of her eye drew her attention.

Alone and wearing an unnervingly grim expression, Emily lay on the sofa, propped up on a pillow. Her fingers played with the hem of her shirt in an unconscious sort of way, but her eyes had a distant look to them that was anything but casual. And they were turned in the direction of the upstairs as if she was listening for something. She started when Kat moved to the doorway.

"Sorry," Kat told her.

The girl turned her eyes downward.

"Head better?"

Her answer was a silent nod.

She was about as chatty as Kat usually was. Was it DNA that made them so similar, or something else? "Emily..."

The little girl didn't look up.

Kat came the rest of the way into the room and sat down on the other end of the sofa, barely. She perched on the very edge of it, several inches of space still between herself and her half-sister, and still she felt awkward at the close proximity. If Emily did, though, she didn't show it. "You didn't leave your skate out, did you?"

Emily's head came up, and she shook it with wide, startled eyes, then winced.

"Stuff like this..." Kat faltered and tried again. "Have there been other times like that?"

Instead of answering, Emily glanced back upwards and then around the room as if afraid of eavesdroppers before resuming her nervous twisting of her shirt's hem.

There was no one else there, not even hovering in the doorway, but Kat dropped her voice to a whisper anyway. "Have there?"

After a moment, the girl nodded.

"Like what?"

"Things get broken, or lost."

"What kinds of things?"

"My toys. The ones I like the best. Mom says I need to be more careful with them, but I *am* careful. I am." Emily's eyes grew red around the edges, and she blinked.

"I believe you." And she did, because it was exactly the kind of thing she'd tried to explain herself to adults when she was Emily's age. Memories came swirling back, vague and fuzzy around the edges when she tried to pin them down.

"You do?"

Kat nodded.

"Mom doesn't. She thinks I just forget things and that's why my toys get ruined and why my kitty went away."

"Kitty?"

"Lucy. She was my birthday present, but she didn't like it here, and she ran away."

And suddenly there was a flash of golden fur in Kat's mind, a wagging tail and soft brown eyes. Rosie. She was meant to comfort Kat in the months after her mother's death, that was why her father had given the puppy to her, his own heartache still written all over his face in spite of his efforts to hide it. A sweet puppy who seemed to take her job as caretaker seriously and even got to sleep in Kat's bed at night, which helped Kat finally sleep better except for the times when Rosie would growl in the dark at things that weren't there. Two weeks with that warm little body curled up next to hers, soothing and safe and warm, until they found her dangling from between two third-floor banister railings with a broken neck. A strange accident, her father had admitted, and one he couldn't ever quite explain. There were no more pets after that. "Ran away?"

"That's what Mom says. She says maybe I can have another one in a few years, but I don't think I want one." Emily had stopped blinking, but her eyes were still red when she looked up at Kat. "I think—"

Her mother bustled into the room then with what looked like ice wrapped in a kitchen towel, and Kat instinctively gave up her place on the sofa to her, crossing instead to the window.

"There now, how's that?" Grace pressed the makeshift ice pack to her daughter's head.

"Good," said Emily, but she grimaced as she said it. Maybe she would have made that same pronouncement no matter what her mother did.

Michael appeared in the doorway and watched his mother fret over Emily, and Kat couldn't help but study both Grace and him for some sign that they felt any kind of unease at all being in the house. The earlier anxiety that had taken hold of her had lifted, but its aftereffects still lingered. Did they really feel nothing out of the ordinary?

Maybe her gaze was more intense than she'd realized, because Michael seemed to become suddenly aware of it. He turned his head to study her back, his frown a question.

The front door opened, slamming shut a moment later, and Alexis popped into view behind her brother. She did a double take at the sight of the group and the ice pack pressed to Emily's head. "What? What did I miss?"

◆ CHAPTER THIRTEEN ◆

ORDINARILY KAT WOULD HAVE retreated to the solitude of her room in the evening, but tonight she stayed in the parlor, and when Grace went to tuck Emily in for the night, Kat made herself stay put until her stepmother returned. Grace was too well-mannered to say anything if she thought Kat's presence there was out of character, but the way she spent far longer than was necessary straightening things in the room and tidying things that didn't need it told a different story.

No need for either of them to squirm any longer than they had to. Kat cleared her throat and broke the silence. "She doesn't seem to like it here much."

Grace looked up from the lamp she was in the process of moving a quarter of an inch closer to the center of the end table on which it rested. "I beg your pardon?"

"Emily. She doesn't seem to like the house." 'Seem to' was an unnecessary part in the sentence. She'd only added it to appease Grace's preference for conversation that was soft around the edges.

Apparently she hadn't softened it enough, though. Grace froze for a moment before forcing a smile that was a little too stiff to be completely sincere. "I'm not sure what you mean. This is a lovely home. We all think so."

"She doesn't."

The smile grew even stiffer, and Grace abandoned the lamp in favor of a potted plant whose few brown leaves were apparently in need of plucking. Her hands moved delicately, but there was a kind of ruthlessness in the way she let nothing less than spotless green remain. "Emily is a sensitive child with an active imagination, that's all. This is a wonderful place for a child to grow up in. Room to play, a beautiful yard to run around in, fresh air..."

"She's afraid here."

Now the smile disappeared altogether. "This is her home, Kat. The place her father wanted her to grow up in. And it's one of the few ties she has left to him."

There was a firmness to her tone that was unfamiliar; Kat had touched a nerve.

"I'm not blind, Kat. I see how she jumps at shadows sometimes, but that's because she's so sensitive. It's not the house, it's her, and she'll grow out of it in time. People do, you know."

"Not all of them." The shadows under Kat's eyes had to serve as an excellent reminder of that fact, and she very pointedly stared at her stepmother to better allow her to see them.

A variety of emotions crossed Grace's face, warring with each other. It was easy enough to guess at what she was thinking.

Yes, but Emily's not like you.

And maybe she *was* thinking something along those lines, but her next words, spoken more softly, caught Kat off guard. "There were good times here, too, Kat. Not just the bad. And they're worth holding on to." Then, perhaps taking advantage of Kat's momentary silence, she raised her voice and forced a little more cheer into it. "Well. I did want to use the good china for dinner tomorrow night, and there are several pieces that need a good dusting at the very least. Might as well get done what I can now. Excuse me."

Kat watched her go without a word. There seemed to be little point in saying anything else anyway. Grace saw what she wanted to see, and clearly the house had no intention of swaying her.

She'd done it again, just now. Attached intention to the manor, as if it was capable of thought or opinion. Maybe more. It was beginning to feel increasingly natural to do so, and the thing that disturbed her the most about that was that she wasn't sure if that meant she ought to be worried about her mind or about the house.

In spite of the relative warmth of the parlor, Kat wrapped her arms around herself and shivered.

There was no reason to wait for Grace to return. Most likely she wouldn't come back anyway as long as she knew Kat was in the room. It had always been like this between them. No open hostility—no hostility of any kind really. Just an awkward sort of distance that was forever present no matter what either did, and to be fair, Grace had probably made more of a genuine effort to cross it than Kat had. Or at least she had when Kat's father was still alive, to please him. Since his death, neither of them had made much of an overture. Why would they? There was no common ground between them, not with him gone. Except now there was Emily.

No, not just now. For six years Emily had been here, and Kat ought to have done something about that sooner. It wasn't that she'd consciously tried to block out this part of her life and the people in it—not any more than she'd done with every other area of her life anyway. It just... happened. And she'd managed to all but forget that there was a little girl living in Delancey Manor who was at least part of Kat's father, no matter how small that part might be.

This was not a good house to be forgotten in.

Kat thought about that as she made herself climb the stairs to her bedroom, and especially as the door to Emily's room came into view at the end of the darkened hallway. A closed door, just as she was sure—almost sure—it had been earlier today. She stared at it a long time before going into her own room and shutting that door as well.

No, this was not a good house to be forgotten in at all. She should have known that, should have remembered that before now. And when Kat finally slid under the sheets, it was with newfound guilt hanging over her.

It might have been guilt that woke her sometime later in the dark, or maybe it was just the usual dreams; she was more than a little surprised that she'd fallen asleep at all. But whatever it was that woke her, it left Kat with a vaguely panicky feeling. Giving in to impulse, she threw the sheets off and stumbled toward the door in the dark, feeling around for the key with which she had locked the door; Alexis was back under the roof, after all. Finding it, she turned it and pulled open the door to burst out into the hallway on silent feet.

There was nothing there, just like there had been nothing there this morning when she'd fled from the house while in the throes of a full-on panic attack. But she waited there anyway, listening and peering into the shadows as far as she could. Her gaze made its way back to Emily's door and to the faint light that glowed underneath it from what must have been a night light. Oh, the memories that conjured up, and none of them were good. Sounds a little girl knew shouldn't be there, feelings that wouldn't go away no matter how hard she—

The light under Emily's door flickered and went out.

Nightlights failed for many reasons. Faulty wiring, broken parts, bulbs burning out... Her own had failed many times, too, and Kat's father had never been able to figure out why, no matter how many times he replaced it. And it would often work fine when he was in the room. It was only later, after Kat was alone, that it would sputter out again. She'd lain awake in that oppressive darkness countless times, terrified and unable to make anyone else understand why the darkness here felt so different to her than the darkness anywhere else. And that was enough to send her hurrying to Emily's door now.

Pausing, she pressed her ear against it to listen and thought she heard the sound of a muffled cry or whimper. "Emily?" she called softly, knocking twice with as little sound as possible—more of a tap, really—to avoid waking Grace up. Getting no answer, she turned the doorknob and thrust her head into the room to try again. "Emily? Are you all right?"

"K-Kat?"

"Yes." It was too dark to see much of anything, but enough moonlight pierced a crack between the curtains for Kat to be able to see the vague outline of Emily's head lifting from its place on her pillow. Too late she realized her own appearance out of nowhere was probably enough to unnerve the little girl all by itself. "I... I thought I heard something. I'm sorry if I scared you."

"My light went out."

"Yeah, I see." Slipping inside the room, Kat shut the door behind her and felt her way against the wall to where the window was, her steps wary in case something like the roller skate might find its way in front of her. Pulling the curtains apart a foot or more, she let in the moonlight and turned to where Emily lay.

Or had lain. She was sitting up now, bed sheets pulled up beneath her chin as if to shield her from something only she knew, and her fingers clutching them like a lifeline. The new light that filtered in made the whites of her small eyes all but glow in the dark, and they were wide with fear.

She was no good with kids. She never had been. So she didn't reach out to touch the girl or even so much as stroke her hair, which might have been the sisterly thing to do. Instead, Kat knelt down beside the bed and looked her in the face. "What is it? What happened?"

"M-My light went out," she repeated, her voice thin and whispery. "And I thought something was in here with me."

Kat's own voice was thin, and her body grew taut. "Why did you think that?"

Emily only sat there, silent and wide-eyed.

"Emily?" she pressed. "What made you think there was something in here?"

Finally, and with what sounded like great effort, the girl answered. "I don't know. I just did." She made a choking sound that Kat didn't recognize right away, and then she realized it was a sob being bitten back. "You think I'm making it up, don't you? You think it was just a bad dream."

No, she didn't, but even she knew it couldn't be a good idea to assure a young child that, yes, she absolutely believed that there was something off about this place. She shifted position so that she leaned sideways against the bed, her eyes on the moon as she struggled for the right words. "This used to be my room," she said finally. "Did you know that?"

In the dim moonlight, Emily shook her head.

"I used to have trouble sleeping in here, too."

"You did?"

Kat nodded.

"Sometimes Mom lets me sleep with her for a little while, but she thinks I'm too big now. She thinks I shouldn't be afraid anymore."

"Some people think a lot of things," Kat said, and she was aware of the bitter undercurrent in her voice. Maybe her little half-sister heard it, too, because she only sat there silently, playing with the bed sheet entwined around her fingers instead of responding. No, Kat was no good with kids. No good at all.

"Sometimes Mom sits with me for a while," Emily said a minute later, her voice soft. "Until I fall asleep. But then I wake up, and... and..."

"I know." And then it would be suddenly dark and cold, and the shadows of things in the room wouldn't seem quite right, and it would feel as if something was watching from a place she couldn't see. Oh, yes, she knew. "I'll stay if you want."

"What?"

"I'll stay. If you want me to, I mean. And I won't leave after you fall asleep. I'll stay and... and keep watch." She would be awake anyway. At least one of them might get a decent night's sleep this way.

"You will?" The relief in the girl's voice was audible. "You mean it?"

There was a bare stretch of wall beside the bedroom door. Since she was already down on the floor, Kat shuffled over to it on her hands and knees and turned so that her back could rest against it. It was hard and cool, not the most comfortable of places to sit, but it had the advantage of being right where Emily could see it past the foot of her bed. All she would have to do was look up from her pillow. "Yes. It's okay, Emily. Go to sleep."

"You won't leave?"

"I won't leave."

"Promise?"

"Promise," Kat agreed, feeling another stab of guilt that she was only just now here, to keep watch or do anything else. That it had taken her six years, she who knew what it was like to be a little girl trapped in this room.

Even with the moonlight, it was hard to see much in the room, but she heard the rustling of the covers as Emily lay back down and burrowed beneath them.

Then all was quiet, and Kat started her long watch.

◆◆◆

"KAT?"

The voice was hushed, and Kat was only dimly aware of it. She became more aware, though, as someone touched her shoulder.

"Kat—what are you doing in here?"

Kat's eyes sprang open to see morning sunlight sifting through the gauzy inner curtains. At some point in the wee hours of morning, exhaustion must have gotten the better of her in spite of the uncomfortable nature of her position. Back stiff from leaning against the hard wall and neck aching from the angle at which her head rested along the doorframe, Kat blinked eyes that felt gritty with lack of sleep and saw her stepmother bending over her, an odd and unfamiliar expression on her face.

Wider awake now, she remembered then where she was and why, and her eyes darted toward Emily's bed even as her hands started automatically bracing themselves against the floor so she could rise from her position. Easier said than done. Her legs were asleep and half-numb from being curled under her, and she was forced to stay where she was.

But it was all right. The little girl was sleeping peacefully, her eyes closed and the blankets over her chest rising and falling with her breathing.

In another minute, Grace's eyes would bore into Kat. Oh, yes—a question. She had asked Kat a question and was waiting for the answer. And suddenly Kat realized what that unfamiliar thing in Grace's expression was. Suspicion.

That was new. And under the circumstances, maybe understandable. "She was having trouble sleeping. Bad dreams." Not quite true, but close enough. "I was keeping her company, and I must have fallen asleep."

She was met with silence. That was new, too. "Well," Grace said finally, her voice still quiet but not so quiet that the stiffness couldn't be heard in it, "you must be very tired then, after a night upright like that. Perhaps you ought to try to catch an hour or two of sleep in your own room." She emphasized the last part of that sentence, and if her tone was not exactly unfriendly, it was not what one would call warm, either. "I'll take over now."

As chastisements went, it was a mild one, but Kat only nodded wordlessly. The feeling was coming back in her legs, so she used the doorjamb to haul herself to her feet and left the way she had come hours ago, sparing one brief backward glance over her shoulder.

Oblivious to the new tension in the room, Emily slept on. Grace, however, was not oblivious, and she shut the door firmly behind Kat as she left.

◆ CHAPTER FOURTEEN ◆

KAT TOOK GRACE'S ADVICE, whether it was kindly meant or not. She had to; her eyelids were too heavy to do otherwise. And she did sleep a little, but only after lying awake for what felt like an hour or more, thinking about Emily and picturing the light sputtering out beneath her door.

A slam of another door woke her later, followed by the sound of Alexis's voice.

"Why the hell are we even paying that stupid internet place? Half the time the damn computer won't even work." Her feet thundered past Kat's closed door on their way to their stairs, and although the words became too muffled to make out, the tone was still petulant.

Kat reached for the watch on her bedside table. A quarter to eleven. Late to sleep in, yes, but she couldn't help but think that the loud show put on outside her door just now might have been deliberate if her stepsister had found out Kat was trying to rest. Was that being paranoid? Maybe. But that happened when a person grew up in the same house as Alexis Fairmont.

By the time Kat crept down the stairs, her footsteps soft and careful and avoiding those places on the stairs that creaked, it was after eleven o'clock. She was not surprised that Grace and Emily were not in the kitchen this late in the morning. Unfortunately, Alexis was. She had a magazine spread out before her on the counter and a bottle of something bubbly and sugary in one hand from which she sipped as she turned a page.

Glancing up at Kat as she entered the room, she let her eyes travel over her and then flicker away in an exaggerated show of distaste. "Heard the lawyer was here yesterday. Did he explain the term 'mentally competent' while he was here?"

Kat passed her to go to the fridge and pour herself a glass of orange juice. "He explained my rights as your landlord." She downed it without preamble. "You might want to have Grace explain them to you sometime. Using little words."

"Bitch," her stepsister returned, turning her attention back to her magazine. "How's that for a little word?"

Ignoring her, Kat took an apple from out of a bowl of fruit sitting on the counter and exited the room.

She heard a voice in the parlor and stopped in the foyer before she could see or be seen through the doorway. It was Grace, praising Emily for some bit of number practice with flashcards, and at the moment Kat felt strange about seeing either one of them. The air in the house was oppressive under the best of circumstances; Grace's disapproval only made it worse. Careful to step lightly on the wood floor for fear of it creaking, Kat slipped past the parlor doorway and out the front door.

The brightness of the sunlight made her blink and put her free hand up to shade her eyes. Even on overcast days it took a moment for her eyes to adjust to the lighting; the dark paneling just inside the doorway always seemed to have that effect. Had it been up to her, she would have put in something lighter. With a start, she realized it *was* up to her now, and she descended the steps to look up and imagine for a moment what it would be like to take a wrecking ball to the place, or a torch.

She immediately felt a moment's shame over what seemed like disloyalty to her father, given how much he'd loved the place. But only a moment's. And anyway, there were other options that were less destructive, and one in particular that had taken root in her mind ever since the visit from the lawyer. One that Emily at least would appreciate.

She turned away and drew in a deep breath, grateful to be outside. At least out here she could breathe properly. Did Emily feel the same way?

Closing her eyes, Kat pictured the small beachfront cottage that belonged to her grandparents, missing it—and them—so much just then that it was almost painful. The warmth, the safety, the peace it represented. Her nights were restless even there, but at least she didn't go to bed feeling as if she was surrounded by the enemy, or wake up that way, either.

Away. She needed to get away, if only for a little while and if only by foot. A run might have helped restore her equilibrium, but there was no good place to do that here. The grounds were extensive enough, if lacking paths, but they were also riddled with uneven spots and loose stones that were a twisted ankle waiting to happen. A walk would have to do, and although she had little appetite, she made herself eat the apple as she went.

This time she made sure to keep well away from the manicured gardens and the pond and instead stuck to the more natural landscape on the other side of the manor, mostly gentle hillside and trees. Gradually the sun thawed the chill that she hadn't been aware permeated her skin until now, a coolness she'd gotten used to feeling whenever she was inside the house. Out here it felt like it really was summer after all, warm but early enough in the season that everything was still green and lush. Anywhere else, and even Kat would have acknowledged that it was a beautiful summer day.

But even though lovely, something seemed off about it, and as peaceful and quiet as it was, it was hard to pin down why until it finally struck Kat as *too* quiet. True, she was used to the near constant background noise of the ocean waves back home, and it was natural for anything else to feel different, but still...

She paused and listened, and she heard nothing but the faint rustling of leaves overhead as a gentle breeze stirred them. Surely there ought to be more signs of wildlife? Or *any* signs. The snap of a twig as a squirrel darted over it, or a bird calling out—something. But there was nothing, not even the soft buzz of insects flying about. Had it always been so quiet here? Maybe it had, and she'd just never really noticed its absence of sound and activity until she'd gone to live with her grandparents in a place that was surrounded by life everywhere she turned. She couldn't remember now.

Peace and quiet ought to have been relaxing, not unsettling the way it was here. A prickle went down Kat's spine. She continued walking, deliberately heading deeper into the trees, and after a while, she started hearing those sounds that had been so conspicuously absent closer to the manor itself. The presence of people in the house might have been what made the local wildlife keep its distance. *Might* have been, yes. Man had that effect on nature, after all.

Maybe she was looking for problems where there were none, too ingrained in her ways when it came to Delancey manor to do anything else. And yet after her most recent spooks in the house and the way her senses sometimes seemed to deceive her, it was getting harder to tell the difference between paranoia and a true gut feeling.

Eventually, and with great reluctance, she turned and left the soothing sounds of bees and twittering birds behind; she couldn't avoid either the house or Grace forever.

Unfortunately.

◆◆◆

GRACE WATCHED HER STEPDAUGHTER approach the house from beyond the far side of the driveway. What, had she been traipsing around in the undergrowth? Why? There was nothing that lay that way except untamed nature, no paths to follow and no manicured landscape.

She turned away from the window. An odd girl, that one, and finding her in Emily's room had been odder still, and disconcerting. Yes, Emily had defended her presence there when asked, and it was true that Grace's youngest did suffer from nighttime fears occasionally, but Kat was nearly always shut up in her own room away from everybody and seemed to prefer it that way. Her room was farther away from Emily's door than Grace's was, too; if Emily had made any sounds of distress in the night, Grace ought to have heard them before Kat.

She would have sworn she caught Kat studying her half-sister more than once since she'd gotten here. Natural enough maybe, considering that she had never seen the little girl before this visit and had already commented once on her resemblance to Jonathan.

A pang went through Grace at the thought, but she didn't let it distract her. There was something more than mere curiosity in the way Kat watched Emily, and although nothing about it seemed obviously ominous, it was still... unsettling.

Well, she would talk to Emily about it more later, and she would keep an eye on things in case they changed, but for now there was still a dinner to plan and prepare, and for now she would still play the hostess and peacemaker. For Jonathan's sake. And then perhaps Kat would decide she'd had enough of the manor for now and return to her home on the west coast.

She heard the sound of the front door opening and placed herself in the parlor doorway to meet Kat. "Been out walking?" It was inane chitchat, but that was the kind of thing she fell back on whenever Kat was in the room.

Her stepdaughter stiffened as if she'd been caught with her hand in a cookie jar and did a double take at the sight of her before nodding.

"Lovely day for it."

Again a nod. Could the girl not even try to meet her halfway?

Grace gave up on casual conversation but did her best to keep her tone pleasant. "Dinner will be at six tonight, unless you have any objections." She waited, heard none, and continued, "I thought we all might dress up a bit, since it's a special occasion. I mean, that is, if you packed anything, well..." She trailed off uncertainly, eyeing the jeans and t-shirt the younger woman wore that seemed to be her regular uniform and seeing her mental image of a lovely formal dinner disintegrate. Maybe she'd been foolish to try for it in the first place, but formality did sometimes serve a purpose. If nothing else, it offered a kind of reassurance and comfort. To her, anyway. "But it's not important. Anyway..." She cleared her throat. "Six o'clock."

"Six," Kat acknowledged, which was downright chatty for her. And then she started up the stairs.

Letting out the breath she hadn't realized she was holding, Grace retreated to the dining room. There were place settings to create, more china to wipe down, and seating arrangements to think about—putting anything less than a continent between Alexis and Kat was going to cause problems. But with a little effort, it could still be something like the beautiful occasion for which she hoped, and with a little luck since the paperwork was over and done with... maybe even a kind of farewell dinner.

Her spirits lifted, and she began humming under her breath.

◆◆◆

WHEN SHE'D PACKED FOR this visit, she'd had many things on her mind. A dress code was not one of them.

But the look of trepidation on Grace's face as she eyed Kat's clothes was impossible to miss, no matter what reassurances she'd offered that attire wasn't important. To Grace it was and always had been; more accurately, propriety mattered to her. It seemed to be the guiding force in her life, which struck Kat as bordering on ridiculous after what had happened to them both. Etiquette and manners... flimsy and foolish things when one had the kind of past Kat did. What did they really matter?

But considering the subject that she planned to broach tonight—best to do it when everyone was together and get it over with—ignoring Grace's wishes for the evening seemed churlish. Which presented a problem, since she hadn't packed anything much other than jeans and shirts. Alexis would sooner set her wardrobe on fire than loan anything to her, and the thought of wearing something of hers made Kat's skin crawl anyway.

There was one other possibility, though.

Skipping the second floor landing, Kat continued up to the third. This floor was full of bedrooms, too, plus a bathroom. The staircase ended here, and she paused, but there was another one further back that led to the attic. It was possible that what she wanted had been moved into there by now, but it seemed just as likely that no one had seen fit to disturb anything up here. The entire floor had an eerie sense of desolation to it, long empty of any guests.

She was staring, she realized then. Staring at absolutely nothing but a deserted hallway as if she expected something or someone to appear. Searching her memory, she turned her attention to the last door on the right and moved down the hallway.

The floor creaked beneath her feet, expressing its age. One of these rooms would have served as the nursery years and years ago, a place where children could be reared by a nanny without being seen or heard at undesirable times, or at least that was what she thought her father had told her once. A different age, and a very different way of life. Somehow the thought of young children spending much of their time shut up on this floor made her shiver. Granted, part of that might have been due to the fact that with the rooms closed off as they were now, the hall was full of shadows that lent the space a grim feel, but even so…

Kat let the thought go unfinished as she stopped in front of the door she wanted and tried the knob. Unlocked. Turning it, she opened the door and peered into the gloom inside. There was no furniture in this room to speak of other than a couple of stacked chairs; instead it held several large cardboard boxes; things had been left undisturbed as she'd hoped. Crossing the room, she opened the curtains to allow in some light before turning her attention back to the boxes.

There were no labels of any kind on them. Maybe her father couldn't bring himself to write her mother's name on them. Some of Lily Delancey's things had been sent to Gran, but the rest had been packed up and stored here. Picking one at random, Kat opened it up and looked inside. Sweaters. Not what she was looking for. She paused to run her fingers over the topmost one, though, finding it vaguely familiar but unable to picture her mother in it. Too long ago, she supposed. Setting that box aside, she picked another one.

This one held more promise. The clothes in them were lighter, more appropriate for summer. She searched through them, lingering longer on the ones that she could remember her mother wearing. Had her father been the one to fold these up so carefully and pack them away, or had Gran done that after the funeral? Either possibility seemed suddenly painful; maybe this hadn't been a good idea after all. But then her hands closed around folds of white, and she pulled out a simple but timeless sort of sundress that she remembered seeing her mother wear in a photograph. She'd been smiling so happily in that picture, an infant Kat on her lap as they soaked up dappled sunshine together in a place that might have been a public park of some kind, or maybe even someone's backyard. A beautiful moment captured in time.

Giving in to impulse, Kat closed her eyes and buried her face in the fabric as if she might somehow catch a whiff of her mother's perfume on it. There was nothing but the stale smell that came from sitting around in boxes for so many years. Of course. To expect anything else would be silly, so it made no sense to be disappointed. Shaking the dress out, she held it up before her. It looked like it would be a reasonable fit. Wrinkled, though. She'd have to give it some attention before dinner, and a few minutes of time spent hanging out her window maybe to air it out, but it would do.

Closing up both boxes, she returned them to their original places before closing the curtains again and leaving the room the way she'd found it. And then she very gladly left the third floor behind her.

◆ CHAPTER FIFTEEN ◆

A MERCEDES APPEARED AROUND the bend of the driveway and parked in front of the house. Michael was here.

Kat watched from her window as he got out of the car. His posture was that of a man accustomed to success, and his suit alone probably cost more than Kat had ever spent on clothes in a single year, let alone on a single item. She'd seen too few pictures of his father to say for certain, but Michael looked so little like Grace that he must have taken after the elder Fairmont. In looks and in business. He'd majored in the same field and had gone to work for his father's biggest competitor in what seemed like only moments after graduating. That much she could remember.

He opened the door for his passenger, a blonde woman holding a bottle of wine. She was attractive but seemed somehow out of place here—her dress was nowhere near as expensive-looking as Michael's suit—and although she laughed at something Michael said, there was a nervous quality to it. Almost as if she was out of her element and she knew it. With Michael or the manor? But it was only idle curiosity that made Kat wonder, so she turned away from the window to run a quick brush through her unadorned hair and then left the room with only a cursory glance in the mirror and a fervent wish to get the evening over with.

Halfway down the stairs, she paused as she heard the front door open and then the sound of voices. Habit made her linger where she was, safely out of view.

"Hi!" said an unfamiliar voice that could only belong to Michael's date. It was bubbly and full of what struck Kat as falsely confident cheer. "Nice to see you again, Miss Fairmont."

So Alexis was the official greeter then. Too bad for the new arrival. Kat was not surprised to hear thinly-veiled disdain in Alexis's voice when she responded. "Uh huh. Dinner's on the table."

"Thank you. I'll just run this in to Mrs. Delancey, then."

The click of high-heeled shoes on the floorboards signaled the woman's departure.

"You dog," Alexis said, a smirk in her voice. "Isn't that Daddy's secretary?"

"She has a name, Alexis." Michael's tone was cool and crisp. "It's Stacey."

"Like you care about that. What makes you think I won't tattle on you to Daddy?"

"What makes you think I don't want you to?"

Alexis laughed, almost as if in approval, and then the sound of footsteps let Kat know brother and sister followed after Stacey.

No, there was no love lost between Michael and his father, was there? Maybe that was just the natural outcome when a father threw his son's mother over for a string of firmer and prettier twenty-somethings.

Kat remained where she was a minute longer. She was just stalling now. No way out but forward. Steeling herself, she made her way down the rest of the stairs and turned to enter the dining room. The soft green of the walls went beautifully with the polished wood of the dark wainscoting, and Grace had covered the table with an array of food that was so pretty that it looked like something off of the cover of a magazine. She'd washed the good china until it gleamed and had even set out the heirloom silverware. This really was an occasion then. To Grace, at least, and that was something that boded poorly for the night ahead.

No one noticed Kat right away, standing silently in the doorway as she was, particularly since Alexis was busy looking at something on her phone that she clearly considered more interesting than anything else around her, and Michael was in the middle of introducing Stacey to his mother, conveniently leaving out the part about her working for his father.

Her palms were sweating. Kat wrapped her fingers in the folds of her mother's dress as if drawing courage from it somehow. Foolish, really. What good were the dead to her? It was the living she had to deal with now.

Emily sat motionless in a chair to the left of what must surely be Grace's place at the head of the table. Hair brushed within an inch of its life and her starched dress's collar looking like it was threatening to choke her, she looked like someone's perfect little doll. Maybe to Grace she was. Catching sight of Kat then, the girl brightened and offered a shy smile.

"How do you do? So glad you could join us this evening," Grace said to Stacey perfectly politely if not effusively.

"My sister Emily," Michael said then, nodding his head toward the little girl by way of introduction, and then he seemed to notice her attention was directed elsewhere. He turned his head to see what it was and met Kat's gaze. The look he gave her was guarded, neither warm nor cool. "And this is Kat," he added after a moment, pulling out a chair for his date.

"Ah," said the blonde to Kat with determined cheerfulness and a slight furrowing of her brow. "And you are...?"

"The crackpot daughter of the guy our mom married ten years ago," Alexis put in without deigning to look up from her phone. "Normally we try to keep her away from guests, but I guess tonight we're rolling the dice, eh, Mom?"

Grace stammered and turned pink, and Michael gave his sister a look. "Button it, Alexis," he said with a tight jaw, and then he took a seat at the other end of the table with a somewhat taken aback Stacey on one side and Alexis on the other, presumably where he could help keep her in check.

Kat behaved as if no one had spoken and only sat down in the empty chair on Grace's right, across from Emily.

"Well. Shall we dig right in?" Grace suggested in what was probably an attempt to hasten past the awkward moment, and for the next few minutes the only sounds in the room were the clinks of silverware and serving spoons.

Seated beside Kat, Stacey made some complimentary comment about the meal, something trite and typical, but Kat didn't really hear her. She didn't really taste her food either, and was only half-aware of what she was eating. What she was aware of was being watched, and she didn't have to look up to know that it was by Michael. Assessing her. Wondering, maybe, if a straitjacket would be appropriate after all and waiting to see if she would start hearing voices at the table or otherwise offer evidence that she was indeed off her rocker.

Yes, well, he could get in line.

Dinner conversation was strained and carried mostly by Grace and Michael, although Stacey made a valiant effort to help. But there were only so many polite things that could be said about the flavors of the food or the décor of the room before they began to sound a bit desperate. After a while, Kat wasn't sure who was more uncomfortable at the table, herself or the secretary. She was used to awkward company though; Stacey, it seemed, was not.

After a few minutes of mostly silent chewing, Kat glanced up in time to see Grace throw her son a pleading look.

He cleared his throat and took another stab at conversation. "So, Kat, I understand you're at Seattle State. What are you studying there?"

"Clinical psychology."

Alexis started to laugh.

Her brother narrowed his eyes at her but continued speaking as if she hadn't made a sound. "Good for you. Some people I know are still struggling to go two consecutive semesters at the same university without flunking out."

The smirk on his sister's face vanished, and she glared at him instead. He paid her no attention and took a bite of his mashed potatoes.

If Grace wasn't already regretting her decision to host this meal, she probably would be before much longer. One of her eyelids began to twitch, and she put a hand to her temple momentarily as if she was getting a headache. "I'm so glad we took care of all that legal business yesterday," she said after a moment with more brightness than she could possibly be feeling just then. "Kat, I'm sure you're anxious to get back home and start enjoying the rest of your summer."

Translation: go away. Although much more politely put.

"Yes, Kat, how long will you be visiting this time?" Michael asked, and it seemed to Kat that every set of ears at the table perked up with the exception of Stacey's.

Kat met her young half-sister's eyes briefly across the table. There was a bite of chicken on her plate that Kat had been pushing around idly just to have something on which to focus her attention. She abandoned it now and set her fork carefully on the edge of the dish. "I'm not sure," she said finally. "I might stick around a few days longer than I planned."

"Oh?"

"Yes." There was no point in tiptoeing around it, so she continued, "I've decided to sell the house."

The room grew so quiet and still that her words seemed to echo in it. Only Stacey smiled politely at the announcement, and then hastily wiped her smiled away as she seemed to realize it was not the happy news she thought it was.

The color drained from Grace's face as she stared at Kat. "Sell the house? You can't mean that."

"I do."

Her stepmother began to stammer. "But… but it's…"

Alexis was sufficiently startled by Kat's news to actually put down her phone and stare at her, while Emily merely blinked at her with wide open eyes as if she wasn't sure if what she heard was true. Michael, though, recovered enough from his surprise to grow angry. "In case you hadn't noticed, Kat, there are people living their lives here in this house. Is this you trying to be funny, or are you really that cold?"

"Nobody has to pack their bags tonight. And of course you can stay here, Grace, until you find someplace else. But I am selling."

"But you can't sell it," Grace protested, growing more agitated by the minute. "This house was built for Delanceys. It should stay in the family."

Her palms were sweating again. She hated this, hating having all eyes on her. "My father left the house to me, Grace."

"Yes, and the last thing he'd want you to do is sell it!"

That was probably true, but Kat didn't respond.

"Think about Emily. Whatever you think of me, she's a Delancey by blood. It's her heritage, too! I—"

"I am thinking of Emily. I know what it's like to grow up in this house." And then, partly to mollify her stepmother but also because it was what she'd intended to do anyway, Kat added, "She can have half the proceeds from the sale."

Pushing her chair back from the table, Grace stood up. She was trembling, though, and had to hold on to the table for support. "I don't care about the money! I care about what Jonathan would have wanted. I care about protecting our daughter's rights to her family's legacy. I care… I …"

Michael shoved his own chair back and went to his mother—rather surprisingly, Alexis did, too—as if afraid she might faint. Maybe she would have. Kat had only ever once seen Grace even remotely this upset before, and that was on the day Kat's father fell from his ladder to his death. That Grace was not happy with Kat's decision was not a surprise; that she was this unhappy was, though.

"Is this your idea of a homecoming?" Michael said tersely to Kat, easing his distressed mother back into her chair again while she clutched at Alexis's arm as if for support. "Waltz on in and drop a bombshell? She doesn't deserve this from you, Kat."

Kat's pulse grew thready. "This isn't the rotten stepchild looking for a way to screw her stepmother over, Grace. My decision has nothing to do with you."

Grace was too upset to respond. Michael did it for her. "Well, that's the problem here, isn't it? Because after everything that's happened in this house, a decision like that should have something to do with her. Or did that thought not even cross your mind?"

Dinner was clearly over, and probably the kindest thing Kat could do for everyone else now was simply leave the room. Maybe she had been overly blunt in her delivery—typical—but it was too late to change that now. Leaving her napkin on the table, she stood up. "I understand your reasons for disagreeing with my decision, and I'm sorry if you're upset. But it is my decision to make." And then she turned and headed for the door, increasingly queasy.

Behind her, she heard Stacey clear her throat and say softly, "You know, I think I'm just going to call myself a taxi and head home, Michael." Any response he made was too low for Kat to hear, because by that time she was in the hall and heading straight for the front door.

Air. She needed some air.

She fumbled with the door handle before finally getting it open, and then she realized her hands were shaking. Small wonder. Stepping onto the front porch, she was quick to close the door behind her and breathe in deeply.

That could have gone better. Much better. She sank down to sit on the topmost step. Granted, she probably could have found a gentler way to break the news, but it would have been the same news all the same. Grace would have been unhappy either way. Was she really so attached to the house? For someone who disliked it as much as Kat did, the concept seemed foreign. She would have thought losing her husband here would have spoiled any real attachment Grace could have had to the place. Apparently she was dead wrong.

Kat held one hand out and saw that it was still trembling. Clenching it closed, she wrapped her arms around herself and just breathed in and out while she waited for her nerves to return to normal.

When she finally went back inside the house, she passed the secretary on her way out to wait for the taxi. The cab had yet to arrive, but it wasn't really surprising that she might prefer to wait for it outside. The woman avoided direct eye contact and merely nodded once as she slipped out through the front door. Michael wasn't with her; no doubt he was still with his mother. The sound of their voices behind the closed parlor door quickly confirmed it.

Grace was still quite upset; her words might be muffled, but her tone was not. Eavesdropping on her after what had happened seemed in very poor taste, so Kat didn't even try. Besides, she really didn't need to. She could guess well enough what Grace was saying, and she was sure it wasn't flattering. Michael seemed to be doing his best to try and soothe her, but so far it didn't seem to be going well.

Kat hesitated. Should she knock? Go in and try to make some sort of amends?

No, not now. Not yet. Knowing her own social ineptness, she would only make things worse. Tomorrow, maybe. Once everyone's heads were cooler. Grace had been her father's wife, after all. For his sake, Kat ought to try.

Light spilled out from underneath closed doors to both Emily's and Alexis's rooms when Kat reached the second floor. It was a relief, really. Closed doors were welcome right now and far preferable to having to deal with people. Pulling the key to her room out of the pocket in her mother's sundress, she unlocked the door and went inside.

Something crunched beneath her shoes. Switching on the bedside lamp, she gasped when she saw bits of broken glass strewn on the floor. Above the bureau, the mirror looked like someone had taken a baseball bat to it. Cracks spiraled out from the center, distorting her reflection as it stared back at her, openmouthed.

For a moment, all she could do was stare at it in surprise. Then shock gave way to anger, and she stormed back out the way she had come to go pound on Alexis's door.

A muffled expletive on the other side of it greeted her, followed a moment later by Alexis as she threw open the door. The consternation on her face turned to a glare when she saw Kat. "What—giving my mother a heart attack wasn't enough? What the hell do you want now? To evict me?"

"You set foot in my room again, and you're damn right I will!"

"What are you talking about? I haven't been anywhere near your room, you freak."

"Like hell you haven't. What did you do, pick the lock?"

In response, Alexis rolled her eyes and started to shut her door in Kat's face.

Kat shoved it open again with one hand, trapping Alexis between it and the wall nearest to it. "You think I'm crazy, Alexis? Keep pushing me, and maybe you'll find out just how right you are."

She stared, unblinking, into Alexis's wide eyes a moment longer to let her know she meant it before turning to go, and then she stalked back downstairs long enough to grab a broom and a dustpan from the kitchen.

Alexis's door was closed again by the time Kat got back upstairs. Just as well. Kat's anger bubbled perilously close to the surface still, and it would be a shame to add smacking her eldest daughter around to the list of ways she'd offended Grace tonight.

She swept up the shards of glass as thoroughly as she could, checking under the bed to make sure she didn't miss any that might cut her later if she swung her feet over the edge to stand up. Damn Alexis and her pettiness. That mirror had been a lovely piece, and although Kat had no more sentimental attachment to it than she did for any other piece of furniture in the house, she knew the wanton destruction of it would have pained her father. Six years gone, and he still seemed present somehow in the halls of Delancey Manor. Maybe that should have been comforting, but it was not. Cutting ties with this place would be a welcome relief.

After everything that had happened that evening, she didn't quite have the courage to take the broom and dustpan back downstairs and risk running into either Grace or Michael. Instead, she set the items in question over in a corner to be dealt with in the morning and then sank down onto the end of her bed.

God, she was tired. Less than a week here, and she already felt like she was fracturing. Not unlike the mirror. She stared at her reflection in it again, and it stared right back at her in a way that left her feeling disturbed. It was just the cracks, she decided, and the violence that had put them there. That was why the sight of her distorted face bothered her so much. Either that, or the shadows she saw beneath her eyes when she looked closer.

Lying back on the bed, she closed her eyes as much to shut out the broken image as to try and relax. Breathe, she reminded herself, falling into the familiar pattern she'd been taught before. In and out, slow and steady.

In and out.

A kind of drowsiness settled over her as her breathing slowed, and she felt the tension in her body begin to flow out of her.

In and out…

◆◆◆

SOMEONE'S MOUTH WAS ON hers, forcing oxygen into her lungs. A moment later, Kat began to cough up water and then choke in deep breaths of air on her own, shocked and disoriented. Panic took her over.

Water?

"Damn it, Kat, what are you trying to do?"

The voice was Michael's, but the question might as well have been gibberish, because it made no sense to Kat's foggy mind. Still coughing and gasping, she clutched wildly at whatever was nearest for purchase, which turned out to be Michael's dripping arms; he was on his knees and leaning over her. She lay on something hard and uneven, not her bed at all. Why wasn't she on her bed? And she was soaked, her mother's white dress clinging wetly to her body.

"Breathe," Michael instructed her, his tone sharp as he rolled her onto her side.

No more water came up, but that didn't seem to stop her throat from trying to cough up more in a reflexive action. The breath she drew in was ragged and harsh. Digging her fingers into the ground—the ground?—she pushed herself up on shaky arms and saw a familiar bit of stonework two feet away from her. The edge of the pond. She was outside in the gardens, lying in a puddle on the ground and hardly more than an arm's length from the place where her mother had died.

Her breath rattled in her throat again, and this time it had nothing to do with water she had swallowed. "W-what happened?"

"You tell me! You really are a head case, you know that?"

Kat stared numbly at the pond, not noticing Michael was helping her to her feet until she was standing on them.

She was outside. And at the pond. How in God's name had that happened?

"Come on. You and I need to have a talk." Michael held firmly onto her arm and started toward the house.

Fresh terror filled her when she realized where he was taking her, and she pulled back so abruptly that she lost her balance. She would have fallen if he hadn't recovered from his surprise quickly enough to catch her. "No!"

He stared at her as if she'd lost her mind. "Kat—"

"Please—" Her hands clutched at the front of his shirt as fear took over her completely, and she began to shake all over. In another minute she was going to be sick. If Michael had any doubts before about her sanity, she was giving him plenty of reason to sweep them aside now, but she didn't care. All she knew was that she could not face going back inside that house. Anywhere else, just not in there. The house, the gardens, they were all wrong, every inch of them. Her skin was crawling, and she didn't care that it didn't make sense. All she cared about was getting as far away from there as possible. "Please get me out of here." The words were practically a sob, and if she had been more in her right mind, she would have been ashamed.

Her reaction seemed to take him aback, but it also seemed to soften the edges of his anger toward her. "You're soaking wet, Kat. You need to get dried off."

"Not in there. Please, Michael. *Please*," she begged again, and something in her manner must have swayed him, because he finally nodded even if it was with obvious reluctance.

"Have it your way. But we are going to talk." His suit jacket lay on the ground nearby; he must have shed it earlier. Picking it up, he draped it around her trembling shoulders and helped her around the house to where his car waited in the driveway.

◆ CHAPTER SIXTEEN ◆

IT WAS THE SOUND of the back door swinging shut that alerted him, and he'd come this close to missing it altogether.

After finally calming his mother down enough to the point where he felt that he could leave, Michael had to resist the urge to slam the front door shut behind him as he made his way to his car. Stopping beside it, he'd glanced up at Kat's window with a surge of fresh anger, wondering at her coldness, and had seen the glow of her bedside lamp flicker as if the electricity was threatening to fail.

Where did she get off? Tragic history or not, she was not earning herself any admirers in this house. And for a fleeting moment, he'd considered returning to the house just to light into her about it. But cooling off first might be the wiser thing to do; he hadn't gotten as far as he had in life by being ruled by impulse. And then he'd opened his car door with the intention of getting in and roaring off down the driveway.

Which was when he heard the back door.

It was the inappropriateness of it that had caught his attention. Late as it was and dark, no one should have been out for a jaunt in the backyard. So finally, wondering if he was about to stumble onto Emily sneaking out for God knew what, Michael closed the car door again and started toward the back of the house.

He'd called out once, maybe twice. He couldn't remember now. All he knew for sure was that there had been no answer. Then he heard a splash, much too large to be a pebble tossed into the pond. And when he rounded the corner and was halfway to the pond, he realized with an unnerving jolt that there was something floating in it. And when he realized that it was a person facedown and not moving, he'd broken into a run.

It was her dress that he recognized first, so white that it almost glowed in the moonlight as it and her hair floated around her. He'd had a momentary flashback to finding her unconscious on the bathroom floor, and then he was hauling Kat out of the water and toward the edge of the pond, his pulse thundering as he searched for signs of hers.

Now, her back to him, she sat in his apartment only a few feet away from where he stood watching her, curled up in borrowed sweatpants and shirt that were too big for her and so still that she might have been made of stone. Had she moved even once in the last ten minutes? Not that he'd seen, unless shivering counted.

Well, his own hands weren't the steadiest either right now as he poured something into a mug for her to drink. Nerves of steel in the boardroom were one thing; this was another altogether. The wrong kind of excitement seemed to follow Kat around, and he was getting more than a little tired of it.

Time for her to explain herself.

◆◆◆

SHE COULDN'T GET WARM.

Dry clothes and all, with forty minutes gone by since Kat came to beside the pond, and she still couldn't shake the chill that enveloped her. The water hadn't even been that cold, and certainly the night air was mild enough. But the chill seemed to go deeper than her skin.

Because she was terrified. Small wonder. Maybe she'd had the lines between reality and hallucination blur a few times in the past when her mind played tricks on her, but not like this. Never like this.

Except for once, and that scared her all the more because of what had nearly happened then.

She'd lost time. Not much of it, but lost time nevertheless. And hours of it weren't necessary in order for it to be disconcerting. As it turned out, five minutes worked just as well for that to be true. How could she not remember anything about leaving her room, about wandering outside—about falling into water, for God's sake? Shouldn't that alone have brought her back to… to, what? Reality? The waking world? What in God's name had happened to her?

Hands trembling, Kat wrapped them around herself in a kind of desperate hug that was as much to comfort herself as to try and warm up. At least here in Michael's apartment she could think about what had happened without dissolving into a puddle of fear, because here she felt as if the oppressive weight of the house didn't press on her quite so much. It still lingered there in the back of her mind, as it always seemed to do no matter how many miles she put between herself and that place, but she could breathe at least. Literally and figuratively.

His apartment was rather like Michael himself. It reeked of modernism and the kind of designer taste that only money could buy, but there was something impersonal about it. Aloof, even. The only personal touches evident were a couple of framed photos of Grace as she stood between Alexis and Emily, her hands resting on the shoulders of both. Not surprisingly, there were none of his father. Or Kat's.

No, the place was nothing at all like the manor. That alone was reason enough to like it.

"Drink," she heard a voice say crisply to her right, and she turned her head to see Michael holding out a mug of something that steamed. He had changed into drier clothes, too—jeans, and t-shirt—and somehow it was jarring to see him in anything more casual than a suit.

The sweatshirt and drawstring pants he'd pulled out of a drawer for Kat to wear were much too big for her, and she had to pull back one sleeve in order to take the proffered drink from him without the cuff getting in the way. "What is it?" she asked, and her voice sounded odd even to her own ears, almost as if it wasn't working properly. Maybe it wasn't, after what had happened.

"Tea. With a shot of something stronger. You're still shaking." He settled into a chair across from her.

She took a tentative sip and had to work hard not to grimace. Stronger was right. She was not a party girl on campus, but she was familiar enough with beer and wine to know that whatever Michael had added to the tea was much stiffer than either of those.

"Better?"

Not really, but she nodded anyway. Once.

"Good. Then let's talk." He leaned forward as if to read her response more closely. "You want to tell me what the hell happened back there, Kat?"

The subject was an uncomfortable one to discuss with anyone, let alone Grace's son, but this question was one she could certainly answer honestly enough. "I don't know."

The reluctant patience he'd displayed up until this point, including when she'd dripped all over his leather upholstery, seemed to be wearing thin now. "Try again."

"I don't know," she repeated, her tone just as terse as his. "I have no idea how I ended up in the pond. I don't even remember leaving my room."

"You don't remember leaving your room," he repeated, his face a mask.

"No, I don't. The last thing I remember is lying on my bed."

At first she thought he didn't believe her, but then he fixed her with a penetrating gaze and asked a question that took the conversation in a different direction than she expected. "Tell me the truth, Kat. Are you on something?"

She blinked. "On something?"

"Did you take something? Swallow it, inject it, whatever—"

"What? No!"

"Because if you did, you probably shouldn't be drinking that, and we should probably be on our way to an ER right about now."

Her face grew warm, but more with anger than embarrassment. "I'm not on anything, Michael."

"This is no time to lie about something like that. If there's something in your system, you need to have a doctor check you out."

"I said I'm not on anything. Not unless your mother slipped something into the food tonight. Or maybe Alexis. You want to grill them, too?"

His eyes narrowed.

"Maybe I am a head case like you said, but I've never been into drugs. The only pills I've ever taken are the ones my doctors made me take."

"Oh, I think we both know that isn't true. Don't we?"

It took her a moment to realize what he meant: the overdose, the pills she'd swallowed years ago at her father's wake. A low blow in her opinion, and also an unjust one, although he had no way of knowing that. No one did, because she'd never told them the whole truth, any of them. About the blankness around that day, an utter blankness after she'd numbly left the mourners downstairs that lasted right up until she felt someone shaking her in an attempt to wake her, heard someone speaking to her.

Wake up, Kat… Kat...what did you do…

Michael's voice, she suddenly realized. "It was you."

"What was me?" he asked, sounding increasingly frustrated.

"You're the one who found me on the bathroom floor." No one had told her that part of it. She'd awakened in the hospital after her father's wake, foggy-headed and dazed, and all she'd been told was that she'd swallowed a bottle full of pills but that everything was going to be fine now, just fine. And she was going to go stay with her grandparents for a while where she wouldn't have to be reminded on a daily basis of what she'd lost. Then "a while" had turned into six years.

"Yes, I was. And one experience like that was more than enough, Kat. I really didn't need another one."

She could have done without it herself and would have said so if his comments hadn't made her wonder just then about something she hadn't thought to ask before. "Tonight—how did you know to come looking for me?"

"I didn't. It was purely dumb luck, and if you're not going to finish that, I will." Taking the mug from her hands, he drained it in a matter of seconds and without any sign of the grimace she'd had to suppress. She was not the only one unnerved tonight.

"How did—"

"I heard a noise," he said abruptly. "While I was on the way out to my car. I'd finally gotten my mother calmed down, no thanks to you—" Here he gave her a hard look. "—and I was ready to go home and call it a night. And then I heard the back door swing shut."

The back door. Try as she might, Kat couldn't remember anything about slipping out through the back door. On her own or—as her paranoid mind whispered to her in its frantic search for possible explanations—with help. For a moment she seized on the possibility that someone in the house was to blame for all of this, that they'd done something to her out of anger over her announcement at dinner. And made her forget it all how? With a five-minute roofie? Sure. She might be crazy, but she wasn't that crazy. Besides, she was all too familiar with the aftereffects of sedatives. What she felt now wasn't that. She almost wished it was.

"And since Emily should have been in bed already, and since Alexis would only go hang out in the backyard if the house was on fire—and maybe not even then—I decided to check it out. Then I heard a splash come from the direction of the pond. And I think you know the rest." He glanced at the mug he had taken from her and sighed as if sorry that it was empty. "All right, let's say for the sake of argument that I believe you and that it's not drugs that made you go for a swim tonight. What was it then—a blackout? Sleepwalking?"

That wasn't it at all. She didn't suffer from either and never had except for the day she'd swallowed all those pills. She nearly said as much but stopped herself just in time. An admission that something like this had happened once before would get her nothing but trouble in the form of more doctors and maybe a stay in a psych ward to determine if she was a danger to herself. She would not go down that road again. That was why she'd never told anyone the truth before, that she had no memory of opening the bottle of pills and taking them.

And if you are *a danger to yourself?* that little voice whispered in her head.

She had no answer for it.

Michael must have taken her silence as an affirmative. "Seriously? Don't you think you ought to have warned us about that? My God, Kat, there's a little girl living in that house with you."

Kat bit her tongue again and merely averted her eyes.

"All right, so maybe I can understand not wanting to make a general announcement of it around Alexis—and certainly not Emily—but you should at least have said something to my mother. Why didn't you? Were you embarrassed?" When he still got no reply, Michael sank back into his chair and ran his hands through his dark hair in obvious frustration. "Why are you doing this?" he asked finally.

That startled her into answering. "Doing what?"

"Why did you even come here? No one seems to be unhappier than you are that you're back at the house—it's like a shadow follows you around. Even I can tell that much. Considering what you've lost there, that's understandable. What doesn't make as much sense is why you'd want to come back."

"You wouldn't understand."

"No? You're not the only one that house has a hold over, Kat." He shook his head, looking suddenly tired, and his voice grew cooler. Bitter, even. "That place is like a mausoleum, everything kept just the way she thinks he'd have wanted it. Your father."

Kat stiffened, wary.

"You know, personally I don't think your idea to sell Delancey Manor is half bad. Then you could get the hell away from it and get on with your life, and maybe my mother could, too. I don't want her to spend the rest of her life tending a dead man's grave. But she'd sooner cut off both of her legs than see that house leave the family of the sainted Jonathan Delancey. Oh, relax," Michael added when he saw Kat open her mouth. "I'm not going to start disparaging your father. In fact, I'm going to make both you and my mother happy in one fell swoop. You want to unload the house? Fine. I'll buy it from you."

His words caught her off guard. She stared at him. "You'll what?"

"I said I'll buy the damned place. Then you can go on your merry little way, and my mother can keep living there. Problem solved. I can call the lawyer up tomorrow or we can do it through a realtor if you want, I don't care, but—"

"No."

Now he was the one caught off guard. "No… what?"

"I'm not selling it to you."

"And why wouldn't you want to sell it to me?" he asked in a voice that was growing progressively icier. "Think I'd expect a family discount?"

"We're not family."

"No kidding, sweetheart. So why wouldn't you want to take my money?"

"You said it yourself," Kat answered, picturing Emily trembling in fear beneath her bedcovers as her nightlight gave out, and then thinking of the door to her room that she still wasn't sure hadn't opened on its own. "We'd all be better off away from that place."

"Ah." He set the mug down on a nearby end table with more force than was necessary. "So you're trying to do my mother a favor, not stick it to her. Sure, Kat. What the hell have you got against her anyway? She lost him too, you know."

"I'm not trying to stick it to anyone." Rising from her chair, Kat turned her back on Michael to go over to the phone she saw resting on his marbled kitchen counter.

"What are you doing?" he asked irritably as she picked it up.

"Calling a taxi."

He was out of his chair and at her side before she could dial. "Oh, no," he told her, putting his hand on hers to stop her. The unexpected contact made her flinch, but if he noticed, he gave no sign. He put the phone back where it had been. "I'll drive you back."

The last thing she wanted right now was to be stuck in a car with him for the next half hour. "I don't need your help."

"I'm not helping you, I'm keeping an eye on you. There's a difference. And if you think I'm leaving you alone another night with my family after what happened tonight, you really are nuts."

"You don't honestly think I'm going to hurt somebody?"

"Well, you almost hurt yourself tonight, didn't you? Maybe next time you'd take a tumble down the stairs and try to slap some ridiculous lawsuit on my mother. Who knows? Point is, we're not going to find out."

His close proximity unnerved her after everything else that had happened tonight. She took a step back, needing the distance. "What are you talking about?"

"You and I may have spent a couple of Christmases in the same house when you were a kid, but we don't really know each other, do we? In fact, all I really know about you now is what I've seen tonight, and that doesn't exactly inspire a whole lot of confidence. So basically what I'm saying is, give me five minutes to pack a bag."

They stared at each other like it was high noon, and then he added,

"Because as long as you're staying at the house, I am, too."

◆ CHAPTER SEVENTEEN ◆

GREY LIGHT FILTERED AROUND the edges of the curtains in Kat's room. Sunrise. It had taken forever to get here. She'd lain awake most of the night, afraid to close her eyes and checking every so often to make sure that the door was still locked and that the chair she'd braced in front of it was still in place. And then checking again.

She was less concerned with keeping someone out than she was with locking herself in. Whatever happened last night, she was increasingly sure it had involved herself alone. She would have heard someone trying to get in, or she would at least have some sort of recollection of someone else's presence, or… *something*, surely.

Could sleepwalking have been the answer? People were known to do all kinds of things in that kind of state, weren't they? Including, perhaps, using a key to unlock a door. It seemed unlikely, considering she had no history of it, but just in case, she'd buried the key deep in the back of a drawer after locking herself in for the night.

But sleepwalking certainly didn't explain what happened six years ago when she'd wound up with a bottle of prescription pills in her stomach. She was grasping at straws right now, and she realized it, desperate for an explanation that would mean anything else besides her mind cracking up, because what else could it be? She'd been fine back home—well, not fine, but not seeing or smelling things that weren't there. It was this place, this house. Something about it was doing this to her, surely.

But why there? Why the pond? She was repulsed by that place, not drawn to it. Of all the places her subconscious could have led her to—if indeed it had—virtually any other place on the estate made more sense. But the pond, the pond was loss. The pond was death. At least that was what *she* saw every time she looked at it. She would never go there of her own free will.

She shivered beneath the covers. The room had gone cool again, in spite of the fact that she'd kept the windows closed and locked. It ought to have been stuffy. She hated the way the house did that and always had. Her mother hadn't cared for it either. Maybe Kat was more like her than she realized.

In life *and* in death, a voice in the back of her mind taunted her.

Her hands clenched reflexively, and she wrapped the covers tighter around herself.

But maybe the answer lay with her mother after all. Or even her father, although her mother seemed more likely considering the odd circumstances surrounding her drowning. Maybe there was a family history of this kind of behavior.

That her parents had neglected to mention to her? Her grandparents, too? Unlikely. And her mother's accident had occurred in the middle of the day when she was supposed to have been working in the garden. No sleepwalking there.

Kat closed her eyes and reached back into her memory as far as she could. No encounters with her mother roaming the halls at night in her sleep, no odd behaviors that could be linked to something like—

She opened her eyes again.

Wait, there had been something, hadn't there? Just once, and a very long time ago. So long ago that she was half-afraid she was remembering it wrong. An evening in the parlor. A cold evening, because the fireplace was lit up brilliantly with crackling flames, so it must have been during that first winter. Kat played on the floor beside the sofa with some toys, but she couldn't remember which ones now. What she did remember was that something made her glance up at where her mother sat curled up beneath a blanket on the sofa. What had it been?

Something about the quiet in the room, that was it. Somehow the silence had been disturbing and wrong. And when she looked at her mother's face for reassurance, she saw the strangest look in her eyes. Something so blank that it unnerved her, and she'd put her small hand on her mother's wrist intending to shake her out of it.

But the moment her daughter's hand touched her skin, Kat's mother had blinked, and the foreign look dissipated. And her mother patted her hand as if nothing was amiss before returning to the crossword puzzle on her lap, and the evening had continued.

Was it real? Her mind had already proved that it couldn't be trusted. Add in her state of exhaustion and what nearly happened last night, and the line between truth and fiction was impossible to see.

But it *felt* real.

Her head began to ache. If she wasn't crazy yet, she was going to drive herself crazy wondering about such things. Maybe Gran had been right after all. Maybe this trip was a bad idea. If she had hoped to achieve closure and peace of mind, she was failing miserably. All she really wanted to do was run screaming from the house, but she couldn't leave. Not yet. Because now there was Emily to consider.

The light outside brightened further. It was more reassuring than the darkness of night, but Kat still lay rigid in her bed. Finally, she threw back the covers. Sleep was a lost cause at this point, and she was more than a little afraid of what might happen if she closed her eyes anyway. No telling where she might wake up this time, or if she'd even wake up at all.

Stepping carefully in case she'd missed any pieces of broken glass the night before, she stopped in front of the bureau to pull out some clothes and caught her reflection in the fractured remains of the mirror. She was not surprised to see shadows under her eyes, but she was taken aback by just how dark they were, and by the hunted look in her eyes themselves. It was almost like looking at someone else, so foreign did her own face seem to her just then.

Hunted. An odd choice of words for her mind to produce.

Her sleep-deprived mind was running away with itself now. Time to get out of here, at least for a little while. If she couldn't jog, she could still get some fresh air.

Dressing quickly, Kat undid the makeshift barricade in front of her door and unlocked it. The house was still and quiet, and she was careful where she stepped in the hall. The floorboards tended to creak, and although she couldn't avoid the rest of the household forever, she was loathe to wake any of them before she had to.

No one stirred on the second floor. Reaching the landing, Kat glanced upward towards the third. Michael was up there somewhere having moved into one of the bedrooms late the night before, and she frowned instinctively as she thought of him. Which was unfair of her, she knew, especially after last night. Of course he was concerned about her being in the same house as his family. She'd given him every reason to be. And considering that she would have been dead twice over if it hadn't been for him, she was hardly in a position to be churlish about it.

But that was easier said than done after the sleepless night she'd had. Frowning came naturally. After listening for a moment longer and hearing no signs of wakefulness from the third floor either, Kat crept downstairs and into the kitchen.

Her stomach was in no condition to handle food yet this morning, but she needed something. Not coffee; more jitters would not be helpful now. But juice would be enough to keep her from getting lightheaded while walking, so she got a glass from a cupboard and rummaged through the refrigerator until she found what she was looking for.

Then she closed the refrigerator door again and nearly jumped out of her skin when she saw Emily standing in the doorway. "Holy—"

Stifling the rest of what she'd been about to exclaim, Kat willed her heart back down from her throat. "What are you doing up so early?"

The little girl studied her gravely. "I heard a noise."

So much for Kat's tiptoeing. "Sorry. I thought I was being quiet."

"It's okay. I wasn't asleep."

"No?"

Emily shook her head, and for the first time Kat noticed faint shadows under her eyes as well. "Where are you going?"

"What do you mean?"

"You have your shoes on." Emily pointed at the sneakers on Kat's feet. "Are you going outside?"

"Just going for a walk, that's all."

"Can I come?"

The request took Kat by surprise. "With *me*?" she asked, which she supposed sounded about as stupid as it really was, but she couldn't help herself. She was not used to being found interesting by young children. Or by most other people either, really. "Oh." Glancing up at the ceiling as if she expected to hear Michael's feet on the stairs, hastening to check if she was pilfering the silver—which was ridiculous since it technically belonged to her anyway—Kat pictured the expression on his face if he were to hear Emily's request. "I don't think your big brother would be too happy about that."

And then she told herself that it was because of the disappointed look on her half-sister's face that she reconsidered, but it was impossible to ignore completely the spark of satisfaction she felt when she pictured Michael's frown of displeasure.

"I'll give you two minutes to get dressed."

Emily's eyes lit up.

◆◆◆

THE CHILD MUST HAVE taken Kat at her word, because she was up and back down the stairs again so quickly that Kat had little time to do more than scribble a short note and put it on the refrigerator. It was nothing much, just enough to say where they were going if someone should stumble onto Emily's empty room and start to panic. This early, though, that seemed unlikely.

Kat's feet seemed to know where she wanted to go even before she did. They took her out through the back door and toward the hill with the Delancey family plot, which meant going through the gardens to get there. She gave the pond a wide berth, sticking to the farthest edges of the landscaped grounds. If Emily noticed, she gave no sign and merely trotted contentedly beside her older sister. Reminding herself that the little girl had much shorter legs, Kat slowed her own pace down.

Neither of them spoke as they walked up the hill, and Emily seemed just as comfortable with silence as Kat was. Was that common for someone so young? Maybe it was when one was raised as an only child, or nearly so as the age differences in Emily's case meant for her. Or maybe it was growing up here that did it. As hard as she tried, Kat couldn't imagine the sounds of happy children at play anywhere on this estate.

The iron gate creaked as they went through it, and it almost seemed as if the wind picked up at the sound. It swept a few loose strands of hair into Kat's eyes, but she ignored them as she came to a stop by her parents' graves. She wasn't sure why she'd come. Maybe she'd hoped to feel her parents' presence in this place, foolishly wishing for some sort of comfort from them after what happened last night. She was much too old to be soothed by something so simple as a stroke of the hair or a kiss on the head, but for just a moment she was sorry that she was not five years old and could not run to their arms for reassurance. Her father's lap had been the safest place in the world when she was little. Now no place was.

Emily stared somberly down at their father's grave. "Mommy says he was very nice."

"Yes," Kat agreed, feeling a sudden pang that the little girl would never know it for herself. "He was." Her voice caught in her throat, and she didn't dare say anything more for fear of it giving out altogether.

"She looks at pictures of him a lot. Sometimes she cries, but only when she doesn't know I'm there."

Somehow that revelation was surprising, although maybe it shouldn't have been. Of course Grace would miss him, maybe even as much as Kat did. It was so easy for her to forget that sometimes. In spite of the fact that her father had openly cared for Grace, she'd still always felt on some level that her stepmother was an intruder into their lives. Well, not an intruder maybe, but certainly an outsider. And if Kat felt it, maybe Grace did, too.

She studied her father's headstone with a flicker of guilt, noting again the way his grave and her mother's were so carefully tended. Clearing her throat, she tried to speak with more lightness than she felt. "Your gardener doesn't miss a weed, does he?"

"Mommy does it."

Another surprise. Grace was not outdoorsy, and the image of her on hands and knees in the dirt was hard to conjure up. "She does?"

Emily nodded.

Which meant Grace had also been the one to tend the grave of Kat's mother. Because it had been important to Kat's father maybe. And suddenly Kat wished that she'd broken the news of her plans for the sale of the house much more gently last night.

"We're supposed to bring flowers," her sister said from beside her. "I'll get some." She wandered off toward the edge of the fenced-in plot to gather what might have been wildflowers but were most likely just flowering weeds.

Kat let her go, grateful for the reprieve from guarding her emotions. But it wouldn't last long, so she allowed herself a single shaky breath and then moved on past the headstones.

She'd noticed her great-uncle Thomas's headstone before but paid no special attention to the ones beside it. Today she did. His wife, she realized, reading the name and dates on the first one. And the others… Good God, had all of his children died before him? She supposed it made sense now that she thought about it. Why else would he have left the manor to her father? He had no direct descendants of his own left. And they had all died relatively young although at different times, she realized with growing nausea as she examined the dates more closely. And she'd thought her own losses here tragic. Not that she'd expected a graveyard to be a happy place, but still…

She glanced up and around her. Considering that the house had been built in the middle of the nineteenth century, there seemed to be an unfortunately large number of graves in the family plot. Shouldn't more Delanceys have moved away, spread out into the world and started their own branches of the family tree? Granted, disease and war might have claimed more than a few before they were of an age to start their own families, especially in the home's earlier years, but other families survived and even thrived despite harsh circumstances. Why had this one been so unlucky?

Her eyes traveled over the many headstones. The ones furthest back were the most overgrown with weeds and brambles, probably the oldest. Curious now, Kat made her way over to them, careful not to step on any of the graves themselves.

Thorny vines covered much of what had originally been inscribed on the oldest stones, and moss covered some of the rest. It might have been wiser to come back later with gloves on, but curiosity made her impatient. Truth be told, she wasn't sure how much longer she dared stay at the manor anyway. She might not come back to the graveyard before she left. So she grasped the vines as carefully as she could and pulled.

They hung on to the stones tightly, but she persisted until they finally began to give way. A thorn sliced into one of her fingers, and she dropped the bunch of brambles that were in her hand. It was bleeding, and she held it carefully away from her as a few drops of red fell to the ground, her attention focused on the headstone before her.

"Richard John Delancey," she read aloud. Born in 1854, died in 1910. And below that, *Beloved Husband and Father.* The first Delancey, or at least the first one to live here. And right beside him…

Charlotte Hoyt Delancey. 1866 - 1889. Beloved Wife and Mother. Another one who died young.

But even worse were the three grave markers beside hers, smaller and with childlike cherubs carved into them. Her children? Kat turned away, her stomach churning at the thought.

Her gaze landed on the grave on the other side of Richard's and would not have lingered there except for part of the name that caught her attention. *Miranda Hoyt Delancey.* The same maiden name as Charlotte's. Sister or cousin? She read the rest of the inscription. *1864 - 1904. Beloved Wife.* So Richard had buried two wives and three children. No—maybe four, because there was another tiny headstone beside Miranda, too covered in moss and vines to read. Kat's hand wouldn't appreciate any more attempts to clear brambles, and she didn't really care to read about another dead child anyway. She turned away, sorry she'd looked at all.

And saw Emily heading toward her, a fistful of yellow wildflowers in her hands. Kat hid her injured hand from view.

Not quite fast enough, though, because the little girl asked, "What happened to your hand?"

"Nothing. Just a little cut. I'll fix it up when we get back to the house."

"We have Band-Aids."

"Good to know," Kat said, surprised by a faint urge to smile.

Wordlessly, Emily held out half of the flowers she'd picked. Taking them in her good hand, Kat followed the girl back to their father's grave and watched as her little sister placed hers very carefully just so on top of it. She then looked at Kat expectantly.

It was awkward using just one hand, but Kat managed to set some of the cheery yellow blossoms first on her father's grave and then on her mother's.

"Who is that?"

"My mother," Kat answered, looking down at the headstone.

"Oh."

"Come on, we should get back now."

Kat held the gate for Emily and then closed it behind them. When she turned to start down the hill, she was startled by the feel of Emily's small hand slipping into her own, the uninjured one. The little girl did it quite naturally and seemed to think nothing of it, and after a moment, Kat curled her fingers around her sister's.

They walked in companionable silence the rest of the way back, and when they reached the gardens—whether it made sense or not—Kat was careful to keep herself between the pond and Emily.

◆ CHAPTER EIGHTEEN ◆

GRACE WAS WAITING FOR them when they walked through the back door and into the kitchen. She sat on a stool at the kitchen counter, already dressed for the day and with a cup of coffee sitting in front of her. From the look of it, she had not touched it yet. Kat's hurried note was next to it.

Emily's hand was still in Kat's, so Kat felt the way the girl tensed up as soon as she saw her mother. She was not the only one to do so. While Grace's face was almost carefully expressionless, the look in her eyes when she looked at Kat was decidedly cool.

"Your shoes are dirty, Emily. Please go upstairs and change them."

The girl nodded at her mother's request and withdrew her hand from Kat's. Glancing uneasily between her mother and her sister, she plodded out of the room.

Grace rose from the stool, her body rigid with tension. "I don't want you and Emily alone together again. Ever."

"I see Michael talked to you."

"Kat—"

"Understood," she returned crisply. It was not unexpected. The dismay she felt was, though. Mostly regarding Emily, but to some extent Grace as well. They had never been friends, but they had never precisely been enemies, either. It was Kat's own fault, but it had never been her intention. Even if things hadn't turned sour, no mother in her right mind would be thrilled to have her daughter hanging around someone prone to odd blackouts. Had their positions been reversed, Kat would likely have drawn the same line in the sand, and probably with more bluntness.

So she didn't protest. She did, however, bring up something that would likely be a sore subject—not because she knew it was sore, but because she felt an increasing need to wrap things up with the house and get herself on a flight home as soon as possible. In the end, they'd all be grateful for that.

Grace was just turning to go when Kat's words stopped her. "Dad used to have some old family records. Books and things."

"Yes," Grace acknowledged coolly.

"Do you know where those would be?"

"Probably in the attic." Her stepmother's expression turned wary. "Why?"

For a moment, Kat considered not answering, or at least not answering truthfully. But she was not a skilled liar, and earning more suspicion at this point might be worse than earning more enmity. "A history of the family and the house might appeal to buyers."

Grace turned and walked out without another word. Remembering the carefully tended graves on the hill above them, Kat watched her go with a twinge of regret.

Her words had been a half-truth; her interest in appealing to buyers was only part of the reason she'd asked about family records. There was a wrongness to this house, despite the dismissals of therapists and family alike. A kind of shadow over her childhood, her parents... Herself. But there were a lot of graves up on that hill besides those of her parents—a startling number, really, and so many tragically brief dates on the headstones. History, her father used to say—this place was full of history. Maybe it had more to tell her than he'd ever realized.

Her hand was still bleeding. Not badly, but it did need attention. So did the rest of her since the walk had only done so much to wake her up after her restless night. Fresh air hadn't been enough, but maybe a shower would be. Cradling her injured hand, Kat left the kitchen.

◆◆◆

THE SHOWER DID LEAVE Kat feeling more alert than before, but she suspected the effect was only going to be temporary. Past experience taught her that. But at least her hand felt better once she'd cleaned it up. Emily was right; they did have Band-Aids. They were decorated with Sesame Street characters, but they were Band-Aids all the same. It took three to cover the cut, but at least the cut wasn't deep. They made her think of Emily, which might have been why she didn't immediately see Michael when she stepped out of the bathroom and into the hallway.

His reflexes were faster than hers after her lack of sleep, which was probably the only thing that saved them from colliding with each other. Both were quick to put space between them.

His eyes flickered over her, and he glanced at her bandaged hand. "Should I ask?"

She ignored the question. "Didn't waste any time tattling on me, did you?"

"Well, I did consider gambling with the safety of my mother and sisters just for the sake of good manners, but then I decided… what the hell. Screw Emily Post."

That deserved even less of a response than his initial question, so Kat stepped around him and headed for the third floor stairs.

"Where are you going now?"

"Oh, I don't know," she returned crossly, over her shoulder. "Set fire to the house maybe, or throw myself off the roof. You never can tell with crazy people."

Judging by his expression, he was not amused.

She didn't care. It was her house, after all. He might have reason to keep tabs on her after last night, but she'd be damned if she was going to report her every move to him.

The floorboards creaked; he was following her. Fine. Let him. With any luck, he'd get tired of it soon enough and leave her alone, at least when she wasn't around the rest of the household.

The third floor wasn't her final destination. She reached it and proceeded down the hall to the stairs that led up to the attic. She got no more than two steps up those stairs before the air grew suddenly so cold that her startled breath came out as visible as if it had been a frosty winter's day, and she almost missed her step.

The chill was gone so quickly that it would have been easy enough to dismiss it as another trick of her mind. But it wasn't. It couldn't be. There were still goose bumps raised on her bare arms, and the effects of the drop in temperature still lingered on her skin in spite of the return of warm air. She wasn't—she *wasn't*—imagining things this time.

The hairs on the back of Kat's neck rose.

"What are you doing?"

The sound of Michael's voice as he came up right behind her made her jump and gasp out loud. She was lucky it was only a gasp and not a shriek, and she clutched at the bannister for balance.

"What the hell—" he started.

She cut him off. "Did you feel that?"

"Feel what?"

"The cold." Although that simple a word seemed insufficient to describe what she'd felt.

"All old houses have drafty spots. Wear a sweater," he returned, eyeing for just a moment the tank top she wore but then abruptly turning his attention to a place somewhat higher. He frowned a moment later, studying her face. "Kat, sit down. You look like you're about to pass out."

"I'm not going to faint."

"You're white as a sheet. Sit down before you fall down."

Obviously he had not felt the same thing she had. If he had, he would not be so unaffected. She wasn't about to provide him with more excuses for painting her as unhinged, so she said nothing more about the odd chill. "I'm fine. I just didn't eat any breakfast."

"Is that supposed to be reassuring? Because it's not."

Turning her back on him, Kat started up the stairs again. Behind her, Michael muttered something under his breath that she guessed was about her and rather unflattering, but she didn't pause.

She kept expecting at every moment to be hit with that unnatural cold again, or maybe something worse this time, but she made it to the top without further incident. Now she did pause, her hand on the doorknob of the attic's entrance, and she felt her heart pound in her chest.

The wrongness of the house was so strong. How was it possible that anyone could spend five minutes in it and not feel it? Let alone spend the entire night as Michael had done.

Because he's not the one who's a certifiable loon...

Her knuckles turned white where her grip on the doorknob tightened.

She was not crazy. Exhausted and worn through so thin from sleepless nights that sometimes she was amazed there was anything left of her at all, but she was not insane. She was *not*, she told herself, and maybe she would actually find something in the attic that would help convince everyone else of that. Or at least convince herself.

She took a deep breath and turned the knob.

It was not locked, but the door remained closed. Putting her shoulder against it, Kat shoved hard. It still stuck. Considering the age of the house, warped wood was a perfectly reasonable explanation. And yet there was a paranoid part of her that couldn't shake the feeling that warped wood had nothing to do with it.

Taking a step back in preparation to ram the door with her shoulder, she jumped again when she felt Michael's hand on her arm.

"You're going to hurt yourself," he said shortly, and he moved her out of the way enough that he could apply his own shoulder to the door instead. With a grunt, he threw his weight into it, and the door finally gave way. "Happy?"

Not really, because he was standing too close. Not intentionally, she was sure, and probably no one else but her would feel uncomfortable. Certainly Michael didn't seem to think anything of it, but she wasn't like Michael. She wasn't like anyone else she knew, really. And so the best she could do was manage a stiff nod, hoping he would step away from the door now that he'd opened it for her.

But maybe Michael's curiosity got the better of him, because he remained where he was in spite of the fact that the air that wafted out from the attic was stale and dusty. He peered into the gloom, and since it didn't appear as if he was going to step back anytime soon, Kat finally drew closer to him so she could see inside as well.

There was no light switch here. Whatever upgrades had been made to the house over the decades, modernizing the attic was not one of them. The only light available filtered through tiny windows that were covered in so much grime that it was a wonder any light penetrated them at all. The cobwebs didn't help either.

A particularly thick one hung right before their faces. Michael brushed it away with one hand, and a small dark shape skittered away. He grimaced. "Lovely. This place hasn't seen the light of day in years, Kat. What do you want with it anyway?"

"Those," she said, spotting several boxes in the gloom. Behind them sat a tremendous assortment of trunks and old furniture, none of which looked familiar to her.

"Why?"

"Family records, I hope."

"You're trying to uncover your family tree?"

"No, the house. I want to know more about the house."

He continued to eye the room with obvious distaste. "Since when?"

"Since now." Steeling herself, she brushed past him and into the room. "Don't you have a job to go to?"

"I've cleared my schedule for the next few days, so… no. You're my job right now."

"Are you planning on babysitting me all day?"

"Pretty much, yes."

Any papers that had been her father's were most likely to be found in the boxes nearest to the door, but it was entirely possible that there might be other family things buried in the attic that would tell a story all their own. Giving the boxes a cursory glance, Kat bent to examine a stack of books further back. It was filthy with dust up here and not the kind of place a person would enjoy exposing themselves to willingly, and maybe that was why she couldn't resist tossing back over her shoulder, "You're going to have a hard time doing it from the doorway."

She heard a mutter from over by the door that was quickly drowned out when she bumped against a couple of stacked chairs and inadvertently sent the top one crashing to the floor nearby her.

"Are you *trying* to kill yourself again?" Michael asked with a frown in his voice, and a moment later he appeared beside her, grimacing at the grime surrounding him.

Upon closer inspection, the books turned out to be children's books from a few decades ago. Sad, considering what she'd seen in the family burial plot, and not very promising either. Kat abandoned them and moved deeper into the piles of things around her, smothering a cough at the dust. Older items would be further back and further in, like the rings of a tree. That was what she wanted.

"What are you looking for back there? Besides tetanus, I mean. I thought you wanted those boxes over there."

"I do want them. If you're going to stalk me all day, you might at least make yourself useful and move them out by the stairs for me."

A huff of mirthless laughter escaped him. "You're a piece of work, Kat." But he rolled up his sleeves and hefted the first box as asked, shaking off a few more spiders as he did so.

Anything could have lain buried up here, there was so much stuff stacked up on every side. No, not stuff. Remnants from people's lives, some pieces more poignant than others. Some of it looked like potentially valuable antiques, although Kat's untrained eye couldn't tell for sure. It hardly mattered. She had no interest in the monetary value they represented. What she cared about more were drawers and cabinets she caught glimpses of in the gloom that might hold surprises in their nooks and crannies. A desk peeking out from behind a china hutch looked interesting. So did the china hutch, actually. But getting to them would be no easy feat. She'd have to move a lot of things to clear a path to them first.

Good thing she'd started early.

◆◆◆

"YOU MIGHT HAVE MENTIONED we'd be moving furniture." Michael glanced down at his clothes that were now streaked with dust and sweat. "This is a two-hundred dollar shirt, you know. Or at least it used to be."

Kat strained to push an old trunk nearer to the light of a window. "Two hundred dollars for a shirt? And you manage other people's money for a living?"

"I do all right."

"Better than your dad?"

It was a sore subject, and she knew it. A shadow flickered over Michael's face. "I really wouldn't know," he returned, refraining from helping her this time.

That was fine by her. If she was prickly enough, maybe he'd leave her alone altogether. She finished shoving the trunk over to where she wanted and knelt to rummage through it. "I guess not, working for his competition." Nothing but moth-eaten clothes and blankets. She let the lid fall back closed, disappointed. "Found any other ways to give him the finger lately?"

"You disapprove? Not all fathers were the saint that yours was, Kat."

Well, well. Kitty had claws of his own. Kat straightened to stretch her legs. "My dad wasn't a saint."

"Really? Try telling that to my mother."

The bitterness in his voice caught Kat off guard. She turned to face him. "He was good to Grace."

"Was he?" Michael shrugged and rifled without interest through a stack of yellowed magazines. "Well, he didn't toss her aside like an old pair of shoes the way my father did, so I suppose that's a step up."

"A big step up, from the sound of it. What exactly is your problem with my dad, Michael?"

He fixed her with a steely gaze. "My problem is that I watched my mother compete with a dead woman for your father's affection, and I think she always knew that she came in second."

"You're upset because my dad loved my mom? Are you serious?"

"I'm tired of watching my mother live her life for everybody except herself. Frankly, I think moving away from this place would do her a world of good. I just don't like the way you're pushing her into it."

"I'm doing her a favor. This house is poison."

He stared at her, and she realized a second too late that the words came out more vehemently than she'd intended. "I know you hate this place, but it's just a house, Kat. Bricks and wood."

"Really? Have you checked out the Delancey graveyard?" She pointed in the direction of the hill. "Because it sure seems like an awful lot of us die young."

"So… what?" His expression turned wary. "You think the place is cursed now? Please tell me that's not where you're going with this."

Of course not, not really.

And yet...

His voice lost some of its edge. "Kat—people die. That's just the sad truth. Your family's no different from any other that way."

Maybe he was right. Maybe not. Turning away from his gaze, Kat ventured back into the depths of the attic's questionable treasures. So far she'd found only a handful of old papers that looked even remotely personal—a few letters, some old newspaper clippings—but there was still plenty of unexplored space up here. She put her shoulder against a chaise lounge that had seen better days and started to shove.

A few boxes of old clothes tumbled down practically on top of her as a result, but she barely noticed because the slight movement she'd been able to manage was enough to reveal something new. The outline of a doorframe along with a rusty knob and keyhole. Maybe she ought to have realized that the footprint of the attic room in which they stood was too small to match the floors beneath it, but with all the things stored in here, the true size of the room had been impossible to tell. Servants' quarters maybe, from the manor's earliest years? Or had this floor always been used for storage? In any case, the sight of that door sent a prickle down her spine. If the oldest family mementos were stored in the back as the layers had so far suggested, then perhaps in this room…

She reached for the doorknob only to find it locked.

"Kat, wanting to sell this house because of painful memories is one thing," came Michael's voice from behind her as he approached, "but if you're doing this because of some craz—I mean, archaic notion of a curse—"

"Would Grace have the key to this?" Kat asked without turning around.

"What? I don't know. She's probably never even seen it before. Did you even hear a word I said?"

Frustrated, Kat rattled the doorknob uselessly. "Emily hates this place, too."

There was a pause before Michael responded, as if the words had caught him off guard. "Emily is six. Please tell me you haven't been putting ideas of a family curse into her head. Damn it, Kat, of all the irresponsible things!"

"I haven't said anything like that to her. I'm crazy, not stupid, remember?" Giving the door one more frustrated and fruitless yank, she turned and then gasped as Michael abruptly grabbed her and hauled her away from her recent discovery. She heard him grunt in pain and then heard the sound of something heavy crashing to the floor.

Dazed, Kat looked down to see a large, metal figurine lying in the place where she had been standing a moment ago. She had a vague recollection of seeing it perched up high on top of several other things earlier and could only stare at it now, along with the deep gouge it had made in the floorboards. If Michael hadn't pulled her away—

But the floor was not the only thing to have been damaged by the falling statuette. Frozen with shock in Michael's arms, Kat could only stare at the bleeding gash on his forearm that hadn't been there a moment ago. *That should have been my head* was the only thought that seemed to be able to form in her mind just then, and she stared up at him with wide eyes.

He noticed the gash first, and then her expression. His turned wary. "Don't even say it. It was just an accident, Kat, not some sort of curse from beyond. You were shoving furniture around like a bull on steroids—"

A sudden squealing sound interrupted him, and they both staggered back from the sight of a pair of rats squeezing out from behind stacks of furniture in one dark corner. And then what had only been two turned into a steady stream of them, pouring out from the shadows as if running from a raging fire. The appearance of rats out of the blue would have been bad enough in and of itself, but when the creatures seemed to veer straight for them as if herded that way, Michael and Kat bolted toward the exit at the same time as if on cue. They burst out into the hall, and then Michael slammed the door shut behind them, muttering a particularly foul expletive under his breath.

"Well," he said, giving his arm a cursory inspection and grimacing, "we don't need an exorcist, but we definitely need an exterminator."

Kat didn't answer. She just sank down onto one of the boxes he'd carried into the hall earlier and stared at the closed door.

◆ CHAPTER NINETEEN ◆

IT WAS THE BLOOD that jarred her from her current state. It was pooling in the cut on Michael's arm, and in another minute, it would start dripping on the floor. He altered the angle at which he cradled the injured limb as if suddenly becoming aware of that fact himself.

"If it's all the same to you, maybe we could call it a day as far as the attic goes." The look he gave her dared her to protest.

She didn't. After what happened, she couldn't. And when he gestured at the stairs in expectant invitation, she took them without a word. He followed closely behind.

He seemed surprised, though, when she went into the second floor bathroom ahead of him and began rummaging in its cabinet for something to bandage his arm. "I can clean it up myself," he said, and she wondered how cold she must really seem to other people that he would find her intention to help so unexpected.

In spite of his comment, she fished out a bottle of something for disinfecting. "It's your right arm, and you're right-handed."

"Oh, I'm very versatile."

She'd offered, and he'd said no. Walking away would have been perfectly acceptable now, but she stayed where she was anyway. He was the enemy and yet he was not, and the line in the sand didn't seem as clear as before. Something in her face must have shown the turmoil she felt, including no small amount of guilt, because he finally held out his arm for her and let her doctor it.

She tucked her hair behind her ears so it wouldn't interfere with her examination and then leaned over his arm. The cut wasn't as deep as she first thought, and it stopped bleeding almost as soon as she finished cleaning it. She tore off short strips of tape and fastened a patch of gauze over it.

"Ah, damn. I had my heart set on Elmo."

With a start of surprise, she realized he was referring to the Band-Aids on her hand. Was that a joke? It was a mild attempt at humor at best, and rather dry, but it was still so unexpected that she was at a loss as to how to respond. And when she glanced up just in time to see his gaze flicker away from where it had been resting on a stray lock of her hair that had escaped its place behind her ear, she was even more discomfited.

Maybe he was, too, because he flexed his arm as if testing it and then spoke with what seemed like forced cheerfulness. "Well, that takes care of the arm. Now excuse me while I go burn the shirt." And then he left the bathroom, and Kat, muttering something to himself about two hundred dollars going up in smoke.

And she was left contemplating the empty space where he'd stood.

◆◆◆

THE MORNING IN THE attic left her so grimy that Kat took her second shower of the day. She might have been better off waiting until after she retrieved the dusty boxes that sat outside the attic door, waiting for her, but her mind was not at its sharpest right now. No matter. If nothing else, she could always search through them right where they were and bring the most promising items back to her room for closer inspection.

But she was reluctant to return to the topmost floor. Whether it was the rats or the unearthly draft of icy air she'd felt before that most disturbed her was impossible to say. Neither helped the situation much, but it would have been of some comfort if Michael had at least felt the unnatural cold, too; she was left instead to agonize as she always did over whether or not she could trust her senses. Had it been real or not? She spent a long moment at the base of the attic steps just staring upward before finally ascending them.

There was no strange chill this time. One for one, she thought as she reached the landing, and then she paused and listened for sounds of movement.

Nothing. No squeaking, no scratching of small claws against the wooden floor. She was two for two, although she didn't try to tempt fate any further by opening the attic door. Instead she knelt beside the nearest box, painfully conscious of how even something so slight as her arm accidentally brushing the lid of the box could make her tense up with fresh anxiety. Shame ate away at her, and she all but tore the first box open as if to prove to herself that she had not been rendered a complete basket case after all.

She half-expected something to jump out of the box at her, be it four-legged or eight, but nothing did. Inside was a mix of books, notebooks, and folders full of papers. She recognized her father's writing on one sheet that stuck out and reached for that folder first.

He'd been working on a family tree, by the look of it. A detailed one. No mere list of names and dates, this one included snippets about whatever he'd unearthed about Delancey lives at the time. He'd started at the most recent birth—Kat's—and had been working his way backwards; maybe information further back was harder to come by, at least in the kind of detail he appeared to have preferred. Or maybe he'd just been saving the best for the last since he'd always had a particular fascination for the man who'd built the manor. In any case, the oldest names had little written about them. He'd died before he could finish it.

She'd take it with her to read later. Setting the folder on the floor beside her, she dug further through the box. A few photos fell out of a sheaf of papers she flipped through. Some looked to be from the 1930s or 40s by the look of the clothes in the black and white images. One or two looked even older than that. Turning one over, she saw that it had been labeled, although not by her father. This was someone else's writing. The light was poor up here, but she was finally able to make out the faded, spidery scrawl.

Charles Delancey, August 1912.

One of Richard's two surviving sons. The eldest, according to her father's unfinished family tree. He looked grim in the photo. Given everything that had happened to his family, she couldn't blame him. The other photo that might have come from the same era was of a small group of people, too small for her to make out their faces very well. With a start of recognition, she realized they were posed in the gardens, although the landscaping was far less mature than what existed there now. But there was no doubt it was the backyard; she recognized the edge of the pond on one side. Unable to suppress a shudder, Kat thrust the pictures into the folder beside her with less care than she should have, given their age. Later. She would look at those later. Not here on the shadowy attic landing.

Some of the books in the box were of no help at all. They were not specific to the house or the family, but were either histories of the region or on the subject of genealogy in general. From what she could tell, her father had merely marked passages he found interesting in and of themselves, because they had little or nothing to do with the Delanceys. Those she left in the box.

The other boxes were even less helpful and had nothing inside them about family history at all. Well, it had been a gamble. Junk, she thought, leafing through it briefly. Someone's old personal items—things in such poor shape that they couldn't be donated but perhaps too personal to just be thrown out with the trash. An old shoe-shine kit that had seen much use by the look of it, a photo frame so badly smashed that she could barely make out faces in the photo within it, a broken watch…

Picking it up, Kat turned it over and saw initials engraved on the back: T.W.D. Thomas William Delancey. Her father's great-uncle, and the man from whom he'd inherited the house. Had her father been the one to pack up these things? He would have been too respectful to merely throw them out, so it might have been him, or even her mother.

She was about to close that box up when she saw what looked like the edge of a newspaper clipping beneath the wrecked picture frame. Careful not to break it any further, she lifted the frame out of the way. There were two news clippings. One looked like an obituary for Thomas, and the other more like a general article about his death. She glanced over the first and saw that what she'd guessed in the graveyard was correct; his wife and children had died before him, although no details about their deaths were given. The second clipping made her go cold.

> *Tragedy struck one of the area's oldest homes Tuesday night when reticent local William Delancey was killed in an accident in the library of the Delancey family manor. Local authorities say that one of the grand home's heavy bookcases fell on top of Delancey, and the ultimate cause of his death was trauma to his head. He was not discovered until the following afternoon when a business associate came around to learn why Delancey had missed a morning appointment. Evidence at the scene suggests that a candle may have caught a curtain on fire, and investigators are speculating that Delancey may have knocked the bookcase over somehow while attempting to put out the fire. Considering the most recent loss that Delancey had suffered, one acquaintance speculated that the fire might not have been entirely accidental. The official report is still pending.*

Kat's stomach turned over. She'd *played* in that room, curled up in a chair to read, and run across it countless times to greet her father or to play explorer. And a man had died in it? Was that why her parents hadn't let her go in there when they'd first moved in? And why her father bolted every bookcase to the wall? Her parents had mentioned an accident, but this was no mere bump or fall. This was... gruesome.

Maybe this was the real reason her mother always preferred the parlor; maybe the cold had nothing to do with it at all. Accidents happen, her father said pragmatically more than once over the years. Would he have overcome his distaste for the site of a man's death so easily if the house hadn't been in the family for generations? Surely if it was any other place, he would have just sold it to the first buyer willing to take it. But maybe that was the nature of old things. The longer you possessed them—or the longer your family did—the more they possessed you.

She stared at the words and reread them, particularly one part.

> *... Evidence at the scene suggests that a candle may have caught a curtain on fire, and investigators are speculating that Delancey may have knocked the bookcase over somehow while attempting to put out the fire. Considering the recent losses Delancey had suffered, one acquaintance speculated that the fire might not have been entirely accidental...*

The ruined curtain. She remembered that burn mark. It had been at an odd location. Too high up for whatever had lit it to have been sitting on the floor, but no furniture nearby on which a candle or anything else might rest. Had it been put to the curtain deliberately by an old man grieving for his family and tired of life? The author of the article hadn't quite been bold enough to do more than imply—worried about libel, maybe—but there was enough there nestled between the lines on the page. The reporter needn't have worried about any backlash. There was no one left except Kat's father to worry about a smear on the family name.

Well, no one but Kat's father and Kat. According to her father's notes, they were the last branch on a family tree that had all but died out. And now it was just Kat.

No, not quite. There was Emily, too. Kat would have to add her name to the list and finish what her father had started. There was something very unsettling about the chart of names, though, and the way it looked less like a spreading tree and more like a fire that was slowly being extinguished.

Adding the news clippings to the pile of things she'd pulled out of the boxes, Kat scooped them up in her arms. She gave the attic door one last uneasy glance before heading back down the stairs and wondered if the air around the attic landing momentarily darkened or if it was just her imagination.

◆ CHAPTER TWENTY ◆

HER NIGHTS OF INSUFFICIENT sleep took their toll on her, because in spite of her best intentions to read through every page she'd brought down to her room from the attic floor, Kat had to fight to keep her eyes open. At some point in the afternoon, she must have lost that fight, because she woke with a start that sent papers tumbling off her lap and onto the bed—and an eerie feeling that something was reaching for her.

Her first instinct was to look at the door. Although she'd locked it out of habit, she'd neglected to prop the chair in front of it. Why would she? Napping hadn't been part of her plan. Panic flashed through her before a quick perusal of the room reassured her that she hadn't been running amok in some sleepwalking state. Nothing was out of place or disturbed.

Just her.

Her pulse slowed back down to normal. Maybe the nap had been a godsend, then. She needed sleep, and somehow sleeping seemed less dangerous during the day than it did when the house was dark and quiet. And the few nights she had left in this place were unlikely to be any more restful than the others, including this one. She glanced out the window at a sky that was already beginning to grow grey with twilight and felt a familiar dread descend.

Her stomach growled, breaking her line of thought. No wonder. She'd skipped breakfast and slept through lunch. Hunger seemed like a small and inconsequential thing after the past few days, only really catching her attention when it finally grew too severe to ignore. She was loathe to go downstairs, though, and even went so far as to rifle through her bags for any snacks left over from her flight. There wasn't much, just a half-empty bag of stale pretzels. But it was enough to take the edge off. She could wait a little longer for real food and lessen her chances of running into anyone else in the kitchen, and that included Michael. Maybe especially him.

She would have waited until twilight turned to full-fledged evening, but before it did, she heard a creak from the floorboards outside her door. And then another one, as if whoever stood outside there couldn't quite make up his or her mind about whether or not to knock. Or do something far less civilized, Kat thought, picturing all manner of nasty little surprises Alexis might leave outside her door.

But her stepsister hadn't crossed her path since Kat confronted her about the smashed mirror, and Grace was too upset to be so hesitant to walk in. That left only Michael and Emily, and when a folded piece of paper appeared beneath her door, she suspected it was the latter. It wiggled slightly as if whoever was trying to slide it under was having trouble. A moment later it came all the way through the crack of space beneath the door, and by the time Kat made it off the bed and to the door to open it, she thought she'd missed her unexpected visitor. But then she saw the top of Emily's head and then her eyes, blinking at her, as the girl climbed back up a few of the stairs to which she'd retreated.

Grace's warning from that morning rang in Kat's ears again, and she froze, uncertain whether she ought to acknowledge the girl's presence or not. But then Emily climbed another step and—after a furtive glance down the stairs and at the floor below—flicked her hand in such a shy wave that Kat couldn't ignore it.

"Dinner's over," the child said, her voice low and hushed; Grace must have given Emily a similar speech to the one she'd given Kat. There was too much guilt in Emily's posture for it to be otherwise. "You can come down now, if you want."

So serious for such a young age, and perceptive. "Thanks," Kat returned after an awkward pause. And then because she couldn't think of anything else to do, she bent to pick up the folded piece of paper from where it lay on the floor near her feet. She opened it and saw a hand-drawn picture in crayon of what might have been the yellow flowers Emily picked that morning, along with other blossoms that had to be works of her imagination; color combinations like those didn't exist anywhere in nature. Bemused by the unexpected gift, Kat stared at it for a long moment.

Emily must have taken her silence the wrong way, because she fidgeted on the stairs and said, "I'm better at cats, but flowers are prettier."

"They're very pretty," Kat agreed, realizing belatedly that she should have said so right away. Her inexperience with children was showing through. Was it meant to be a thank-you? An expression of her delight at the prospect of moving? Whether it was or it wasn't, it seemed to mean *something* anyway, and Kat suspected it was as meaningful a gesture as a child of five could make.

Late as they were in coming, her words must have been the right ones, because Emily's expression relaxed into one of pleasure. Only for a moment, though. It was replaced by anxiety when she heard Alexis's voice behind her.

"What the hell do you think you're doing?" The older of Grace's two daughters came into view as she climbed higher on the stairs. "You know perfectly well Mom doesn't want you talking to her. Get back downstairs right now. She's going to go ballistic, you know," she called after the child with satisfaction as Emily hastened to comply.

If Grace was going to be angry at anybody, it was more likely to be Kat. She knew it, and she was sure Alexis knew it, too. But trust Alexis not to miss an opportunity to make someone tremble.

Defending the little girl would only make her more of a target, so instead Kat hid the picture Emily had drawn from view and only said, "Started packing yet?"

It was enough of a dig to make Alexis's eyes lose their glimmer of satisfaction. Her response was a raised middle finger.

"Guess not." Locking her bedroom door, Kat walked down the stairs and past Alexis's glower as if the other young woman wasn't there.

But Alexis didn't return the favor. "You look like crap. Rough night?" Judging by her tone, she already knew perfectly well that it had been and was delighted by that fact.

Kat ignored her, but her hand on the banister was not as steady as she would have liked. She heard Alexis laugh and knew she'd noticed it as well. No help for it now, though.

She heard the door to the parlor open and close again before she reached the ground floor: Emily, no doubt, returning to her mother's side as ordered. The door was open long enough for Kat to catch a snatch of voices, and the tones of them were clear even if the words were not. Grace was not happy with Michael.

She should have taken advantage of this opportunity to slip into the kitchen and grab some food while no one else was in there, but instead Kat was drawn to the parlor door as if she couldn't help herself. Knowing there was a good chance she'd regret it, she pressed her ear against the door anyway.

◆◆◆

GRACE WAITED UNTIL EMILY was busily absorbed in her coloring again on the other side of the room before speaking to her son again, and when she did, her voice was even more clipped than before. "Perhaps you'd like to help her send us packing."

Michael sighed and ran his fingers through his hair. Dark, thick hair that reminded Grace all too well of his father's. "Mother, you're being ridiculous. All I did was move a few boxes around that she would have moved on her own anyway."

He might have been right, but that fact did nothing to improve Grace's mood. She raised her teacup to her lips and took a sip instead of responding. It was one of those lovely heirloom pieces she'd admired for years, the same pieces that belonged to Kat now—in reality always had. The sudden urge to smash the thing into tiny pieces against the wall caught her by surprise. She set it down again before she could give in to the impulse.

"Do you really want her running around here unattended? I'm just keeping an eye on her."

"Oh, believe me, I noticed that," she returned, ice in her tone.

He blinked, and for a moment—just a moment, but it was long enough, and telling—he looked away.

Just like his father, a voice in her head whispered at her, astonishingly bitter. So much so that even she had to admit it couldn't possibly be directed toward Michael alone. No, she wasn't being fair to him, and she knew it; he'd been the rock she'd leaned on ever since Jonathan died, but still...

For a man who despised his father as much as Michael did, he took after him in more ways than he realized. Biology rearing its ugly head. Perhaps it was unavoidable. Oh, not that he was so very like the elder Fairmont; he was not the cold and calculating figure that Steven was, after all. Except, perhaps, in matters of business. But when it came to women—

Well, they both had an eye for pretty things, didn't they? And Kat did look so much like Lily. Maybe that was what made it sting most of all.

The only sound in the room was that of Emily's crayons against her paper. Maybe the little girl noticed that fact then, too, because she glanced up at her mother and Michael with a tiny furrow in her brow.

Grace picked up her dainty teacup again and took another sip. And then she pressed her lips together tightly and looked out the window in deliberate silence.

◆◆◆

KAT DREW BACK FROM the parlor door, not waiting to see if Michael had a response to his mother's accusation. This was why it didn't pay to listen at closed doors. Whatever was overheard was likely to be confusing at best and unsettling at worst.

Glancing up to make sure that Alexis hadn't witnessed her eavesdropping, Kat retreated to the relative safety of the empty kitchen.

◆ CHAPTER TWENTY-ONE ◆

THE THOUGHT OF BUMPING into either Grace or Michael just then filled her with such anxiety that Kat's dinner turned into something more closely resembling a mad dash than an actual meal. She scooped something out of a dish that was in the fridge, some chicken thing that was possibly past its prime—no real worries, though; Grace would never permit bad food to remain in the house—and slapped it between two slices of bread so that there would be no dishes to necessitate another trip down the stairs. One had been more than enough.

Dinner in hand, she locked herself in her room again. This time she remembered to barricade the door with the chair. She barely tasted the food, and in spite of her hunger, had to force herself to finish it.

A floorboard creaked—the second story landing. Footsteps sounded outside her room, slowing by her door for a moment before continuing on past it. Or were they returning to the stairs? They were too heavy to be Emily's, too heavy probably for all but one person in the house.

She held her breath until all was quiet again, not completely sure that she was more relieved than disappointed and not enjoying the confusion that inspired.

The chicken didn't sit well in her stomach. Or maybe it was the day itself, and if the future held more of the same unsettling sorts of things, continuing to stay on at the house made little sense. Tomorrow she could speak to a real estate agent and maybe establish someone local to handle the on-site details of putting the house up for sale. Maybe she could pack up and go home then, sooner than she'd first thought. Gran was right; this was the twenty-first century. All kinds of business matters could be handled from afar. Why not the sale of a house?

Gran. She was overdue to call her. After what happened last night, she was almost afraid to. Would Gran hear something in her voice and demand to know what had happened? Or worse, hop on the first plane out here in spite of Kat's insistence that both of her grandparents stay away?

Kat picked up her cell phone, eyed it for a minute, and then returned it to its place on the bedside table. No, not yet. Not until she was sure she could do it safely. Waiting was the lesser of two evils. Soon enough she could be back home, and then Gran could keep tabs on her to her heart's content.

She glanced at the mess of papers and books on the bed. There was no reason why she couldn't pack them all up and take them home with her. She could finish the family history her father started and send all or some of it to the real estate agent later, if he or she thought it would be beneficial. Sell the house and do her sisterly duty to Emily from afar.

And leave this place and sleepless nights behind her, God willing. Even just the prospect of it filled her with a kind of desperate hope. She'd made an honest effort, after all, and made the trip itself. Maybe the result had not been as promising as she'd hoped—understatement of the year, that—but maybe it would be enough to let her put the past behind her. It would have to be, because staying any longer seemed downright reckless. Facing her fear of the house was one thing; letting it quite literally be the death of her was another.

Her absence might be the kindest thing she could give to Grace anyway under the current circumstances, and after her bluntness last night, Kat owed her some sort of kindness. The sale of the house would go forward; she would not change her mind about that. But there was no need to rub salt in the wound with her continued presence in the house. The only one who might be sorry to see her go would be Emily, but at least the little girl would have the sale of the house to look forward to. Better to leave now before she unraveled anymore than she already had; that wasn't something Emily ought to see.

The night that lay ahead seemed just a little less daunting in light of her new plan. Not much, but at least it offered her a light at the end of a very dark tunnel. Barricading herself in for the night and burying the door key in the back of the drawer again, Kat slipped into a nightshirt and slid under the covers to examine more of the morning's find. It was bound to be a long night as they always were here, and reading was as good a way as any to pass the time.

Her new collection was a mixed bag, some things far more dull than others. One book turned out to be little more than an old business ledger that had belonged to Richard Delancey. Not much of interest there, although she did leaf through the whole thing just to be sure.

And couldn't help but grimace at some entries near the end.

Burial costs. Judging by the dates, they must have been for the first of his children to die. The ledger ended before the deaths of the other two, and those of his wives, which was something of a relief. There was something very depressing about reading references to caskets and other burial expenses, especially when they pertained to young children. And it was perhaps even more depressing because the entries were so impersonal, mere notations devoid of any emotion.

Then again, these were business papers. Words of loss and lament belonged in something more personal, like letters to family and friends—

She looked up.

—Or a journal, like the one she'd recognized in the library her first night here and carried up to her room with her. How had she forgotten about that?

Because it was no longer sitting on the bedside table where she'd left it, that was why. Out of sight, out of mind. Stiffening, Kat pushed aside books and papers to get out of bed and double check that the journal was indeed gone.

Alexis? Had she taken it the same evening she'd smashed the mirror? For the life of her, Kat couldn't remember when she'd last seen the leather-bound book there. All she could really remember was setting it down in the first place. Maybe it—

Then she spotted it, almost entirely hidden from view where it appeared to have fallen off the table and beneath the bed, halfway tucked between a bedframe leg and the wall. If she hadn't gotten down onto her hands and knees to search, she would never have seen it. She stared at it. The angle seemed wildly improbable for it to have wound up there on its own, even if it had been inadvertently knocked down in passing. Again, she thought of Alexis, but Alexis would likely have hidden the book farther away than that if she really wanted to drive Kat crazy.

Could she have done it herself? Possibly during that brief period last night when she'd lost time? If she'd been able to unlock a door and walk herself to the pond in her sleep, moving a book would be nothing in comparison. Well—it was unsettling, but nowhere near as unsettling as trying to drown herself.

She reached for the book and discovered it was actually wedged into its spot. Tugging on it at first had no effect, and the hairs on the back of her neck prickled as it seemed increasingly unlikely to her that the journal could have fallen there on its own. The force it must have taken to jam the thing in there… It had to have had help, although why either Alexis or Kat's own subconscious self would go to such trouble was a mystery. And she was getting damned tired of mysteries.

The book finally came free, although a part of Kat couldn't help but think the bedpost released it with great reluctance. The leather cover was damaged now, with scuffs and scrapes that she was sure hadn't been there before. For a moment Kat started to reach to examine the place where it had been caught, still wondering how it had gotten there, but a sudden dread of the bed somehow trapping her fingers there stopped her. It should have been a ridiculous thought, but after everything that had happened under this house's roof, somehow it wasn't.

So instead Kat climbed very carefully into her bed and opened the book on her lap, tensing up as she did so as if something might suddenly happen to stop her.

Nothing did.

Maybe her imagination was reading too much into things. No one was trying to keep the book from her after all, no one and no thing.

It was a strange turn of phrase to enter into her mind, even as an afterthought, and it lingered on the edge of Kat's awareness as she began reading the journal of Richard Delancey.

It was from later in his life, closer to the end of the nineteenth century than the middle. Somehow that didn't surprise Kat; her father would have been less fascinated by the romanticized ramblings of a younger man who was still wet behind the ears. Then again, the more she read the more Kat found it unlikely that Richard was ever all that sentimental, no matter what age he was. The journal began with little more than detailed accounts of his investment strategies and business dealings, and she began to worry that its pages were a waste of time after all. But then references to his first wife, Charlotte, crept in along with some of his children, and by that time there was enough to read between the lines that Kat decided her first impulse had been wrong. He was more than just a stoic businessman after all.

It was an entry about the third child's death that struck her as the most emotional one, almost as if he'd held it in as long as he could but that third one had finally broken him. The writing was still formal and even reserved, but the words were clearly those of a grieving man. She reread them, thinking of her parents as she did so.

We buried our dear Christopher today. It is still so terribly hard for me to grasp. My boy, my dear boy, lies cold in the ground beside his sisters, and I begin to wonder if God has seen fit to punish me, although I know not for what. Three children gone, and this last one my beloved Charlotte's heart and soul.

The small headstones and their cherubs appeared in Kat's mind, and she couldn't suppress a shiver of revulsion. Three children, one no older than Emily was now. Yes, that could be enough to make a man wonder if God had turned His back on him.

She bent her head to keep reading and found that the next passage disturbed her even more, but in a different way.

I do not know if she will survive this most recent loss, or if her grief will finally overwhelm her. Were it not for her sister's devotion, I think she would have succumbed long ago. I fear sometimes that the shock I see in my wife's eyes verges on madness.

Kat looked up from the book and stared unseeingly before her. Madness, mental illness—whatever name it went by, maybe it was no stranger to the Delancey bloodline. Maybe Kat was not the first in her family to draw whispers and stares. It wasn't the kind of reassurance she'd hoped to find in these pages. Should she trust her senses more or less now? After all, crazy people didn't question their own sanity, did they? And she questioned her own nearly every waking moment.

Her gaze lowered again, landing on the old photos she'd found that morning and tucked in amongst other things. They spilled out now, peeking out from beneath loose papers. She started to look away from them and back to the journal, then stopped and glanced back. The bedside lamp cast a brighter light than what little had made it through windows to the shadowed attic landing earlier. There was something in the photo of young Charles Delancey that was so faint she almost missed it again, in spite of the better light here. Setting the journal aside on the bedside table, Kat reached for the photo and held it closer to the lamp.

There, behind him in the photo. At first glance, it appeared almost to be a smudge, but it wasn't something *on* the photograph; it was *in* it. A sort of wispy blur, small and faint. Almost like some thing caught in mid-movement, but not a thing that was visible to her eyes. Something there and yet not there. She peered closer, trying to get a better look. Maybe her eyes were just too tired to focus—

Something hit her window with a loud smack, startling a gasp out of her and making her drop the photo. It tumbled from her fingers and onto the floor as she looked up at the window in time to see what might have been a flap of wings as something vanished into the darkness. She scrambled off the bed to try and get a closer look, but whatever it was, it was gone too fast. Most likely a bird or a bat, something perfectly ordinary and normal… and yet her pulse still thundered in her ears.

Drawing the curtains on both windows closed with such haste that it was a miracle she didn't tear them, Kat returned to the bed and bent to retrieve the picture. Despite having just closed the curtains, she felt an urge to hide herself and couldn't burrow back beneath the covers fast enough.

Coward.

Frightened of things that went bump in the night. Just like that little girl who'd come to the house sixteen years ago and then never felt quite safe again. Was this anything like what Emily felt, too? God help her if it was. They would both be well rid of the place, the sooner the better.

But until then, the key would remain in the lock, the chair would continue to act as sentry, and the light would stay on.

All night.

◆◆◆

SOMEONE'S FINGERS BRUSHED HER hair, and Kat's eyes flew open.

She'd fallen asleep.

Even with the light burning and her heart jumping at every sound, somehow Kat had finally fallen asleep. That light flickered now as if the electricity was considering going out, and Kat's eyes darted around the room in search of whoever it was who was in the room with her.

Because someone *was* there. At least, someone had been there a moment ago. She was sure someone had touched her and could have sworn she'd heard an echo of a voice as she'd been startled awake.

And the room—the room was so cold.

"Who's there?" Her words, hoarse in her throat, came out in a fog of frozen breath just like what she'd experienced on the attic stairs.

She pulled the covers up and around herself, starting to shake from more than just cold. Her breathing sped up, but as suddenly as it had settled over her, the chill was gone again. The light stopped its flickering.

A trick, just a horrible trick. It had to be. Never in her life had she wanted so desperately to look up and see Alexis standing in her doorway with a smirk of malicious glee on her face, but Alexis wasn't there. No one was.

But she might have been a moment ago, so Kat threw back the covers with the intention of yanking the door open and catching Alexis out in the hall. She froze, though, when she spotted the bureau and what lay on top of it.

The journal.

She stared at it. That was not where she'd left it. Maybe her senses couldn't be trusted, and maybe she might even conjure up hallucinations from midair, but she was sure she'd left the journal on the bedside table. Quite sure.

Shaking herself out of her stupor, Kat all but fell out of the bed in her haste to check the door. It was locked, and the chair was still braced against it. Alexis had not been in here playing tricks.

Then the real trembling began, and Kat sank back onto the bed before her legs could give out on her.

Someone had been there, in the room with her.

Not possible.

It wasn't possible, she repeated to herself, her shaking growing worse. She heard a sound like the whimpering of an injured animal and realized it was coming from her.

And she wondered just how crazy she really was.

◆ CHAPTER TWENTY-TWO ◆

RUN.

Where?

Anywhere. Just as long as it was somewhere away from the house. She wouldn't even need to pack. Forget the clothes, forget the bags. They could be replaced. Just board a plane and put as much distance between herself and the manor as possible.

But she could hardly just run screaming into the night, so she forced herself to breathe more slowly until the shakes finally went away. Then she yanked open the bureau drawers and upended what little that was in them into her bags.

First thing in the morning. She could call a taxi or even beg Michael to drive her to the airport.

She faltered in her packing. No, not Michael. A taxi would be simpler. Cleaner. Although he probably would be happy to oblige if it got her the hell away from his family.

And if there were no seats available on the next flight out?

Well, then she would wait. Even spend the night at the airport if she had to. And the next night, too. Anything was better than spending another night in this house—

Her hand brushed the picture then that Emily had made for her.

Kat's hands slowed their mad haste and then abandoned packing altogether. She reached for the picture.

An image appeared in her head then of Emily floating face down in the pond instead of Kat, and Kat's hand convulsed around the paper, inadvertently wrinkling it. She thrust the image from her mind.

She's not like me.

But thinking it didn't make it necessarily true. Maybe the little girl *was* different, and maybe Kat was the only thing that was really wrong with this house.

But if she wasn't…

Kat stared at the picture in her hand and then slowly smoothed out the wrinkles she'd made in it.

And then she pulled her clothes out of her bags with less than steady hands and put them back in the bureau drawers.

◆◆◆

SOMEONE WAS TAPPING ON his door.

At this hour? Good God, was it even morning yet?

Michael cracked open one eye to peer out from where he lay facedown on his pillow and muttered a curse under his breath. Maybe he'd imagined it, or better yet, dreamed it. Maybe it he just closed his eye again and went back to sleep, he—

Another knock sounded, tentative but louder than the one before. No, he hadn't dreamed it. Someone really was outside his room at—

He reached for his watch and squinted at it, then muttered some more.

This early in the morning he would have thought it must have been an emergency, but the hesitation of the person outside belied that possibility. So he didn't panic or make a mad scramble out of bed. Instead he threw off the covers—still muttering—and stumbled half-asleep to open the door with his watch still in his hand.

Kat stood in the hallway, hand raised in what would have been her third attempt to rouse him.

"Are you aware of what time it is?" Michael asked, rubbing the sleep from his eyes with little success.

"I..." She averted her eyes and seemed to struggle to find a good place to let them rest.

Really? Because he was only wearing pajama bottoms? Surely not. Just how sheltered was she?

"Sorry. I couldn't sleep."

Sleep deprivation made Michael irritable. "I could."

"I need a ride into town. I didn't know who else to ask, and a taxi—"

"At this hour? You're kidding, right?"

Now she did look at him, and her forehead furrowed with confusion. He held his watch out to her wordlessly. She peered at it, and then color bloomed in her cheeks. "I didn't realize how early it was. Sorry."

Two apologies in one morning. How unlike her. Given recent circumstances, he wasn't inclined to accept either one, but enough of the drowsiness finally left his brain to allow him to notice how deep the shadows beneath her eyes were this morning, so deep that it was hard to summon up any real hostility toward her. "You look terrible. Did you even sleep at all last night?"

"Not much."

"Up all night thinking about family curses?"

She flinched, and he felt a stab of shame at his flippancy, especially when he realized she was trembling. "What is it, Kat? What's wrong?"

Her mouth opened as if to answer him, but nothing came out, and her eyes were as guarded as ever.

He softened his voice and tried again. "What's happened?"

"You won't believe me."

"Maybe not, but try me."

"Last night…." She trailed off, then started again. "Last night, I could have sworn there was something in my room."

"Something like…?"

The breath she drew was ragged, and there was misery all over her face as if the last thing she wanted to do was confide in him, but something—desperation, maybe?—overrode her inhibitions. "I... I don't know. Things had been moved around, and I thought I felt..." She trailed off and shook her head. "At first I thought Alexis was screwing with my head."

It was, unfortunately, Alexis's style. Funny, but he felt a stab of guilt at that, too. She was more brat than anything else these days, at least when she thought someone was watching—or maybe more accurately, if she thought it would *make* someone watch her—but she hadn't always been that way. It wasn't the first time he'd wondered what things would have been like with his sister if he'd stuck closer to home and family after finishing school instead of throwing himself wholeheartedly into getting back at their father. "Reasonable assumption." He grimaced. "Look, I'll talk to Alexis—"

"It wasn't her."

"What?"

"It wasn't her. My door was locked last night. From the inside."

Her words sent a prickle of warning down his spine, because he didn't like where this was heading. "What are you suggesting?"

Maybe his tone was more wary than he'd intended, because Kat only pressed her lips together into a thin line instead of responding.

"You don't mean—what, like a *ghost* or something?" Oh, hell. What must it be like to live inside her head? "Kat—"

"Yeah, I know. One more checkmark in the crazy column," she returned bitterly. "Forget it. I'll call a taxi. Screw the cost." She turned as if to go.

He caught her arm before she could. "Just hold it a minute, all right? I don't think you're crazy, Kat, but I do think you're a little suggestible." A lot suggestible, actually, but he was attempting to be conciliatory. Someone in this house had to be.

Kat stiffened; maybe she'd heard that line from a lot of people. "I didn't imagine a book being moved."

"Maybe you were sleepwalking again."

"I wasn't—I don't do that."

"How can you be so sure? It's not like you had any witnesses. One of the many perils of sleeping alone, I'm afraid."

She stared at him. Too late he realized that the words carried an undertone of suggestiveness. He released her arm as if it had burned him. "So," he said after a minute. "A ride into town. I'll find you after breakfast."

For a moment, all she did was blink at him as if she hadn't really expected him to say yes, but then she nodded. Just once. And then she hurried away without another word.

Michael stared at the empty space where she had been for a long moment before finally shutting his bedroom door again and returning to his bed.

In vain, because he was wide awake now.

◆◆◆

SHE'D BEHAVED LIKE AN idiot, and probably sounded like one, too. Tripped all over her tongue and blurted out things in a way that only made her seem crazier than she already did, and awkward. It had been a mistake to go to Michael instead of calling a taxi, and part of her had known that, but...

The need to tell someone had been overwhelming, to speak to another living, breathing human being about her fear before it took her over completely. Even now her pulse was still faster than it should have been.

Kat forced herself to slow her pace on the stairs as she descended them back to the second floor, lest she trip, but she was neither as graceful nor as quiet as she ought to have been. The door to Alexis's room opened just as Kat's feet reached the bottom steps, and when she glanced up, she saw her stepsister staring at her.

Alexis looked at the third floor steps leading up to her brother's room, and then looked back at Kat with narrowed eyes.

This isn't what it looks like. The words sprang to Kat's mind if not to her lips. There was little point in saying them aloud. Bad enough that she was sneaking downstairs from Michael's floor in the early morning hours; protestations would only make her look more guilty. Alexis would think what she wanted to think anyway, particularly if it made Kat come out looking bad.

Forget it. She continued past Alexis without saying anything and returned to her own room, feeling her stepsister's eyes glare daggers into the back of her as she went.

◆ CHAPTER TWENTY-THREE ◆

KAT WAITED FOR MICHAEL in her room.

This morning the small space felt less like a refuge and more like a cage, and she spent much of her time pacing or staring out the windows. Downstairs would have been no better, especially not if Alexis had already whispered in her mother's ear about the morning's encounter on the stairs—and if Grace had learned that Michael had agreed to drive Kat into town. If she'd been unhappy with her son before, she was unlikely to feel any warmer toward him now.

Which he had to know, surely. But maybe he wasn't really doing Kat any favors. Maybe he was just keeping an eye on her like he'd warned her he would do. His motives didn't really matter, not so long as Kat got the ride into town that she wanted.

And then?

Kat abandoned the windows and sat down on her bed, her fingers running over the quilt that had most likely been made by someone further down the family tree. A ghost, Michael had said, incredulity all over his face, and although Kat hadn't at that point allowed the word to form itself in her mind, it was certainly there now.

Ghosts. Spirits of those long dead and buried. Of course Michael had looked at her like she'd lost her mind. Restless souls haunting the living? Mental illness made far more sense. It would be insanity *not* to think that.

And she hadn't thought so, not really, not until he'd said it. A hundred different memories came swirling back, all cast in a sudden new light. It was a mean house. It always had been.

What if...

Last night—or perhaps more accurately this morning, given the hours she'd kept, unable and unwilling to drift back to sleep—she'd poured over everything she'd brought down from the attic. It had not been useful. Oh, there had been plenty of dry facts, the kinds of things that her father might have used to flesh out the family tree, but all of that offered nothing to Kat but the sad proof that if the Delancey family was indeed haunted by something—natural or unnatural—it had likely started a very long time ago.

What could she really expect to find, though? A letter from one ancestor to another complaining about odd noises at night or ghostly apparitions roaming the halls? Maybe a diary entry about a mad aunt in the attic or an exorcism gone wrong? If there had been anything like that, the Delanceys neglected to put it down on paper. Or at least on any papers she had found so far. Sometimes families preferred to bury their secrets rather than shine a light on them.

But maybe... maybe friends and neighbors had not been so shy. People of every era liked to gossip, didn't they? And before telephones became commonplace, they did so through the written word. Letters, notes. And that was why Kat needed a ride into town.

A knock on her door made her jump. "Kat?"

Michael's voice. Pausing just long enough to tuck a particular one of her attic finds in her shirt and out of sight, Kat unlocked her door and opened it to see Grace's son on the other side.

He looked grim, and she couldn't blame him. "Ready?"

She nodded and locked the door behind her. He noticed but made no comment, maybe because he knew his sister just as well as Kat did.

He led the way downstairs, and she followed him without a word, her eyes darting this way and that as if to catch a fleeting glimpse of something that was only half there.

She felt other eyes on her as she and Michael passed the parlor on their way to the front door: Grace watching them from the sofa inside the room. Disapproval radiated off of her, and the coldness with which her eyes met Kat's reminded her of the chill last night.

"She's upset with you," Kat noted aloud as Michael closed the front door behind them.

"No, she's thrilled," he returned shortly, and she let the subject drop.

The upholstery of the passenger's side of Michael's car bore faint reminders of the last time Kat had been in it, spots of discoloration from the water. A shiver went down her spine at the memory, and a momentary tremble in her fingers made her struggle to get her seatbelt fastened properly. Even so, she felt mostly the familiar relief that descended whenever she was outside of the house, and her eyes watched it in the mirror as Michael got in the driver's side and searched for the right key.

"So where exactly am I taking you?"

Her attention remained on the manor as she answered him, almost as if it might do something behind her back if she let her guard down. "A historical society, if you've got one here."

He paused as he was about to put the key in the ignition. "You mean you don't know?"

"There's an antique store on every corner—" She remembered that much about the city. "—and genealogy is like a second language around these parts. How could there not be a historical society? Or something like it. If nothing else, the library must have a section on local history. Probably."

"You woke me up at five in the morning for 'probably'?" He frowned. "It takes less than five minutes to find something like that out online."

"Sure, if you have a computer."

"Alexis has a computer. You could have asked…" Michael caught the incredulous look Kat gave him and trailed off with a faint trace of color in his cheeks. "Yeah, I heard it," he muttered. Pulling out his phone, he held it up for a moment before grimacing in defeat. "No signal. Hardly ever is out in this godforsaken—" Catching the way she was watching him, he cut himself off midsentence and started the car. "We'll find out in town."

The car started down the long, winding driveway, and the manor shrank in the mirror.

"Attic wasn't enough for you?" Her lack of a response didn't seem to deter Michael much, because he continued, "Kat, why are you doing all of this?"

"I just want to see if they have anything else about the house, that's all."

"That's not what I meant."

She spared him a glance then before focusing her attention on the mirror again.

"I mean even coming here in the first place, and then staying here. Digging up the past like this. What is it that you really think you're going to accomplish? Why not just let it go—all of it—and just leave? Get on with your life."

His tone was less antagonistic than it was baffled. Maybe that was why she answered him. "You ever go through an entire day and then wonder at the end of it if everything was real or if your mind made parts of it up?"

"What? No. Of course not."

"Then you wouldn't understand." They rounded the bend in the driveway, and the house disappeared from view entirely. And suddenly she could breathe freely again, as if the air was clearer and less suffocating—well, until she imagined Emily watching from a window as the car departed. Standing alone, no one watching over her...

It was possible that Kat's words disconcerted Michael enough to silence any more questions, or maybe he just pitied her enough to let the matter drop. She could only guess blindly, because she turned her face toward the side window instead of looking at him for a reaction, watching idyllic trees and grassy fields go by. He didn't speak again until they were in sight of the city, and then he pulled the car over to the side of the road and tried his phone again. "Woodburn Museum," he said after a moment, his voice clipped.

"What's Woodburn?"

"Apparently the name the city used to be called way back when it had a population of about twelve, which probably included a couple of mules. Will that do?"

It would have to. She nodded.

Wordlessly, Michael punched an address into his car's GPS—state of the art, just like everything else he owned—and pulled the car back onto the road. There was a tightness to his jaw that she hadn't seen there earlier, but the look in his eyes was distant rather than cold. Troubled might have been a better word for it. She'd said little to him in the car, but maybe she'd still said too much.

They passed the museum by completely once in spite of the navigational aid, which was understandable since it turned out to be in the middle of a mostly residential area and was housed in a typical piece of charming two-story Victorian architecture that blended in with everything else. Had it not been for the small hand-painted sign posted outside, they probably would have passed it a second time and continued circling. A dubious lead. Could Michael just be fobbing her off on a second-rate excuse for a historical society to shut her up?

But there was nothing shifty in his manner as he pulled his car up to the curb to let her out. "I'll be back for you in about an hour. Maybe closer to two. Will that be enough time for whatever you...?" He gestured vaguely.

She got out of the car and bent down to look back through the open window. "I don't know." It was an honest answer, not an attempt to be evasive. She might find all sorts of buried bits of family history, or she might walk in to find little more than a collection of old quilts and doilies. Curiosity got the better of her. "Where are you going?"

He averted his eyes for a moment, then looked squarely into hers. "My mother asked me to pay a visit to her lawyer."

Ah. About the house, of course, and about Kat. There was no good response for that, so she didn't try to offer one. Instead, she stepped back to watch him pull away from the curb.

Then she went up the museum's well-manicured walkway to open its door and look for answers on the other side.

◆ CHAPTER TWENTY-FOUR ◆

A SMALL BELL ON the door jingled to announce Kat's arrival.

A stale, starchy smell greeted her nostrils. Quilts and doilies. Yes, there were quite a few of those on the walls, and she was only able to swallow back disappointment at the sight of them because it looked like there was more than that further back. A staircase directly ahead of her was roped off, but a glance toward the room on her left revealed collections of tools and bits of small equipment at whose intended use she could only guess, while the room on her right seemed to be home to things that would have appealed more traditionally to the lady of the house years ago. Clothes, accessories, needlepoint works...

Her eyes focused on one wall.

Family photos. And what looked like faded newspaper clippings. She hadn't even thought of those, maybe because the one she'd found about the fire was rather vague. But maybe, maybe there would be something more helpful in these.

She left the foyer that served as the entryway, brochures and all, and headed right, but she didn't get more than three steps before a voice called out from the direction of the stairs.

"Hello?" A matronly woman with grey hair pinned up around her head appeared at the foot of the stairs and spotted Kat. Her face lit up. "Ah, a visitor. Wonderful. Welcome to the museum. I'm Mrs. Davenport, and I can answer any questions you might have about our displays." Striding forward with a beaming smile on her face, she offered her hand.

Not to take it would have been blatantly rude, so Kat bit back her instinctive urge to decline and put her hand in the other woman's. She withdrew it as quickly as she could without seeming odd, reluctant to risk alienating her before they could even begin to delve into Delancey history. "Kat." And then, curious to see what effect her surname would have on the other woman, she added, "Kat Delancey."

Mrs. Davenport's eyes grew wider. "Not one of *our* Delanceys?" she said proprietorially. "From the manor?"

"Yes."

The older woman clapped her hands together with obvious delight, and for a moment Kat had the odd feeling that this must be what being a celebrity was like. "Oh, but how marvelous! I just love it when someone from one of our old families comes by. But I thought it was just the Mrs. Delancey staying there, with her children. You're not…?"

"She's my stepmother."

"Ah, yes, of course," said her hostess, who tactfully let the matter drop then instead of mentioning Kat's father. "So you're just visiting, then?"

"Yes, visiting. And..." She searched for a socially acceptable excuse. "... getting to know my roots."

The woman beamed again, and Kat knew she'd said the right thing. "It's such a lovely looking place, that old house—not that I've ever actually been inside. I'd give my right eye, though, to see what kind of things might be in that attic. The books alone—"

"Most of them are actually pretty dull, to be honest." Kat glanced at the photo display on the other side of the room in the hopes of inspiring Mrs. Davenport to move in that direction.

But her hostess didn't seem to notice the look. "Oh, no, my dear. You just have to learn to read between the lines, that's all. A hundred years or more ago subtlety and decorum may have been more highly prized than they are now—" Her tone turned wistful. "—but folks back then still managed to find some ways around them. A certain gesture of a fan here, a casual touching of hands during a piano duet... Very juicy stuff, believe me."

They had only an hour. Getting straight to the point before the other woman could go off on a tangent about nineteenth century flirting scandals, Kat opted for bluntness. "I'm more interested in deaths, actually. I know there have been several in my family, but I don't know much about how they actually happened. The original owner of the house didn't leave much information like that behind him when he died."

Mrs. Davenport blinked wordlessly for a moment as if taken aback. "Oh." Recovering, she added, "Well, the Delanceys certainly have had their share of unfortunate passings, haven't they? Right from the start."

"You mean Richard?" Curiosity sparked inside her. Her father's notes only had the date of the man's death, nothing more.

"Yes." Finally the older woman made her way over to a large photograph display in a locked case. She pointed at one very old sepia photo in particular, and Kat leaned forward to see it better. A man and a younger woman in what looked like late nineteenth century clothing. The man, at least, looked familiar. "That's him right there with his first wife, Charlotte. Lovely slip of a thing, wasn't she? Unlucky, though. Bore five children, and buried three of them before dying herself at the young age of twenty-eight."

Images of tiny grave markers flitted through Kat's memory. "How did her kids die?"

Mrs. Davenport moved on to peer at some other pictures, these of children. Kat recognized one of them as a younger version of Charles. "Let's see…" The proprietor squinted as if trying to remember. "The boy had a riding accident, I believe. Supposedly something spooked his horse, but I'm not sure what it was. And the two girls—that one died from some sort of wasting illness. Took weeks, poor thing. And the other girl drowned."

"Drowned," Kat repeated, suppressing the sudden swell of nausea that threatened. "You mean in the pond? The one behind the house?"

Her hostess nodded and clucked her tongue. "So sad. And then the older of the two boys—Frederick—grew ill, and Charlotte took her own life. Overdosed on laudanum. Well," she corrected herself, "they called it an accident, but letters written by family acquaintances and such at that time suggest that most folks didn't really believe that. Not that any of them came right out and said so, but—" She gave Kat a knowing look, and there was a kind of satisfaction to it that suggested she rather enjoyed being able to deliver such gossipy sensationalism.

It made Kat's stomach knot. With an effort, she kept her expression neutral. "But you read between the lines."

"Poor thing probably couldn't bear the thought of watching another child die. Seems that it was the same kind of wasting disease that took his sister."

"Did he die?"

"Frederick? No, thank God. His father sent the two boys away for a time to stay with relatives, and young Frederick recovered."

They were such tiny things in the pictures, one or two of them Emily's age or younger. Tiny and helpless. "And then Richard remarried?"

"He did. I think there's a picture… ah, yes. Here it is." Mrs. Davenport pointed at another photo, this one with a slightly older Richard and a rather plain but serene looking woman. "Charlotte's older sister, Miranda. A spinster until then, if I remember correctly. But she devoted herself to her sister's family, so I suppose it was only natural that she took Charlotte's place when her sister died. But the bad luck continued, because she and Richard had a son, John, but the boy died in his crib the day after his birth."

Kat flinched inwardly. If ever there had been a family that was cursed...

"And then a terrible case of influenza struck the valley a couple of years after that. Richard lost Miranda and nearly lost his two remaining boys, too. He sent them away again, too distraught to do much parenting, I suppose. Can't say I blame him. A few years after that, he died in a fall himself." She glanced at Kat, then did a double take. "You know, I think you have their eyes."

"Whose eyes?"

"The Hoyt sisters'. Charlotte and Miranda. Don't look much alike, do they? But they do have the same eyes. Must have been stronger than the Delancey strain to keep showing up after all these years, eh?"

Her observation might have been intended as a compliment, but it made Kat want to shudder instead to find herself compared to two dead women.

Mrs. Davenport seemed not to notice Kat's discomfort. In fact, she appeared to be warming to her gruesome topic. "After Richard's death, the house got passed along to Delancey after Delancey, but every so often it seems to claim another victim."

"Yes," Kat said with a pointed look. "I know."

Color blossomed in the older woman's cheeks, and she averted her eyes. "Ah, yes, of course. Anyway, we have quite a few pieces of local memorabilia that pertain to your family. Perhaps you'd be interested in looking at some news clippings? We've got some from the nineteen-thirties that are rather, well…" She trailed off, and Kat suspected the word she'd been about to say was "juicy" again.

But gossipy was good right now, and Kat ought to encourage it. "You know a lot about the manor," she stated rather than asked, and she was rewarded with a nod.

"I've always been an enthusiast for local history, yes."

"Are there any stories about the house?"

Mrs. Davenport blinked. "Stories...?"

"Yes, like—" How to put it without being dismissed as a crackpot? "Stories about strange or unusual things happening there?"

Her hostess only furrowed her brow further.

There was no help for it; she was going to have to come right out and say it, consequences be damned. "I mean like... like ghost stories."

Apparently the older woman's idea of what constituted juicy was restricted primarily to matters of society and relationships, because Kat's question seemed to leave her nonplussed. She chuckled uncertainly. "Most old houses do have them, don't they?"

"So there are some?"

"Oh. Well, nothing much. Rumors, I guess, that folks used to use to explain all the bad luck. Superstitious lot, weren't they?"

"What kind of rumors?"

Mrs. Davenport took a step back, which was when Kat realized that she herself had taken a step forward, pressing closer to the other woman. "I... I don't know. Some thought the house was haunted by one or more of the unfortunate Delanceys. Others went further back and blamed all the family deaths on angry native spirits, and still others believed the family had offended the heavens somehow." She gave a nervous chuckle and toyed with the cuffs of her sleeves, plucking at loose threads. "I'm more interested in actual historical facts myself, Miss Delancey."

She was treading on thin ice, but since she'd come this far already, Kat pulled out the one thing from the attic she'd brought with her and held it out to the other woman. "I found this in our attic the other day."

It was the photograph with the peculiar blur. Mrs. Davenport pulled out a pair of glasses from her pocket and examined the picture more closely. "Charles," she affirmed after a moment. "Richard and Charlotte's youngest, yes."

She'd missed the part that Kat couldn't unsee now. She pointed at the wispy shadow. "I've been wondering what that might be."

"What?" Mrs. Davenport adjusted her glasses and peered more closely. Then she relaxed and smiled with what looked like tolerant amusement. "That? Is this what got you thinking about ghosts? Photographic flaws like that weren't uncommon back then, you know. A reflection off of glass, a flaw in the film—I assure you, there is absolutely nothing supernatural about that image."

She clearly meant the words to be reassuring, and maybe they should have been, but they left Kat feeling deflated instead. A problem with the camera had not occurred to her, and even now she still found the blur off-putting, in spite of Mrs. Davenport's confidence that there was nothing odd about it. The opinions of one woman hardly qualified as indisputable proof, but the implication that Kat's mind was seeing what it wanted to see prompted Kat to ask about one other thing. She almost dreaded the answer. "What about mental illness?"

"I beg your pardon?"

"Were there any rumors about mental illness in the family?"

Now the proprietor really looked uneasy. "Nothing so obvious as that. Troubled, I suppose. That's certainly a word more than one person used to refer to the Delanceys in years past. Is that the kind of thing you mean?"

It wasn't, but before Kat could respond, a phone rang somewhere in a back room. The sound made Mrs. Davenport hustle away with what looked like relief. "Excuse me, won't you?" She disappeared into the back.

Troubled. She had hoped to find something more conclusive than that. Nothing but little bits and pieces here and there, which was all that she ever seemed to find when she tried to dig. Anything more substantial always seemed out of reach. Her head began to ache, and she rubbed it.

"It hates, you know. That house."

The unfamiliar voice startled Kat from her thoughts, and she turned to see an elderly woman with white hair pulled back into a tight bun standing a few feet from her. She leaned heavily on a cane and looked so frail that a gust of wind might knock her over, but her eyes were bright—almost feverishly so—as she peered at Kat. "What did you say?" Kat asked, taken aback.

"Your house. The manor." The woman drew closer, her movements stiff and, by the looks of it, painful from arthritis. "It hates."

It was an odd statement to come from anyone but Kat, and to hear something so similar to her own sentiments in the mouth of another made her stare.

Her feelings must have showed on her face, because the old woman nodded with a kind of grim satisfaction. "You've felt it, haven't you? Most people don't. Or won't." Her voice dropped to a near whisper. "It likes to hide, but I felt it, too. A long time ago."

"It?" Kat repeated. The newcomer's intensity was startling considering her infirmity, and it made Kat take a wary step back in much the same way Mrs. Davenport had retreated from Kat a minute ago.

And yet—

Kat froze in place as a strange familiarity became apparent in the woman's frame and face. Something she couldn't quite place, but was hovering just on the edge of her memory, and if she tried just a little harder to remember…

And there it was. "I know you," Kat said, startled. The hair had been grey back then, but the eyes had been just as bright. And desperate. "You tried to talk to my father at his uncle's funeral." Tried and failed, she remembered, picturing her father shaking the woman's hand off his arm and turning to go.

The woman went on as if Kat hadn't spoken, murmuring as much to herself as to Kat. "It likes the dark, and the shadows. It hides there, but we know it's there, don't we?"

"My father. What did you say to him that day?"

"He wouldn't listen to me." A look of anguish crossed the woman's face. "I tried to tell him, but he wouldn't listen."

Long-buried guilt resurfaced. No, he hadn't listened to Kat, either. She hadn't been able to make him understand, and she supposed she would always wonder if things might have been different if she had. "You tried to warn him about the house? What do you know about the place? And what do you mean, it likes to hide? What is *it*?"

She might have had better luck talking to the wall, for all the response she got from the woman. Instead, her wizened face turned aside as if listening, and then the woman thrust out something that Kat hadn't noticed before in her wrinkled hands. "Here, take it! Don't let her see."

It was a book, small and worn. Before Kat could examine it more closely, the woman gestured for her to hide it. Hearing footsteps from the back room, Kat let instinct take over and tucked the book into the waistband of her jeans and under her shirt.

"Sorry about that," said Mrs. Davenport, reentering the room. "It was just—" Spotting the newcomer with Kat, she frowned. "Mother! You should be resting. Go back upstairs, and I'll bring you some tea, all right?"

Some of the iron in the older woman's frame seemed to leave it, and she shuffled in the direction of the stairs, obedient and docile save for the last backward glance she gave Kat on her way out of the room.

"I do hope she wasn't bothering you. She's getting a little senile these days. We live upstairs, you see, and she likes to spend time around these old things." Mrs. Davenport gestured at the displays around them. "Reminds her of her youth, I think. In fact, she used to be a maid in the manor when she was just a girl."

Kat's eyes darted toward the stairs. "She was?"

"Very briefly. The couple living there at the time divorced, and my mother went with the wife when she left with the children. Eleanor, I think it was. Eleanor Delancey."

The name was vaguely familiar from the papers Kat's father had put together. "Can I talk to her? Your mother?"

The question made her hostess do a double take. "My mother? Why on earth—" She frowned again. "Oh. She started in on her bit about the Delanceys, didn't she? My mother is easily excitable, and as I told you, a little senile now. Please don't pay any attention to her ramblings. Nothing she'd have to say would make any sense anyway, I assure you."

Maybe it would, and maybe it wouldn't, but Kat felt a growing eagerness to find that out for herself. "Still—"

Mrs. Davenport's tone was firm and increasingly cooler. "I'm afraid not, Miss Delancey. She's not a well woman, and I wouldn't care to agitate her unnecessarily. You understand."

It was a statement, not a question. Short of shoving the woman aside and barreling past her after her mother, there would be no further conversation with the elder of the two. Not today, anyway.

But there was still the book, the one that Mrs. Davenport's mother had given her, just waiting to be opened and examined. It was possible that the book was nothing more than something random that senility made seem more important than it really was, but it was also possible that it wasn't. *It hates*, the woman had said, and although those words might have made anyone else suspicious of the woman's state of mind, they had a very different effect on Kat. Here, maybe, was someone else who understood at least something of what Kat experienced. It was all she could do to keep from reaching for the book, in spite of the warning she'd been given to keep it hidden.

So when Mrs. Davenport plastered a smile back onto her face and said, "Now, then. How about those newspaper clippings?" Kat merely nodded mutely and followed her into the next room.

• CHAPTER TWENTY-FIVE •

HIS APPOINTMENT WITH HIS mother's lawyer had been an awkward one, both for Michael and, he suspected, for the lawyer as well. The other man's surprise at the nature of the appointment was quite evident, and although he was as tactful as ever, he'd asked several questions about what had happened between Kat and Grace to bring about these new developments. They had not been easy to answer. Simple, maybe, in some respects. But not easy.

His loyalties lay with his mother, naturally. They always had and always would. It was only reasonable for her to ask him to act as her agent in these matters.

And yet the image of Kat floating face down in the pond refused to leave him alone, the fear in her eyes as she'd begged him to get her away from the house... Truthfully, forcing her to let go of the place might actually be the best thing for her.

His head throbbed after the exchange with the lawyer, and he doubted the ache would let up anytime soon. Opening the folder of papers he'd been given by the other man, he studied them in his parked car and rubbed his temples with one hand.

A knock on the passenger's side window startled him into looking up.

Kat looked back at him through the glass, and at the folder he held.

Closing it abruptly, he put it in the back seat before unlocking the door so she could get in.

"Well?" she asked, sliding in. "Get me kicked out of the house yet?"

Was that supposed to be humor or accusation on her part? "I'm not sure you should joke about that."

"I wasn't."

Right. "What about you? Did you find what you were looking for?"

In answer, she pulled a book out from beneath her shirt that he hadn't realized she'd been hiding, something small with no identifying marks on its cover. "I'm not sure."

Good God, was she resorting to stealing now? Michael made a strangled sort of sound. "Please tell me I have not just made myself an accomplice to theft. I'm too pretty for jail, Kat."

"It was given to me, scout's honor."

"You were never a scout." With a furtive look in the direction of the museum, he started the engine and pulled away from the curb.

But not before he saw a curtain move in an upstairs window as if someone was watching them from behind it.

◆◆◆

BY THE TIME KAT'S hour was up, Mrs. Davenport had managed to produce little else about the Delancey family beyond a few mentions in society pages and an old tea set of questionable origins. It might have once belonged to the manor's kitchen, but Kat had a hard time picturing its cheerful painted pansies in the home's stern setting. In any case, it was hardly likely to shed light on her current situation.

She expected the time to fly by, but it did the opposite. After realizing the diminutive museum held little of interest about her family history other than the original photos Mrs. Davenport showed to her, Kat was increasingly worried that the book given to her by the woman's mother would turn out to be nothing more than a collection of family recipes or some other such trivial thing. Her fingers itched to find out for themselves.

Michael left her in the car while he attended to some kind of business at his firm. He offered very few details about it, and Kat hardly heard the ones he did share, anyway. Her attention was focused on the book in her hands.

It was a diary. The name of its owner, Eleanor Delancey, was scribbled across the top of the first page, and Kat dimly remembered the name as little more than a footnote in her father's burgeoning family tree project. His great-uncle Thomas's aunt, if she remembered correctly, and apparently the one-time employer of Mrs. Davenport's mother.

The woman's handwriting was clean and elegant, although when Kat did a quick flip through the pages to see how long the book was, the writing closer to the end seemed less so. Clipped and jagged even, although still recognizable as from the same hand. Curiosity tempted her to read those last entries first, but she made herself start at the beginning, leery of misreading context. Better to let the pieces fall into place in the right order.

Eleanor herself was a Delancey purely by marriage, and the diary began a few years into her happily married state. Her husband, Robert, had recently moved into the manor after inheriting it from his uncle. Charles, Kat realized, reading further. No details about Charles's death were given, but the wispy blur in the photograph resurfaced in Kat's mind in spite of Mrs. Davenport's confident assurances that it must merely be a flaw in the film. Eleanor herself wrote nothing to indicate anything unusual about the circumstances that brought her and her husband to live at the manor. The first several pages contained scattered entries about casual everyday things—local gossip, new recipes to try, mundane trivialities.

Kat's heart sank. Maybe the only kinship she'd felt with Mrs. Davenport's mother had been one forged in shared mental instability after all, because the old woman's desperation to get this diary into Kat's hands seemed to make no sense at all, based upon what was written in it.

And then Kat turned the page.

It wasn't much. Just a mention of the children. Eleanor and her husband had two of them by then, both younger than the age of five from the sound of it, and one no more than a toddler at most. A little girl. An inexplicable accident. No true harm done, just a few bumps and bruises and one sprained ankle, but it was clear from Eleanor's writing that it left her unsettled and shaken. The entire tone of the diary changed.

The driver's side door opened, making Kat jump and draw her breath in sharply.

Her startled reaction made a wary Michael pause as he was getting into the car. "What?"

She only shook her head and pressed her lips together, closing the diary and abruptly self-conscious. He had been remarkably tolerant so far about what she knew most other people considered odd behavior in her—maybe he simply pitied her more than they did—but even he must surely have his limits.

He gave no sign of it, though. Instead, he studied her with an unreadable expression on his face before turning the key in the ignition.

"Where are we going?" Kat asked as they turned the opposite way from the direction that would take them back to the house.

"To eat. It's a little early for lunch, but I love a challenge."

"I'm not hungry."

"Tough."

"Michael—"

"How many meals have you actually eaten in the past two days?"

She looked away without answering.

"That's what I thought," he said crisply. "Suck it up and eat a burger, Kat."

He drove them to a diner, nothing fancy but perhaps more comfortable because of that fact. Maybe it was the smells of food cooking, or maybe it was just being away from the house, but Kat found that she did have some appetite after all. They sat at a booth in the back, away from the few other customers that were dining at this hour, and eyed each other with what Kat thought was mutual uncertainty.

She brought the book in with her, hoping to avoid conversation by reading it. Her plan backfired.

"So whose diary is that?" Michael asked after the waitress left with their order.

"Someone who used to live at the house." Kat's voice was clipped. Not from any hostility, but from that same budding self-consciousness. "In the thirties."

"Exactly what kind of answers do you hope to find in there?"

She didn't know how to reply to that, so she opened the diary with the intention of averting her gaze to it instead.

That plan didn't work either. Michael reached out to touch her wrist, and she had no choice but to look at him. "Close the book, Kat."

She hesitated.

"Please?" he added.

It might have been the softness of his tone that made her comply in spite of the fact that she didn't really want to. She closed the book and waited for him to say whatever it was that was on his mind, her hands clasped tightly together in her lap and out of view.

Whatever it was, he appeared to be struggling with the right words to express it. "Look," he said finally, running a hand through his dark hair and then playing idly with the fork on the table in front of him. "You should know that my mother's lawyer has plans to make you look mentally incompetent, and you're not helping yourself with this obsession you have with the house, and with things like ghosts and curses."

It was not exactly unexpected news. That he would admit it to her was, though. "Why are you telling me this?"

This time he was the one who couldn't seem to answer. Instead, he sipped from the cup of coffee the waitress had poured him.

"Why have you even been helping me at all?" Kat persisted. "I know what your family thinks of me. What you must think of me. Why not just tell me to go to hell like Alexis would?"

"In case you haven't noticed, my sister has issues. Frankly, so do I, but at least I manage to dress them up better for company."

He was avoiding the question. Maybe that shouldn't have intrigued her, but it did. "I know Grace is giving you a hard time. So why go against her wishes?"

"Maybe I'm just a sucker for a hard luck story. Anyway, it's not like she'll hold it against me forever. She'll get over it." He gave her a pointed look. "Once you're gone."

"Seems like things would have been a lot simpler for you if you'd just left me in the pond."

He stiffened. "Is that supposed to be a joke? Because it's not funny."

It wasn't meant to be. However, his reaction to it did lead her to an unexpected realization. Her mouth curved slightly, albeit without much humor.

He noticed. "What?" he asked irritably.

"You. As much as you seem to have a grudge against him, you're cut from the same cloth as my dad."

"And how do you figure that?"

"He was the rescuing type, too."

"I'm not—"

"Sure you are. You rescue Grace when she needs it, and now you're doing it for me. Or trying to, at least. Why else would you be doing this?"

He shifted in his seat. "I don't know. Maybe because as much as I would like to forget finding you lying on the bathroom floor, I probably never will. Does it matter? The point is, you're just digging a bigger hole for yourself every time you bring up things like Caspar. Understand?"

"There's either something seriously wrong with that house, or—" She faltered but forced herself to finish the thought, and the sentence. "—or there's something seriously wrong with me. Do you expect me to just ignore that?"

He must have heard the tremor in her voice, because some of the tension in his frame softened. "I think maybe what's really going on here is that you want someone to blame for what happened to your father. And your mother. You *need* someone to blame, even if it's just a ghost. I don't think you're crazy, Kat. You're just very, very sad inside."

The words hit her harder than she would have expected, and to her surprise, she felt her eyes grow wet. She couldn't even remember the last time she'd cried. She blinked back the moisture and looked away from Michael.

The silence stretched between them for a long time before Michael finally spoke again. "You know, it's funny. You say I'm like your father, but I think it's really you and my mother that aren't all that different. She's hanging on to that house because she can't let go of Jonathan. I think you're hell-bent on getting rid of it for the same reason."

A tear escaped in spite of Kat's best efforts. She wiped it away with a hasty swipe, her face still averted from Michael's.

Mercifully, he let the matter drop. And if the moment was awkward, at least it was made somewhat less so by the arrival of their waitress with their food.

They ate it in silence.

◆ CHAPTER TWENTY-SIX ◆

THE DRIVE BACK TO the manor wasn't much different. This time, though, Kat was able to use the diary as a legitimate escape from eye contact and awkward conversation, for which she was grateful. If Michael had any further thoughts about their lunchtime topic, he kept them to himself. She was grateful for that, too.

And soon the words on the page held her full attention anyway, so that she was no longer pretending to be absorbed by them. Eleanor's uneasiness about the house grew with each entry she made in the diary, and it became increasingly clear that she started keeping her children close to her at all times. Accidents grew fewer and farther between, but there seemed to be a new tension developing.

The thing about diaries was that there was always a possibility that the wrong person might stumble across them and read them. Maybe that was why Eleanor's writing grew vague. A hint of concern about her husband here, an ambiguous reference to a change in his moods or behavior there… Until some dam inside her must have finally given way, because her words and her fears became quite clear in a latter entry in the book, one in which the scrawl was no longer effortless and easy.

Kat read the words on the page and stiffened, so much so that it caused Michael to glance over at her.

He frowned. "What's wrong?"

She started to read, heard her voice crack, and had to clear her throat. She tried again. "'Today something happened that I cannot seem to explain. Robert certainly can't. He doesn't even seem to remember it happening, which frightens me even more. How can a man retrieve and load a pistol without being aware of what he is doing?'"

Michael's hand twitched on the steering wheel. "So… maybe sleepwalking runs in the family." But his voice lacked its usual conviction.

"My mother was only a Delancey by marriage, remember? Did she sleepwalk, too? Anyway, it's more than that. 'I said his name three times before he seemed to hear me. And when he looked at me'—"

"Yes?"

"'I would swear something other than my husband looked back at me.'" Looking up from the pages, Kat watched Michael for a reaction. Other than a slight furrowing of his brow, he seemed to have none, and she suspected his mind was working to come up with a logical explanation. What would it be this time—overexcited imagination of an anxious female, or yet another odd behavior chalked up to the nuts in the family tree? She addressed it before he could. "Are you going to blame this on Delancey quirks? If all this stuff runs in the family, you're going to have to look elsewhere this time. It might explain his behavior, but it wouldn't explain hers."

He gave no answer; maybe he was still working on one. She turned her attention back to the book, but this time she didn't read aloud. The words sent a prickle down her spine.

> *Robert thinks I am imagining things, and I dare not speak of it to our friends, but I think the children feel it, too, young as they are. It is too sly and cunning to be obvious, but there is something in this house that wants to torment us, and I think—I fear it means us greater harm than that. I have tried to fight it, first with help from Father Jameson and then Rose. If*

Robert knew I let that woman in our house, he would be so angry with me, but I did not know what else to do. In the end, none of her candles or herbs worked anyway. I thought at first they did, but I think it *let me hope falsely just to enjoy watching me despair all over again. It does that, waits until we are happy again and then strikes us anew. I cannot stay here any longer. If Robert will not leave, then I must take the children and go without him.*

I can feel that it hates us, but I do not know why.

Kat looked up from the book without really seeing anything through the windshield in front of her, the last words of that entry running through her mind.

I can feel that it hates us…

She closed her eyes.

…but I do not know why.

◆◆◆

THE DAY HAD TURNED cloudy and overcast, lending the manor an especially cold and grey look as Michael pulled the car to a stop in front of it. They both got out of the car, but when Michael retrieved his folder of papers and waited for Kat expectantly, she just stood there, staring up at the house. After a moment, he shrugged and turned to go inside without her, but she thought he gave the house an uneasy glance as he did so.

It wasn't fear that kept her from entering the house, although maybe it should have been. It was more that she was sizing it up, or maybe seeing it through different eyes than she had before. The ramblings of one old and possibly senile woman paired together with a decades-old diary whose deceased author could neither confirm nor deny her state of mind at the time she wrote it didn't exactly make for iron-clad proof, but it was something. Something that meant maybe she wasn't losing her mind after all, and in fact never had been.

There was something there—and she was not crazy after all. The icy fingers that she imagined had awakened her, she hadn't imagined them at all. There *was* something there.

Funny, the relief that thought gave her when it probably ought to have sent her running for the hills.

She reined it in, forcing herself to play devil's advocate. It was what the others would do if she tried to tell them. Just shadows and secrets of an old house playing upon an entire series of suggestible minds, that was all. That was what they'd say.

But that wasn't all it was, her mind whispered at her. The house did hate, and now she knew—she *knew*—she wasn't the only one who believed that.

It likes to hide, the woman had said. Maybe so. But if something was hiding in the dark, in the shadows, maybe it was possible to bring it into the light. No more hiding, no more secrets. And no leaving until she had convinced Grace to take Emily as far away as possible from this place.

Eyeing the house on her way up to its front door, Kat steeled herself and went inside.

"...will do what I have to for my family's sake," came Grace's voice from the parlor, crackling with icy anger. "And it is most certainly not mudslinging. How soon did he say we could start proceedings?"

Michael's voice answered it, calmer and quieter. "I know you think you're honoring Jonathan's wishes, but do you really think he'd want you taking his daughter to court like this?"

From the silence that followed, his words had struck a nerve. What kind of nerve exactly, Kat wasn't sure. In any case, she shut the front door with more force than necessary to let the noise of it announce her arrival.

It seemed to have the desired effect, because someone closed the door to the parlor right away. Michael, probably. Grace would more likely have slammed it.

It was tempting to throw the door open and wave the diary in front of Grace's face and to say something like, *See, see? It's not just me, and you need to pack your things, grab your daughters, and get out. Or better yet, leave the things and just take Emily and Alexis and go. NOW.*

And she very nearly did. She even took a step toward the parlor door, hand outstretched as if to reach for the doorknob, before it sank into her that it would be useless to do so. Worse than useless, because Grace would only see it as more reason to wrest control of the house from Kat. And if she succeeded, if she forced Kat to leave, Emily would be trapped in this house with something no one else believed was there, something that hated. Something—Kat thought of her parents—that killed.

So she bit her tongue, and her fingers tightened their hold on the diary almost as if to keep her from banging on the parlor door with her knuckles or, worse, simply just reaching for the doorknob and barging in.

Not yet, and not like that. But something, she would do something…

Her eyes darted around the gloom in the entryway. She thought of her mother in the pond, and her father lying broken as she'd rushed to his side, and even her own years of misery in this place, and she felt something different from the dread she usually did. Something less afraid and more angry than before.

And she turned slowly, her eyes traveling over the dark, glossy walls, the staircase, and the shadows above them, and she thought,

I know you're here.

◆ CHAPTER TWENTY-SEVEN ◆

AN URGE CAME OVER her to say the words aloud. Not to shout them or call them out with enough volume to bring anyone else in the house running with a straitjacket, but to speak them out loud even if it was only in a whisper.

I know you're here. A kind of challenge maybe, or an act of defiance against something that had tormented her for years. Something to show that it had made a wrong move and revealed itself, first to others who had lived here before her and now to Kat as well, and that it hadn't succeeded after all in driving her mad or into despair or whatever it was that it hoped to do.

She took a slow step forward in the entryway, then another, and then she opened her mouth to let the words come out.

And froze as her gaze landed on the library door.

The writer of the article about Thomas's death had implied that Thomas might have tried to set the house on fire himself, distraught and grieving for the family he'd lost. And maybe he had, maybe he'd wanted to bring the house down around him in revenge, unless it was *it*, the thing in the house itself—but, no. No, it wouldn't destroy itself like that, would it?

But it might defend itself against someone who tried. Maybe it had. Maybe that was what really happened to Thomas that night in his house, because it hated any and all things Delancey. And maybe it would do the same again.

Emily. Where was Emily?

Kat started toward the stairs with the intention of racing up them only to hear a small sound come from the dining room, a kind of clink as something slight hit the table.

Don't run, she thought, suppressing the impulse. *Don't be obvious.* Forcing herself to move normally, she abandoned the staircase as she made her way toward the dining room.

There she was. Sitting at the table, head bent over a coloring book and a boxful of crayons spread out on the table in front of her, oblivious to the fact that she had an audience. The sound Kat had heard was that of a crayon being dropped onto the hard wooden surface. Feeling a rush of relief, Kat put one hand on the doorframe to steady herself.

But the relief didn't last long. She could hardly scoop the child up and run with her out of the house. Grace would have the cops on her in no time, and Emily would wind up right back where she started. Appealing to Grace wouldn't work either; her stepmother already thought Kat was out of her mind. Besides, speaking about any of this aloud with anyone while inside the house where *it* might hear… No, she didn't dare.

She couldn't linger here like this forever either, but she was afraid to go too far away, so she wound up back at the bottom of the stairs, sinking down to sit on the first step.

What if she had said too much already? Yesterday in the attic alone, she'd blurted out plenty to Michael about her feelings about the house and about how wrong it all was. Had she been the one to bring up family curses, or had he? She couldn't remember now. And then outside his room this morning, there'd been more.

But that had all been speculation, and he'd been quick to dismiss it and to urge her to do the same. Maybe it was all right still. Maybe. Because if not...

Time passed with interminable slowness as she waited, unwilling to leave Emily completely unattended and twitching at any creak or imagined movement out of the corner of her eye—oh, God. *Was* it imagined?

So when the parlor door finally opened, she jumped and looked up with wide eyes to see Michael emerge with his mother. They both came to an abrupt stop when they saw Kat.

"Emily's in the dining room," Kat told her stepmother. "Coloring. I didn't go near her." As she'd hoped, Grace went past her to confirm that for herself, her features stiff and cool. When she was gone, Kat looked at Michael again. "Will you come outside with me?"

"Outside? Why?"

"Please."

"Kat—"

"I need to talk with you."

His forehead furrowed. "So talk."

She shook her head and rose to cross to the front door, where she waited for him.

He sighed, and she knew then that he understood exactly why she didn't want to talk inside the house, and that he thought it was foolish—which was fine by her so long as he humored her anyway. He did, and she led the way outside.

"Kat," he started once they were out on the front porch, but she shook her head again and continued down the front steps and toward the driveway. His reluctance radiated off of him as he followed her, and she wondered if he thought he was encouraging—or at the very least enabling—delusions on her part.

How far was far enough? Was there even any distance that was safe? If it could reach the pond, surely it could reach other places as well. But how far?

Her eyes darted around her as she walked, as if trying to catch a glimpse of grass bending beneath the weight of invisible feet that followed her.

Nothing.

Only when she finally began to hear sounds of nature break the silence in the air did she start to think that maybe it was safe, but Michael spoke before she could.

"That's far enough, Kat. What are you going to do, drag somebody outside every time you want to talk to them? You can't."

Turning, she faced him. "You need to make sure Emily is never alone."

He stared at her.

"Please," she pressed. "You can tell Grace you're just making sure she stays away from me—anything, I don't care. But she can't be left alone. And not just inside, but outside, too."

"She rarely is. My mother keeps her on a short leash. Emily even sleeps in our mother's room at night now."

Kat was surprised. "Since when?"

"Since I pulled you out of the pond."

Oh. It stung, but in its own way, it was good news. Emily might be sensitive to whatever it was that was in the house, but it seemed to leave Grace well enough alone. So far, anyway. "Good."

"Why the sudden concern for Emily?"

"Just… keep an eye on her," Kat told him, and then she headed back into the house. She felt his eyes follow her and knew he thought she was acting unstable again. She was not surprised by that.

She was surprised that she cared, though.

◆◆◆

MAYBE THIS HAD BEEN *its* intent all along, to trap her here like this, knowing that it wasn't safe. Because she couldn't leave, not until the others did, too. And maybe it knew that. And maybe it was toying with her.

Kat stared out her window at the pond below. For a fleeting moment, she was sorry Michael had pulled her out of it.

She turned away.

Couldn't speak freely, couldn't take action against the house without risking bringing it down on all of them—which might have been paranoia, but then again, it might not. That was the problem. She didn't know, didn't know what was safe and what wasn't. All she did know was that the house was dangerous, and that there was little hope of convincing anyone under its roof to leave. And all the while, Grace was working toward kicking her out. Her options were not so much poor as nonexistent.

She still held the diary in her hands, and now she opened it up and turned through its pages again. In a moment, she found the words she was looking for.

> *...I have tried to fight it, first with help from Father Jameson and then Rose. If Robert knew I let that woman in our house, he would be so angry with me, but I did not know what else to do. In the end, none of her candles or herbs worked anyway...*

The priest most likely had attempted some sort of exorcism, but the reference to the mysterious Rose was less clear. *That woman*, Eleanor wrote. Someone perhaps not very popular in polite society. Someone who dabbled in the darker arts? Or at least something questionable by the standards of the day. With candles and herbs as her tools.

Neither approach had worked. Did that mean nothing would? But that had been three quarters of a century ago. Maybe now—

Maybe digging in the past was the wrong approach. Maybe it was the present that held the key. There had to be far more literature out there now on the subject of supernatural phenomena than there had been seventy-five years ago, and it was much more accessible, too.

Kat slammed the diary closed. Damn it, she should have gone to the library as well as the museum today, somewhere she could get to a computer since her phone was so spotty. She glanced at her watch. Too late to try to convince Michael to take her back into town now; even if she could talk him into it—and that was unlikely—no place useful would be open now. And anyway, the thought of leaving Emily and the others alone and unwatched in the house left her skin cold, even if she did feel all but ineffective. Someone watching had to be better than no one watching at all.

But maybe, maybe Alexis would venture into town tonight to be with friends and enjoy what little nightlife it had to offer. And leave her computer unattended...

Slim hope was better than none.

◆ CHAPTER TWENTY-EIGHT ◆

ALEXIS STAYED IN. ALL evening, and after loudly voicing her displeasure regarding a recent fallout with a friend—it was a miracle that kind of thing didn't happen every day—she all but locked herself in her room as if everyone else in the house was too dull to excite her interest or deserve her company. There would be no researching tonight.

Tomorrow, then, although every nerve in Kat's body was on edge at the thought of waiting. Somehow, she would have to figure out a way tomorrow, even if she had to break into Alexis's room to do it. Maybe during breakfast, although lunch was more likely. Alexis wasn't an early riser.

Restless, Kat sat rigidly on the bed and finished reading the rest of the diary. There was no further mention of Rose, or of anyone else who might have tried to do something to make the house safe. Only unsettling references to Eleanor's husband in which she referred to him in the past tense despite the fact that—according to the family records—he didn't die until some years later.

The floorboards in the hall creaked every so often as the rest of the household got ready for bed, and then finally it was quiet again. Sleep was impossible, or at least unlikely, so Kat crept to her door with the lights off and opened it. The hall was empty, deserted; the lights downstairs were off. Other than a thin strip of light peeking out from beneath Alexis's door and a single shaft of moonlight shining through the window in Kat's room, everything was dark.

It was tempting to turn on her bedside lamp. It was tempting to turn on lights throughout the entire house, actually, as if that might somehow keep *it* at bay. But even the brightness of daylight hadn't saved Kat's mother. What could a few extra watts do? And besides, the darkness had its own advantages. Whether it actually concealed her or not, it made Kat feel less exposed, and less likely to draw attention to herself. So she left the lights off, but she sat cross-legged in her open doorway and leaned against the doorframe with the intention of remaining there as long as she could stay awake, watching. Just in case.

A wind picked up while she sat there, and the house creaked and moaned with each new gust. The sounds were all too familiar. She'd lain awake many a time as a child, frightened by the noises she'd hear on blustery nights and frightened even on nights that were calm. She shivered once, more from the memory than from the sounds themselves. Still, the hairs on the back of her neck prickled in anticipation, and she forced herself to take a deep breath to ease the tightness in her chest.

It hates, you know. That house...

The light eventually went out in Alexis's room, and although the crack beneath the door hadn't allowed much of the light through, the sudden absence of it made Kat stiffen.

What was she doing? This was crazy. She ought to be somewhere else, anywhere else but here alone in the dark. Just somewhere less exposed than this. Outside even—

She shut off the voice in her head, very deliberately. Someone had to keep watch. Things happened at night when no one was around to stop them, like people wandering out to tumble into ponds and such. If it happened to her, it could happen to Emily.

So she stayed, her nerves too taut for her to even begin to grow sleepy in spite of how the minutes seemed to drag by. An hour went by. Maybe two. She fingered the watch around her wrist, but it was too dark to see it.

The house creaked again. There was no reason that should have caught her attention, except for the fact that the wind had died down some time ago. Still, it was an old house. Old houses creaked all the time—

There it was again, and there was a reason why it drew her ears. It was not a random sound coming from one of the exterior walls or window frames and impossible to pinpoint. No, she knew this one, long familiar from years of experience and memories. It was one of the steps below, the one her father always meant to fix. The fourth one from the bottom.

Her mouth went dry. Maybe she was mistaken. Under the circumstances, her mind and her ears might play tricks on her. Perhaps she'd imagined it.

Another creak. This one even closer. Her hands gripped the doorframe. No, it was not her imagination at all. Someone was coming up the stairs.

It hit her then, the sudden rush of lavender scent. Her stomach turned over, and if she'd eaten anything for dinner, now was the time it would have resurfaced. Hauling herself upright, she stared at the second-floor landing, waiting for someone—some*thing*—to appear and too paralyzed by sudden fear to make a sound.

A flashlight. Why hadn't she taken a flashlight out into the hall with her? Because she had none, that was why, some still rational part of her mind reminded her. She hadn't packed one in the first place. What good would it really do anyway?

The steps continued to make soft sounds as something climbed them. This was why she was here, why she'd been standing guard tonight. In case something like this happened. That was the whole point, she told herself even as her traitorous body seemed to shrink back into her room of its own accord. She had to dig her fingers into the wooden doorframe just to keep herself from closing the door.

Because closing the door wouldn't stop *it* if it was coming for her. And if it wasn't Kat that it wanted—

She forced herself to stay put, and her eyes locked onto the landing again, prepared to cry out at the first sight or feel of something; let them call her crazy if they liked.

Another creak. It was almost here. Then one more…

And it was there. Or at least it should have been. But there was nothing lurking in the shadows on the landing, no signs of movement and no dark silhouette. She was sure that last sound was from the topmost step. Whatever had been on it should have been visible by now.

No power on earth could have compelled her to take a step closer to the stairs to investigate further. She kept her eyes trained on that spot, though, watching for some sign of anything.

Nothing. Absolutely nothing. The lavender scent was still there, but only just barely and fading fast. Had it been a trick, then? No, not a trick. That wasn't the right word at all. Prank was more like it. Something vicious and intentional, meant to terrify her. And it had worked.

She heard another creak then, and her head jerked to face the third floor steps. Another step groaned beneath the weight of something that wasn't there and yet was, steadily climbing towards the third floor.

Michael's floor.

A new fear jolted Kat into action, and she bolted towards the ascending staircase. She gripped the banister railing tightly as if her life depended on it—for all she knew, it did—and raced up the steps, fully expecting to brush against something as she did so and almost shocked when she didn't

Not until she reached the top, anyway, and collided with a solid form. Drawing her breath in sharply for an instinctive scream, she managed to stop herself as she recognized the voice muttering a curse.

Familiar hands gripped her arms in the dark. "What are you trying to do, kill me?"

She couldn't answer. Speech was impossible for her at that moment, and her heart beat so rapidly that it was a wonder it didn't burst from her chest. She was shaking, too, and Michael seemed to realize it at the same time she did.

"What is it? What happened?" He held on to her, which was fortunate because her knees might have given way on her otherwise.

"Are y-you all right?" It came out as a stutter.

"Of course I'm all right. Why? What's going on?"

She tried to speak, failed, and then tried again. "Were you… were you just on the stairs a minute ago?"

"Me? No. I was in my room until just now."

"Did you hear something? Out in the hall?"

It was too dark to see his features, but she could imagine the consternation on them. "Hear something? Like what?"

"Like—" She stopped, thinking *it* might be listening.

"Kat?"

Maybe it didn't even matter if it was listening. Or maybe it did. She couldn't think straight anymore, and, God, she was so tired. But somehow it still seemed unwise to draw attention to it here in the darkened hallway where anything could happen. So far it had chosen not to reveal itself to anyone else in the house. Maybe it was best not to tempt it into doing so.

Which might have been why she panicked when Michael said, "What—you mean like rattling chains? Kat, this has to stop. There are no such things as gh—"

She clapped one of her hands over his mouth before he could finish the word, suddenly sure they weren't alone.

He stood stock still, even when she finally drew her hand away.

"Don't," she whispered.

His eyes were just about all she could make out on his face, and they were fixed quite firmly on her. Maybe a little wider than normal, too.

Think. She had to think. Had to say something plausible. "Sorry, just—I couldn't sleep," she said, her voice still a whisper but sounding somehow much too loud in her ears nevertheless. "The house makes too much noise sometimes."

Michael still didn't respond. Since her knees were steadier now, Kat took a step back, pulling herself free from the hold his hands had on her. "Couldn't sleep," he repeated after a moment, and there was something about the way he said it that made her think he might suspect the real reason why she was up at this hour. And then she was sure of it when he added, almost as if disappointed in her, "Or chose not to?"

She said nothing.

"You *need* to get some sleep."

"I can't."

"Try," he said. "The human body can only take so much, Kat. Cut yours some slack and get some shut-eye."

"I said, I *can't.*"

There was a brief hesitation in his manner, and then he said, "What if I stay up instead?"

It took her a moment to realize what he'd said. "What?"

"I have paperwork I need to do. Might as well do it now. You go back to bed, and I'll—" He broke off in midsentence as if he abruptly realized he'd been about to say the wrong word, then tried again. "I'll stay up. Deal?"

What had he been about to say—stand guard? Keep watch? He read her surprisingly well, including her fears. Too bad it wasn't that simple. Sleep would be impossible tonight.

But to have someone else awake and alert. To know that it didn't all rest on her...

After a moment, she nodded. Dark as it was, he must have seen it well enough, because he turned her toward the stairs and guided her down them. "Good. Look, if you want a sleeping pill—"

"No." Her whisper cut through the air with as much finality as if it had been a shout.

Her response didn't seem to surprise him. He held both hands up as if in defeat and left her at her bedroom door.

"Michael?"

He paused by the landing and looked back at her.

Thank you. The words shouldn't have been so hard to say, but somehow they were, so she just shook her head instead. "Nothing."

Shrugging, he started down the steps. "Geez, it's freezing in here," his voice floated back to her, soft and barely above a disgruntled murmur. "Where is that draft coming from?"

And any tension that had eased out of Kat flowed right back in again.

◆ CHAPTER TWENTY-NINE ◆

MICHAEL DID AS HE promised. The faint glow from the downstairs light that managed to reach its way upstairs along with the occasional sound of him clearing his throat were proof enough as Kat lay in bed all night with her door open just in case there were any more disturbances. There were none, and when the faint grey light of dawn filled her room, she finally closed her door and did sleep. Not for long, but anything was better than nothing.

Or maybe it wasn't, because she could barely drag herself out of the bed later. Michael was right. She couldn't take much more of this.

Michael looked paler than usual himself when she passed him in the hall on his way up to his room to try to catch a little sleep of his own, his eyes verging on bloodshot as he rubbed wearily at the budding stubble on his cheek. "Could have sworn *one* of us was supposed to get some sleep last night," he muttered in passing with an accusatory look, and she knew the shadows under her eyes must have given her away.

There would be no trip to town to find a computer, not yet. Not until he'd rested. She didn't even try to ask. It would have to be Alexis's computer. Somehow.

The door to her stepsister's room was closed now. Still in bed, or enjoying a late breakfast? Lunch would be more like it at this hour.

Creeping down the steps with a death grip on the bannister, Kat listened for telltale sounds from the floor below.

Something moved on her right. Flinching back, Kat realized a moment later that it had simply been her own reflection in the glass of one of the framed family pictures hanging on the wall beside her. Or had it? She would have sworn the eyes that looked back at her from the glass—in that brief glimpse—had not quite looked like her own.

Her hand on the bannister was not as steady as she would have liked, and she clenched it there more tightly to keep from breaking into a run. No running, not yet. She forced herself to continue down the stairs at the same careful pace as before.

A murmur of voices came from the kitchen, and she rounded the doorway to meet the startled and then cool stares of Grace and Alexis.

Kat broke the silence, her voice barely more than a croak after her sleepless night. "Where's Emily?"

"Emily," said Grace, narrowing her eyes, "is none of your concern."

"Is she inside the house?" Kat persisted, tensing.

"Are you nuts *and* deaf, or what?" Alexis snapped, and for once, her mother didn't chastise her. "She said it's none of your business."

"It's my house—at least for the moment—so yes, it is my business. Is she inside or not, Grace?"

"She's in the parlor, where I am about to join her. You will kindly keep your distance from both of us," her stepmother returned, stalking past Kat and out through the doorway.

Which left only Alexis to shoot looks that could kill in Kat's direction. Her expression took on a tinge of satisfaction. "You realize you've totally screwed yourself, right? Mom wants you gone even more than I do now. Wait until some judge gets a load of you. What do you think he'll say—mandatory therapy sessions or a permanent stay at Bellevue? What the hell, maybe both."

Kat said nothing as Alexis brushed past her to follow her mother.

But only in her exit, because—to Kat's dismay—she went up the stairs instead, and her bedroom door slammed shut with an ominous note of finality.

No computer, then. Not yet. She would have to bide her time, all the while feeling her skin crawl at the thought of what might be all around her, watching. Waiting.

So Kat waited, too.

But whatever held sway over the house, both the sunshine outside and Alexis's vanity proved to be beyond its control, because Kat's stepsister eventually appeared in a swimsuit and slipped out the back door with a towel and a bottle of suntan lotion, ignoring Kat altogether. Waiting just long enough to be sure that Alexis was settled in for an afternoon of sunbathing, Kat crept back upstairs to the second floor.

Her stepsister didn't share Kat's paranoia—she had no reason to—so her door was unlocked. Glancing toward the third floor staircase to be sure Michael wouldn't stumble upon her breaking into his sister's room, Kat put her hand on the doorknob and turned it.

"What are you doing?"

The small voice made her nearly leap out of her skin, and Kat spun around to see Emily standing on the second floor landing. She stifled a curse barely in time. "You scared me half to death! Don't sneak up on me like that."

The little girl seemed unabashed by Kat's words, and her eyes even lit up at the obvious clandestine nature of Kat's presence by Alexis's door. She tiptoed over. "Alexis would be really mad if you went into her room without asking."

"That's kind of why I was hoping not to tell her."

"Are you going to put spiders in her bed or something?"

The hopefulness in Emily's tone took Kat aback. Had Alexis been torturing her the same way she'd tortured Kat? "No, I just need to use her computer, and she wouldn't let me use it if I asked her nicely."

"No, she wouldn't," the child agreed, her face falling at Kat's announcement that no spiders would be involved in her activities today. Then she brightened again. "I'll stand guard for you, if you want. In case she comes upstairs."

"Aren't you supposed to be with your mother?"

"She's on the phone. She doesn't know I'm up here."

There was no way that would end well, not if they stood around talking like this and Grace caught them. "If your mom comes looking for you—"

"I won't tell her you're in there, I promise. I'll stand guard," the girl repeated.

She looked so pleased with herself that all Kat could bring herself to do was nod.

Nodding back gravely, Emily took up her post at a window at the end of the hall that overlooked the backyard. Giving her one last glance, Kat slipped inside her stepsister's room.

To say that it was a pigsty would have been kind. The room was a sloppy disarray of clothes, makeup, and magazines. Were it not for the corners of the rolltop desk peeking out from underneath a thick layer of what could only be broadly categorized as "stuff," Kat might have overlooked it entirely. As it was, it still took her a minute to unearth the laptop that was all but drowning in the mess. Something unidentifiable and sticky graced one edge of it. Kat grimaced and wiped her hand before turning the machine on.

It sputtered to life with a soft glow and seemed to take forever to warm up, and when it finally did, a screensaver image of a teenage Alexis and her father filled the screen, the former in the robes of a high school graduate. Her smiling face focused on the elder Fairmont even as his eyes stared blankly at the camera instead of back at his daughter, a hint of impatience in his expression. A sad picture really, whether Alexis realized it or not, but the need for haste drove that thought from Kat's mind before it had time to develop fully. She pulled up a search engine and then paused with her fingers hovering over the keys.

Was it watching? Maybe it always was, but surely it couldn't be everywhere at once. Or maybe it could. What did she know about what the dead could do?

Her tired eyes darted around the room as if she might see something spying on her. There was no drop in temperature, no sickly smell of lavender. Did that mean she was alone?

After a long moment of agonized indecision, she finally began typing, well aware that the seconds were ticking by.

"Ghosts" was much too general to be of any real help. So was "hauntings," although she did glance over one article just to be sure.

...There can be many different causes for ghostly appearances. First, and perhaps most common, is an instance in which someone has either met his or her death at the hands of another but that death has never been properly identified as murder or else he or she is troubled by an improper burial of their remains. This sort of "unfinished business" as it were will often leave a restless spirit behind in its wake.

Kat paused and reread the words. If that was true, there were any number of Delancey deaths that might qualify. Death seemed to haunt the family as much as any restless spirit could.

Sometimes a spirit will attach itself to a location or even an object, perhaps an antique brought home by an unwitting shopper. Perhaps worst of all in that it is so difficult from which to disentangle oneself is that spirit which attaches itself to a person and then follows that person no matter where he or she may go.

God help her if she was dealing with something like that. But whatever it was, it had not seemed to follow her to her grandparents' house. It was *this* house that seemed to be its home, and this one alone. Too bad the fire hadn't taken hold the night Thomas died.

She narrowed her search down further to rumored ways people might rid themselves of ghosts. Some of those results would have been laughable if she was not so far past laughing. Others made familiar references to things like crystals and sage, no doubt the same kinds of things Eleanor's guest Rose had used, to no avail. And when she read, *Probably the easiest way of ridding yourself of a ghost is simply to ask it to leave,* she felt like throwing the computer across the room.

Clearing the results of her search, she started over. Before she could finish typing, the screen abruptly went haywire, jumping around in a bright array of colors before all at once going dark.

Her heart pounded, and she pressed the power key. Nothing. No matter how many times she pressed it, it remained dark. Slamming the laptop closed, she pushed back away from the desk and spun around, half-expecting to see something—she wasn't sure what—watching from behind her.

But the room was empty except for her. Suppressing the urge to curse, Kat covered the computer so Alexis would be less likely to suspect anyone had been in there and then stalked out the door.

Emily looked up as Kat shut the door behind her with more force than was necessary. "What's wrong?"

"This whole house is wrong," Kat returned, her frustration getting the better of her, and then she saw the little girl turn pale. "Emily? What is it? What's wrong?"

"You shouldn't say things like that." Her voice dropped to a whisper, and her eyes darted around. "Don't make it mad. Please don't make it mad."

Before Kat could think of an appropriate way to respond, Michael appeared at the top of the stairs. His eyes immediately focused on Emily's frightened face, and the look he then turned on Kat was not a warm one. "What's going on?" He came the rest of the way down the stairs, thinly-veiled anger in his voice. "Kat? Please tell me you're not talking about what I think you're talking about."

"She's *listening* to me!" Emily burst out, taking him aback. "She's the only one who listens to me!"

He frowned. "Listens to you about what, Emily?"

But instead of answering him, she darted away and down the stairs

Michael turned back to Kat. "Explain. Now."

"You know what she's afraid of, and no, I haven't been putting ideas in her head. She was afraid long before I ever got here." She pushed past him and toward the staircase he'd just descended.

"Where are you going?"

"Attic," she said shortly. She'd found *some* answers up there already, maybe there were more waiting to be found.

She heard his steps behind her. "You already brought down a library's worth of books from up there."

"They haven't told me enough. I may know the 'what' now, but I need to know the 'who.'"

"Kat, wait—"

Just as she glanced back at him, the railing beneath his hand gave way, sending him tumbling backwards, falling and striking his head on the bottom step with a loud crack.

Kat scrambled back down and to his side with a gasp, and he blinked up at her, conscious but with a dazed look on his face. She put a hand under his head in an effort to support him as he struggled to pull himself upright, and her hand came away bloody.

She stared at it, feeling numb, and then she recovered her wits enough to turn around and yell down the stairs.

"Grace!"

◆ CHAPTER THIRTY ◆

IT WAS HARD FOR Michael to tell which was worse, the pain in his head or the way his mother fretted over him in the ER as if he was Emily's age despite the reassurances offered by the doctor who was currently examining him. "See?" Michael told his mother, who hovered close by. "I just need a couple of stitches, so please take a breath before you pass out, all right?"

She seemed barely to hear him and turned her full attention to the doctor while Emily watched wide-eyed from the lone chair in the exam room and Alexis stood close by their mother's side. Funny, but he would have sworn the concern on Alexis's face was genuine, something that touched him more than he expected it to. She'd even stepped up to do the driving while the rest of them piled into Michael's car.

Beyond all of them, Kat watched from the doorway. Grim, pale. She hadn't said a word in the car but only kept a towel pressed tightly to his head the entire ride in to town.

"Doctor, are you sure he shouldn't stay overnight for observation?" Grace asked, the lines in her face more pronounced than usual.

The man in the white lab coat shook his head. "Not necessary. The blood made it look worse than it really was. But he should take it easy for the next couple of days. No more picking fights with staircases."

At the mention of staircases, Michael glanced over his mother's head and at Kat in time to see her open her mouth as if to speak. He shook his head at her once, curtly, and immediately regretted it as the motion started his skull throbbing again. "I'll do my best," he told the doctor through gritted teeth.

The other man removed his exam gloves and disposed of them. "I'll send a nurse in here to prep you for stitches. If you'll excuse me..." Nodding to them all, he left the room.

Grace immediately took his place in front of her son and began fussing over him again. Brushing her hands away from his head, Michael took one of them in his own to soothe her. "I'm fine. Relax. Go find a magazine or something to read until this is all over and we can go back home."

"You can't go back there."

Damn it. He should have known there wouldn't be any way to convince Kat to keep her mouth shut. In a minute she's be spouting God knew what nonsense about haunted houses or family curses. All eyes turned to her, some icier than others.

"I beg your pardon?" Grace asked tightly, and it seemed less like a question than an expression of incredulity.

"Kat," Michael said at the same time, injecting a note of warning into his voice.

It did no good, because she pressed on anyway, the whites of her eyes showing more than usual. "That house is dangerous, and *nobody* should be living in it."

"Oh, God." Alexis rolled her eyes with such disgust that Michael wouldn't have been surprised if her next move would be to spit on Kat. "Now what?"

"There's something in that house, something bad, and I'm not the only one who's felt it. Other people who used to live there—Emily, even—"

"You are a friggin' nutcase, you know that?" Alexis jabbed a finger in Kat's chest. "Why don't you just pack your stuff and get the hell out of here if you hate the place so much? Nobody wants you here anyway!"

Michael pushed himself up from the table to referee, wincing at the headache it caused. "Alexis, calm down."

"No! We were just fine before she got here. Just get out!" she hurled at Kat, her features twisted with far more than just the usual dislike they showed.

"I plan to," Kat returned, and something in her eyes reminded Michael of the look she'd turned on him when she pleaded with him to get her away from the house. Something desperate. "And you should, too."

Alexis drew a deep breath as if to rant some more, but Kat turned to leave before she could.

"Where are you going?" Michael called after her, wincing again and wondering if he really wanted to know the answer.

"I'll be back," was all she said, her voice clipped.

And then she was gone.

◆◆◆

IT WAS STEPPING UP its game, the thing that was in the house. Whether she could convince anyone else of that or not, it was. She knew it was. Drawing closer, showing itself. To her, anyway. The move it had made on Michael today... And it *had* made a move, she was sure. Another accident that was no accident, but that other people would try to dismiss as one because after all, accidents happened all the time, didn't they? Particularly at Delancey Manor.

Yes, well... so did worse things.

They had to listen. She had to find a way to *make* them listen, before it turned into what happened with her father all over again. She would try harder this time, find something or someone that would convince them, *anything*—

Michael's car was not an option this time; Alexis still had the keys. So Kat ran instead, ignoring the curious looks she got from other people, until she passed a taxi and was able to flag it down.

It took the driver a couple of passes to find Mrs. Davenport's museum even with Kat's help. When he finally pulled up to the curb in front of it, she leaped out before he came to a full stop and dashed up the walkway.

And halted as she saw the sign in the window that said it was closed.

No, no—not today. Tomorrow might be too late. Taking a chance, Kat pounded on the door anyway until at last Mrs. Davenport's startled face appeared at the window.

"Miss Delancey," she greeted Kat as she opened the door, looking less than pleased to see her. "I'm afraid we're closed for the day. Perhaps if you came back on Monday—" She adjusted her spectacles and gasped. "Good heavens, is that blood on your shirt?"

"I need to speak to your mother."

"What?"

She barely resisted the urge to shove her way past the woman. "Please, you have no idea how important this is. *Please.*"

If anything, her plea only seemed to make the other woman more uncomfortable. "My mother is sleeping upstairs, and to be frank, I don't like to see her bothered. She was most upset after you left here before."

"You don't understand. If I could just—"

"I'm afraid not. Good afternoon, Miss Delancey." And with a strength and speed that caught Kat off guard, the older woman all but slammed the door closed and locked it again.

Kat beat on the door again. "Mrs. Davenport! Please, Mrs. Davenport!"

But the woman didn't return.

More likely she'd gone to call the police, or at least she would if Kat continued to make noise like this. Pounding and yelling would get her nowhere but jail, and then the others would be at the house...

Perspiration dampened her skin that had nothing to do with the warmth of the air. Options. She needed options. Retreating back down the walkway, she looked up at the second story of the building. Then she leaned down to speak to the cabbie driver through the window. "Wait for me down the street, please. I might be a few minutes."

He gave her a dubious look but nodded before pulling away from the curb. Waiting until he was gone, Kat glanced around to see if anyone was watching.

Then she slipped around the side of the house.

◆ CHAPTER THIRTY-ONE ◆

THE BACK HELD MORE promise than the front. A tall trellis for roses reached all the way to a balcony on the second floor, and if it wasn't the sturdiest looking structure, it was still better than nothing. Testing it for strength and then glancing around one last time, Kat started climbing.

Thorns cut into her skin, and she bit down on her lip, hard, to keep herself from making any noise. Shutting out the stings and slices as she grappled for handholds among the barbs, she hauled herself upward a few inches at a time, testing her weight here... feeling for a place to grip there... Just a few more feet until the bottom of the balcony would be in reach—

The part of the trellis that was beneath her left foot snapped and gave way.

She slipped, but the thorniness of the roses worked in her favor this time and caught her clothes before she could fall far. And caught her skin. Pain made her vision blur for a moment, but she blinked it away and pulled herself up higher until her dangling foot found something to rest on. Higher. Just a little higher...

The fingers of her right hand curled over the edge of the balcony. Pulling with all her might, both upward and against the clinging roses, Kat hauled herself up and over the railing. Ducking down at once for fear of being seen by Mrs. Davenport, she crept closer to the balcony's French doors and peered through their glass panes.

The light was dim on the other side of them. Her eyes adjusted to the light and then settled on a figure nodding off in an easy chair with a blanket across her lap.

Mrs. Davenport's mother.

She was alone in the room. Kat reached up to try the handle of the door closest to her and found it unlocked. Careful not to make a sound, she turned it and edged the door open.

It creaked ever so slightly, so she only opened it enough for her to squeeze through. Slipping inside, she knelt by the old woman's side and gently touched her arm. "Ma'am," she whispered, praying her appearance wouldn't frighten the woman into a scream, or worse, a heart attack. "Ma'am, please wake up."

The old woman woke with a start. She blinked at Kat, and her eyes tried to focus. "Wha…?"

Forcing a smile in an effort to reassure her, Kat put a finger to her lips. "Shh. It's all right. It's me, Miss Delancey. Remember? You spoke to me downstairs before."

The woman just stared at her as if she spoke gibberish. Had senility taken hold? Maybe today she had no memory of Kat at all. Or even the house. As if to confirm Kat's fears, the woman asked in a quavering voice, "*Who* are you?"

Kat glanced at the closed door behind her, half-expecting Mrs. Davenport to walk in at any moment. She tried again, trying not to think of the minutes passing. "Kat Delancey. Katherine. I'm staying at Delancey Manor."

The words had a dramatic effect on the elderly woman. Her eyes widened, and she seized Kat's arm in a surprisingly strong grip. "You mustn't stay there! It's an evil place."

Hope flared. "I know it is, but no one else believes me. Please, I need your help."

That elicited a startled blink. "*My* help?"

"I read the diary you gave me, Eleanor's diary. I know she tried to fight whatever it is that's in that house. Please, is there anything else you can tell me that might help—maybe something that she didn't want to risk putting in any diary?"

The woman pulled her blanket closer and shivered as her eyes stared unseeingly into the distance. "Poor Eleanor. No one believed her. Except me. And Miss Rose."

Tick tock, tick tock..."Who was Rose?"

"Miss Rose used to say that it must have been a woman once, because it hated like a woman." Her voice dropped to whisper. "It likes to hide."

She'd said that before. "What do you mean?"

"All shadows and secrets, never quite out in the open to be seen. They have their limits, you know."

"Who?"

"The dead. That's what Miss Rose used to say. And she would know, wouldn't she? The dead were her business."

"You mean…séances? Like a medium?"

The woman continued as if she hadn't spoken. "She said most would go away if you told them to. Not this one. Oh, no, not this one." There was fear in her voice. "It runs too deep in that house. It won't give up its hold."

Adrenaline had been keeping Kat going so far; now it threatened to desert her. "So there's no way to beat it? Is that what you're saying?'

Mrs. Davenport's mother grabbed Kat's arm again, and her eyes grew fiercely bright. "Make it give up its secrets. Find out why it hides, and then it can't hide from you anymore."

"Did Rose find out?"

There was a sorrowful shake of the head in response. "She tried. Robert put a stop to it. It had him by then."

The words had a chilling effect. "What do mean 'had him?'"

"It gets inside people, the ones that don't know it's there. The ones whose guard is down. Be careful, girl."

Kat slumped beside the easy chair, and her voice dropped to a whisper. "Why is it doing this? What does it want?"

The old woman cupped Kat's cheek in one wrinkled hand. "To see you suffer, you and yours. I don't know why."

Something that hated Delanceys. Something that hated like a woman. Someone, maybe, who had lost much herself and let it warp and twist her. The words from Richard's journal came unbidden to her mind.

I fear sometimes that the shock I see in my wife's eyes verges on madness.

Madness and hate could go together very well. "Is it… is it Charlotte?"

Before the older woman could reply, there was a noise from somewhere on the other side of her door. She stiffened and motioned for Kat to leave. "Go. Hurry. She won't understand."

"But—"

"Go."

She had little choice but to do as told. Slipping back the way she'd come, she closed the door to the balcony only a moment before Mrs. Davenport appeared in the room with a tea tray. Her gaze wandered toward the balcony, but her mother said something that drew her attention back before she could spot Kat.

She didn't dare linger any longer. Back down the trellis she went, feeling the unforgiving thorns bite into her skin the whole way down.

◆◆◆

IT WAS ALREADY TWILIGHT time when Kat made it back to the hospital, and the impending darkness only made her more anxious. Mrs. Davenport would not be pleased if Kat returned with a group in tow, but her displeasure was the least of Kat's problems. So was jail, at this point. If she could just get the rest of them there, if she could get them to listen…

So great was her speed that the sliding doors of the ER barely opened in time for her to pass through them. She started in the direction of Michael's exam room only to come to an abrupt halt when she saw him in the middle of signing paperwork at the front desk instead, a bandage on his head.

He was finished already. Had she really taken so long? "Michael?"

He looked up as she approached him.

"I know everyone thinks I've lost it, but there's someone they need to meet. If she tells them what she told me, maybe they'll understand."

"Sit down, Kat."

"What? No, I—"

He took her by the shoulders and guided her gently toward a pair of empty chairs in the lobby. "Sit."

She did so with great reluctance, her eyes scanning the room in vain for the rest of his family.

"Listen, Kat, I think it might be a good idea for you to stay at my apartment for a few days. Just to clear your head and get some perspective—and some sleep."

"My head *is* clear."

"My mother disagrees. She thinks you're…" He hesitated as if searching for a safe word. "…unstable. She doesn't want you under the same roof as Emily."

Kat stiffened. "Then she'd better pack a bag and move the two of them out of there." Which would be ideal, really. It might not have been plan A, but it would at least be a temporary reprieve. "Because she can't kick me out of my own house."

"She can tell the local authorities that she thinks you're a danger to yourself and others. They won't ignore that."

"Me? I'm not a danger to anybody—it's the house that's dangerous. Why would they believe her anyway? Who's going to back her up—Alexis?" She was about to say that anyone with half a brain would be able to see through her stepsister's vindictiveness, but then the look on his face made her realize Alexis wasn't the only one Michael was talking about. She stared at him as if he'd struck her.

He had the grace to look uncomfortable, at least. "Don't look at me like that. I'm not going to lie for you, Kat. You nearly drowned, remember? And you've had periods of time you can't account for."

"You really think I'd hurt somebody?"

"Not intentionally, no. But…" He started to run his hands through his hair, reached the bandage, and stopped with a wince.

Of course his loyalties lay with his family. She shouldn't have been surprised by that, or hurt.

Shouldn't have.

Her stunned silence seemed to bother him. "Damn it, Kat, what else am I supposed to do? Have you seen yourself lately? The shadows under your eyes get darker every day, you barely eat, and you don't sleep. You need to get away from the house for a while and look after yourself. Please." He looked searchingly into her eyes. "Let me take you to my place, okay? You can crash there for a little while and take a break from things that remind you of your dad."

A new uneasiness crept into her. "Where is everybody?"

"Home. There was no need for them to stick around and watched me get poked with a needle."

Home.

For a moment she couldn't breathe. She stood abruptly. "Oh, God."

"Kat, it's going to be fine."

"No, it isn't," she corrected him, frantic. "Don't you get it? Emily's a Delancey, like me. Whatever that thing is—*who*ever it is—it hates everything Delancey. And—" Her heart constricted.

"And…what?"

"It knows. It knows I plan to sell the house and cut the family's ties to it. That's why it tried to drown me. It knows it's running out of time." She cursed under her breath and rushed toward the exit.

"Kat, wait!"

But she didn't wait. She couldn't. A sick feeling started in her stomach and only grew worse as the sky darkened. Spotting a taxi letting someone out by the curb, she hurried over to it.

Michael called out again, and she knew he was close behind her. Knowing he would stop her if he could, she slid into the back of the startled cabbie's taxi and slammed the door shut. "*Go*," she told him, and her manner must have convinced the man to obey, because he hit the gas pedal in spite of the fact she had yet to give him a destination.

Easily remedied. She gave him the address of the manor and turned her head to look out the back window. Michael would commandeer his own ride back soon enough. Fine by her, just so long as he wasn't able to commandeer this one. Because he would have if he could, she was sure, and he would have directed it to his own place. And all the while convinced he was doing the right thing.

She turned her face forward again and dug her fingers into the palms of her hands, wondering if it was already too late.

And what in God's name she was going to do even if it wasn't.

◆ CHAPTER THIRTY-TWO ◆

ANGER WAS A NEW emotion for Grace. Well, not entirely new. Just one that had gone long unused until now. There had been a kind of wounded anger when Michael's and Alexis's father had sent them all packing, and a raw and helpless rage when Jonathan had died that she'd been careful to keep hidden around other people, but this, this was something else. Something colder.

She bit it back now as she knelt down in front of her youngest and tried to soothe away the anxiety she saw on the little girl's face. This was Kat's doing, this fear in Emily's eyes, and after everything Grace had done to make peace with her—

Bitterness washed through her, and again she forced it back and hid it beneath her best attempt at a smile. "I promise you, there's nothing to be afraid of, sweetheart. Nothing. Kat didn't mean what she said. She just... she has bad dreams some times, that's all, and she gets confused."

"I have bad dreams, too. Like Kat's."

"I know, my darling girl, but that's all they are. Dreams." Lights shone in the driveway, but it was too dark to see the car to which they belonged. Michael in a taxi, no doubt. He'd said he would be along when he could. "Everyone was just upset at the hospital because Michael got hurt, and I know things got loud and scary, but it's all right now. See? That's your brother coming in now, and he'll tell you the same thing."

But it wasn't Michael who burst through the front door and appeared in the parlor doorway. It was Kat. Wide-eyed, she locked her gaze on Emily.

The smile disappeared from Grace's face, and it no longer mattered that Kat was Jonathan's daughter. He'd left another daughter behind, too, and by God, Kat was not going to drag Emily down with her. "How dare you—" Years of habit and good breeding allowed Grace to rein in her fury long enough to get herself back under control again. Just for a minute, but a minute was all she needed. "Emily, go up to your room and close the door right now. I need to talk to Kat. *Alone.*"

Her daughter's eyes were wide as she glanced back and forth uncertainly between her mother and Kat, and Grace felt another wave of heat run through her.

Maybe Kat realized she'd crossed a line, because she held up her hands as if to placate Grace. "No, please—please don't do that. Let her stay down here with us."

Grace's jaw twitched, a nervous tic she thought she'd left behind years ago. "Now, Emily. Go."

"Please, Mommy, I don't want to. *Please.*" Tears appeared in Emily's eyes.

The fragile control Grace had slipped, and she turned on Kat. "Are you happy? I have bent over backwards to get along with you for Jonathan's sake, but no more. How dare you come into this house and fill my daughter's head with such ridiculous ideas! Look—just *look*! She's terrified, thanks to you!"

The sound of the front door opening again mixed with Kat's voice as she insisted, "Not because of me," and Michael appeared behind her.

He was paler than usual and breathing fast as if he'd been running to catch up, but that barely registered as Grace turned her anger onto him. "I told you I didn't want her staying here, Michael! How could you let her come back here like this?"

"*Let* her?" he repeated. "Was I supposed to tie her to a chair or something? I'm sorry. The cracked skull must have dulled my reflexes."

"Grace," Kat pleaded, "just hear me out. I understand that you're upset. I'll make you a deal, all right?" Her eyes darted upward and all around as if searching for invisible eavesdroppers. "I'll go with Michael, I will, if you'll just take Emily and Alexis away for a few days. I swear I will."

"I am not going to uproot my daughters just because you're suffering a break from reality!"

Michael put his hands on Kat's arms as if to lead her away. She jumped but only grabbed onto the doorjamb to maintain her spot. "Grace, please listen to me!"

Again, that frantic glancing around. Good Lord, the girl actually believed there was something there! And to think she'd been alone with Emily. Grace shuddered and clutched Emily to her. "And I'm not going to allow you to ruin the only connection Emily has left to her father. I want her out of here, Michael! Do you hear me? Or I'm calling the police."

"We are not calling the police," he returned, sounding exasperated and on the verge of snapping at someone himself.

"I mean it! I want her out!"

Kat turned a pleading look on Michael, and emotions warred in his expression. It was like a slap in Grace's face, that he would hesitate like this. His father's blood rearing up, no doubt, making him fall prey to a pretty face. And for just a moment Grace resented her son as much as she resented Kat.

But in the end, it seemed he was still his mother's son after all. "All right," he told his mother, and Kat seemed to wilt in his arms. "First thing in the morning. I'll even help her pack myself, and the lawyer—"

"Tonight! I don't want her spending another night here!"

"Enough, Mother! You've made your point. She doesn't have to go skulking out in the middle of the night like some sort of criminal. She won't go anywhere near Emily, I promise."

Pressing her lips together in a thin line, Grace cradled her youngest against her body and turned her face very deliberately away.

"Grace, please!" Kat cried out, but she was no match for Michael's strength as he finally succeeded in pulling her away from the doorway.

Emily squirmed just enough in Grace's arms that she knew her daughter was trying to watch Kat's exit, and that sent a whole new flare of indignation through her. With one hand, she firmly turned Emily's face away.

Kat's protestations faded, and the creak of the stairs suggested Michael was leading her up them. To her room or his? As long as it had a door with a lock on it, maybe it didn't really matter.

Alexis's voice broke the silence from the doorway. "I see the freakshow's back in town. You all right?"

Grace said nothing and only held Emily closer.

◆◆◆

SHE RESISTED AT FIRST, her entire body taut like a strung wire, but to Michael's relief, Kat finally allowed him to lead her up the stairs and to her room. She stumbled once or twice though, as if she was dizzy or dangerously close to fainting, so he kept his arms around her for fear of her tumbling back down the way they'd come.

No, not dizzy. Shaking. She was trembling all over, and as mixed as his emotions were about her, about all of this, he could only soften his voice as he maneuvered her through her doorway and closed the door behind them. "Easy. It's going to be all right."

But she turned in his arms, digging her fingers into them as if for purchase and staring with wide eyes into his. Good God, the shadows beneath them were deep. It was like that was all she was made up of anymore, shadows and sorrow and fear, which seemed just as tragic as everything else about her life. "I know what it looks like, Michael, but it's not me. It's the house! Please, listen—I was just fine before I came back to it. No blackouts, no accidents—nothing like that. It's the *house.*"

Her voice was a whisper, almost conspiratorial, but that she would speak out loud at all about any of this after so vehemently refusing to do so before struck Michael as the most telling thing about her state of mind. A part of him wanted to lose patience with her, even get angry like his mother had done, but he kept picturing the way Kat had looked, bereft and crumpled on the bathroom floor, and anger was impossible. So instead he sighed and tried not to notice how tired he suddenly was or how much his head hurt as he tried to come up with the right words to reach her. "The thing is, Kat, the house was just fine, too, before you came back and started seeing ghosts around every corner."

"Emily—"

"Is six years old and suggestible. No one else saw anything, heard anything... Why do you think that is?"

"It was waiting." Still that hoarse whisper. Her eyes bored into his without seeming to actually see him, not really. "Waiting for me to come back, to come home. To come back here so it could finish what it started, and now it's—" Her eyes widened, and she clapped her hands over her mouth as if she'd only just now realized what she was saying aloud, and not, he knew, because she feared his judgment. No, she was afraid of something else altogether.

Was this what a true mental break looked like?

"Kat, please listen to me. Yes, there have been some terrible things that have happened here, tragic things. But they're *accidents*, that's all. Just accidents. Sometimes bad things just happen."

She just shook her head, and her shoulders slumped as if all strength had left her.

He got the distinct feeling that he was failing her, failing everybody, and he tried again to get through to her. "Your memory lapses, the overdose... even the sleepwalking. That's not a haunting, that's just your mind trying to recover from what you've lost. Please, Kat. I'm trying to help you here."

But she didn't seem to hear him. "My fault. It's my fault."

"What's your fault?"

"I couldn't make him listen—can't make anybody listen. Oh, God, I don't know what to do. What do I do?" She was crying now, and she seemed to only realize it at the same time he did, because she blinked with a start and turned her face away as if ashamed.

He caught her chin in one hand and made her look at him so that maybe she would see that he was being earnest and sincere with her. So that maybe she would actually *hear* him. "You need to get away from here for awhile."

"Can't. I can't. Emily—"

"Emily has other people to look after her. Let someone look after you for a change, all right? Your grandparents—"

Her panic seemed to hit a new high, and her voice rose as well. "No! No, you can't bring them here!"

"Okay, fine. Me, then. I'll do it. I'll take you to my place for a while, and it'll be all right, you'll see."

But she just kept murmuring things under her breath that he couldn't quite make out. He shook her in a vain attempt to snap her out of it. "Kat, you can't really think that... Okay, let's say for the sake of argument that this house really is haunted by some sort of angry spirit or something. Why? Why in God's name would it want to hurt you or Emily?"

"I don't know. I don't know why it hates us, I just know that it does."

"Okay, fine. Say it does have some kind of grudge against Delanceys. How do you explain what happened today? You thought it came after me on the stairs today, didn't you? But I'm not a Delancey. So why me? That doesn't fit with your explanation of all this. Why would it want to hurt me?"

"It does that," she erupted with audible bitterness. "It hurts other people just to make us watch it do it, to make us watch them suffer. To watch us *lose* them. It hurt my mother just to break our hearts, it hurt my dog—that's what it does, Michael. It takes what matters to you, piece by piece."

Her outburst left him momentarily at a loss for what to say, partly because of the level of her agitation and partly because of the implication of her words. "Kat..."

Her voice dropped down to a whisper again, and she gave him a pleading look. "*Help* me."

The part of Michael that took after his father, the part that he often wished he could cut out of himself, became increasingly aware of the way that she clung to him like he was the only warm and solid thing she had to hold on to in this house, which maybe he was. *Bastard*, he thought at himself with shame, and he willed the better part into control again before he could do something stupid and selfish like offer her the kind of solace he was best at offering women, which was not at all what a woman in Kat's state needed right now.

So instead he said, "I will, I promise," and picked her up in his arms to carry her over to her bed and lay her on it. She started to protest, still crying, and he knew she'd never stay there if he left her no matter how much he might plead or cajole or threaten. But she was out of her mind with exhaustion and anxiety, so he lay next to her and pulled her back against his chest, one arm wrapped around her waist securely to keep her there. "Just sleep," he whispered into her ear, his own voice hoarse now, and he tried not to notice the way the pulse in her neck was pounding.

She moved as if to try to leave, to get away and perhaps rush back down the stairs again and do God knew what, but he held her firmly in place.

"I'm trying to do the right thing here, Kat. For you and for everybody else. So just—go to sleep, please. *Please.*"

Maybe he'd finally pierced the fog of fear in her mind, or maybe she just finally gave up, because she stopped trying to free herself and just lay there, shaking.

"It's going to be okay, I promise."

She whispered something back, and it took him a moment to realize what the words were.

No, it isn't.

◆ CHAPTER THIRTY-THREE ◆

KAT DIDN'T SLEEP. INSTEAD she lay in the darkness just listening, and watching. Waiting.

The house grew quiet as the hour grew later. Beside her, Michael stirred, but only for a moment and then he was still again. He had lain awake for a long time, too. She could tell as much by his breathing, and by the tension in his body that was so close to her own, tension that only finally relaxed out of him when he at last fell asleep.

Once or twice she moved and felt him immediately tense again, his sleep too light to remain undisturbed. There would be no getting up and leaving the room, not anytime soon.

So she lay there and waited, not sure what she was waiting for. There was no place for her to go, nothing left that she could think of to try. Her time was up. They would send her packing first thing in the morning and do everything they could to keep her from coming back. Grace had said as much.

Out loud. And she'd said it inside these walls. Where *it* lived. Would it let Kat go so easily?

She lay there in the dark, feeling the cold deepen around her, and knew that the answer was no. No, it was coming.

No, not *it*. *Her*. Because she had a name for it now. Charlotte, who had lost so much herself in life and then lost the rest to the sister who took her place after her death. Driven to the point of madness with grief, and taking it out on every Delancey that came after her. Of course it was her. That was where it had all started, after all, the family's misfortune. With her first child's death.

And now there was just one child left. Emily. Would it keep her around for a while, just to torment her in the way it had done to Kat? Or would it finish off the entire bloodline in one fell swoop? It had had its sadistic fun, dragging things out over decades, but maybe now the fun was done.

The floorboards creaked outside her door.

Kat froze.

It could have been innocent enough, someone getting up to walk to the bathroom maybe, or even downstairs to the kitchen. But it wasn't. Somehow she knew it wasn't.

Another creak, but this one was fainter. Whoever it was, it was moving further away.

Toward Emily?

Kat's gut tightened. She slid Michael's arm from around her waist, slowly and careful not to wake him, and slipped out of the bed to creep toward the door. Opening it as quietly as possible, she looked out into the hall.

The stretch heading toward both Grace's room and Emily's was empty. Turning her head to look the other way, Kat saw a silhouette in the darkness at the head of the stairs. Her heart nearly stopped before she recognized it as that of her stepsister.

"Alexis," she whispered. "What are you doing?"

She would not have been surprised to have been greeted with a stream of profanity or insults in general, but there was none of that. Alexis didn't move or acknowledge Kat's presence in any way. Edging slowly forward one wary footstep at a time, Kat approached her in the dark, expecting at any time to feel the unnatural chill that would mean they were not alone.

There was no chill, but when Alexis finally turned around, Kat froze as if there was.

I would swear something other than my husband looked back at me…

The words from Eleanor's diary made sense in a way now that they couldn't have before as Kat stared into her stepsister's eyes and saw something that wasn't Alexis looking back at her.

She stumbled backwards and away from it, and the thing that was inside Alexis grinned. The features were the same as always, but the smile was not.

Sounds with no explanation were one thing. So was the scent of a flower that wasn't there or air that felt like ice against her skin even on a warm summer day. But to be faced with an actual presence was another thing altogether, something that followed her movements with eyes that seemed to glow from within. It made Kat's skin crawl, and it was all she could do to keep from turning and bolting.

But there was no place to run to, not really. Wherever she ran, it could find her. And the others. And Alexis—

There was no love lost between the two of them, but the thought of this *thing* being inside her stepsister.... Kat's stomach roiled violently. Was Alexis aware of its presence? God, she hoped not.

The thing's smile grew wider and more malicious, but it came no closer to her. Why? It gets inside people, the old woman had said. The ones who didn't know it was there. Well, Kat knew it was there, more than anyone else had in a long time. Was that enough to keep it at bay?

She'd have tried anything now that others said might work if she could have, the sage, the crystals—never mind that they hadn't worked for Rose. Here with the thing itself in front of her, anything would have been better than nothing. *Simply ask it to leave*, she'd read, but that had not worked for Rose either. But then, Rose hadn't known who it was.

"Charlotte." Kat's voice was only a whisper, but it was a miracle that she was able to get anything out at all. She clutched at the wall with one hand as her legs threatened to buckle beneath her. "Charlotte, get out of her. Get out of her and leave. Now."

Alexis's mouth twitched as if the thing inside her was amused.

"Get *out*," Kat repeated with more force, having to choke the words out because her mouth was so dry.

Still, it didn't move. And then just as Kat opened her mouth to cry out for Michael, Alexis turned.

And threw herself over the banister.

It was impossible to tell who screamed first, Kat or Alexis, because Alexis did scream—a genuine shriek of terror—a moment before there was a sickening cracking sound that Kat knew, even before she made it to the edge of the railing to look down, had to be bone.

It was dark, but not so dark that Kat couldn't make out the shape of Alexis's crumpled form on the floor near the base of the stairs. And her neck—

Memories of her father's death rushed to the surface, the horrendous angle of his head, and Kat's stomach again threatened to heave. Perhaps the only reason she didn't was because the door to her room was thrown open then, and light from the bedside lamp streamed out as Michael came running.

"What is it? What's wrong?" he demanded, his eyes wide and unfocused as only those of someone who had just been startled awake could be.

Shock took hold of Kat. She stared down at her stepsister's body, unable to answer.

Another door opened, this one the one to Grace's room. She emerged in a nightgown, her hair mussed from sleeping and her face wan. "What on earth is going on?"

Michael reached the bannister before she did. "Oh, my God…"

His mother came running over. He tried to stop her from looking but wasn't fast enough, and she let out her own shriek of horror as she saw what lay below.

Michael finally succeeded in pulling her away from the railing and stared at Kat. "How? Kat, what—"

She had no chance to respond, because Grace tore herself free from Michael's hold and lunged at Kat, her face contorted in grief and rage. "You did this!" she screamed at her, trying to claw her face while Kat fell backward and struggled to fend her off. She was only partially successful, and her cheek stung from where Grace's nails raked it.

"No, I swear—"

"Stop it!" Michael pulled his mother off of Kat. "Just stop it!"

"She did this! I told you… I told you to get her out!" And then Grace slapped her son across the face before staggering down the stairs. He reeled back as if stunned and didn't try to stop her.

Kat struggled to get her feet back under her. "Michael, listen to me—"

Her voice jolted his attention back to her again, and he pulled her back into her bedroom, although she was too numb to realize what he was doing until they were in it. The walls threatened to spin again. "Michael—Michael, it wasn't me. I didn't do this."

"Wait here," he told her hoarsely.

"I'm telling you—"

"Kat!" The sharpness of his tone took her aback, and his eyes were red and wet. "I have to go call 911. Please… just wait here."

Then he was gone, closing the door behind him, and Kat was alone.

◆ CHAPTER THIRTY-FOUR ◆

THAT SCREAM, THAT AWFUL scream...

Alexis had been awake when she tumbled and hit the floor. Awake, or herself again, or whatever it was she'd been before that thing had taken her over. It had let her come to just in time to realize what was happening to her. It was sick. Cruel.

Kat's gut began to turn over again.

She closed her eyes but could not shut out the image of Alexis's broken body, the odd and unnatural angle of her neck.

Her hands trembled violently, and she held them up before her and stared at them as if they belonged to someone else. Useless, empty things. She should have moved faster, made a grab for her—

She clenched her hands into fists and cut off her train of thought. Dissolving into a puddle of tears and fear was not an option right now, because the night wasn't over yet. Bad as it was already, it was only beginning. She could feel it.

The door opened, and Kat looked up to see Michael. He stood there in the doorway for a long moment, a shadow of his usual self, before finally turning to close the door. His movements were slow and heavy, as if even that small amount of exertion cost him dearly.

He didn't look at her right away. Instead, he put one hand on the closed door, still facing it, as if using it for support. "Kat," he said, his voice very quiet and his tone strange. "You need to tell me exactly what happened."

"I heard a noise out in the hall. I went to check it out."

Now he turned. His eyes were fixed on her. "I didn't hear anything."

"You were asleep."

"Why didn't you wake me?"

"Because you wouldn't have let me up. You would have told me that it was nothing and to just go back to sleep. I know you would." He was silent, and she couldn't tell if it was in acknowledgement of her point or in disagreement with it. "I got up to see what it was, and I saw Alexis." Her palms grew clammy. "But it wasn't—it wasn't really her. I mean, it was, but it wasn't."

He just stared at her, and she knew she sounded like a madwoman, babbling. Of course she did. There was nothing sane or normal about what she'd just seen. She tried again, her desperation growing. If she couldn't make him understand… "There was something inside of her, Michael. Something controlling her. Possessing her. It smiled at me—" She was going to be sick in a minute, so she forced the image from her mind. "—like it was glad I was watching. And then it made her jump."

And then that scream...

Michael closed his eyes and shook his head, and she knew he wasn't hearing her. She was failing, failing miserably. Pushing herself up from the bed, she crossed the distance between them in the small room to look him in the eyes and plead. "We have to get out of here, all of us. Right now. Because it'll come after everyone while it still can. It knows it's running out of time—"

"Kat—"

"I'm telling you, it was that *thing*."

"Kat, did you hurt her? I need to know the truth."

His words hit her like ice water. "What? No!"

The expression on his face was one of pain. "Were you afraid no one would take you seriously unless… unless…"

A new chill of realization went through her. Oh, it was clever—not just vicious, but devious, too. "Michael, it wasn't me! Something took her over, something—someone—who used to live in this house. It made her jump, and it knew, it must have known you'd all think I—"

Michael grabbed her by the shoulders. "For God's sake, Kat, stop it! That's enough! She was my sister. I know what a piece of work she could be sometimes, but she was my *sister*. And she didn't deserve this."

"Of course she didn't deserve it! Neither did my mom or my dad, but that didn't save them either, did it? And it won't save us. We have to get out of this house. Now!"

"Oh, no. Forget it.—The police are coming. No one's going anywhere until they get here."

The police. It wouldn't want an audience, would it? No, it liked to hide too much. Which meant time was running out even faster than she'd thought. "Emily—at least get Emily out of here!"

"Emily is safe downstairs with her mother," he told her tersely.

"Safe?" A huff of hysterical laughter escaped her although she felt like crying or screaming, or both. "Safe? No place in this house is safe. God, why won't you listen to me?" His expression darkened. "You have to stop this. This house is not cursed, and it isn't haunted. Nothing is going to—"

The door flew open, and Grace burst into the room, wild and wide-eyed. "Where is she?"

Startled, Michael released Kat's shoulders from his grip. "Where is who?"

"Emily! I left her a moment, only for a moment, to be with Alexis. And when I came back—" She made a lunge at Kat, but Michael intercepted her. "Where is she? What did you do with her?"

Emily…

Oh, no, no, no, no…

Michael forced his mother back toward the door and away from Kat, even as she continued to struggle against his hold. "Mother, stop it. Stop! Kat hasn't done anything to Emily. What are you talking about?"

"Yes, she has!" Giving up for the moment, Grace clutched at her son's arms. "I can't find her, Michael. I can't find her anywhere. She must have done something to her!"

Again she tried to get past him, and again he held her back. "Listen to me. Kat's been in here with me since I left you downstairs. There's no way she could have done anything, all right? It wasn't her. It—"

He stopped abruptly and turned to look at Kat, and it was if he was seeing her for the first time. Or maybe seeing something else. The color drained from his face.

The warmth had drained from hers a long time ago. "It's taken her."

"It's not possible," he whispered, his eyes wide.

"You're insane," Grace spat at Kat, trying unsuccessfully to free herself from Michael's grip. "Give me back my daughter!"

But something must have finally clicked enough into place for Michael that he grabbed her arm and began to propel both her and his mother toward the bedroom door. "Out. Everybody outside, right now."

His mother sputtered at him. "You can't seriously believe any of her nonsense!"

"I don't know if I do or I don't," he returned. "But let's just get outside first, and then we'll argue about it, all right?"

"Michael—"

They were met with an icy chill the moment they stepped foot into the hall. Kat opened her mouth to issue a warning, and her breath came out as fog.

It was here.

◆ CHAPTER THIRTY-FIVE ◆

MICHAEL AND GRACE BOTH saw Kat's icy breath at the same time and stared. "What the hell—" Michael started, but he didn't get a chance to finish his sentence.

Something unseen slammed into Kat with the force of a hurricane wind. It knocked her to the floor along with Grace and sent Michael hurtling through the air, and she had just enough time to see him hit the railing with a sickening crack and go tumbling down the stairs before the side of her own face smacked against the floor so hard that it left her stunned.

For the briefest of moments, all she was aware of was the pain in her head, and then a scream of pure terror to her left jolted her back to awareness.

Grace.

The stars cleared from Kat's vision, and she saw her stepmother huddled in a ball beside her, quaking with fear. She screamed again as the walls of the house rattled around them.

Michael. Where was Michael?

Still lightheaded from her fall, Kat dragged herself on her hands and knees toward the stairs to look over the edge of the topmost one.

He lay crumpled lower down on the steps, his head turned away from her. And he lay absolutely still.

Oh, God...

Instinct made Kat stay low to the ground as much as possible even though it might have been completely useless to do so; it was hardly as if she was trying to evade a sniper. Scrambling down to Michael in her awkward crouch, Kat felt the side of his neck with her fingers. There was a faint beat. Disturbingly slow, but it was a beat nevertheless. And she could see now that he was breathing, if very shallowly. He was alive, at least. For now.

Out. They had to get out.

She put a hand on the nearest railing to pull herself upright and then let it go as if it had burned her. It hummed and vibrated as if the house sat on a fault line that was about to become active. Something was coming.

It would be dangerous to move him, after a fall like that, but it would be far more dangerous not to. As gently as she could, Kat turned Michael over. His eyes were open. Thank God. She opened her mouth to say his name, but then froze. He wasn't looking at her. His eyes were open, but he wasn't seeing anything. He didn't blink, he didn't move. Not even so much as a twitch. "Michael—" She waved her hand before his face and still got no response. Frightened, she risked shaking him. "Michael!"

He gave no sign of being aware of her at all.

It was an unnatural sort of stillness, far more disconcerting than even the blankness she'd witnessed years ago in her mother. Eyes were not meant to look that empty and glassy, and the sight sent s new chill through Kat.

What had it done to him?

The railings up and down the length of the staircase rattled harder, making Kat flinch away from them. There was no time now to worry about Michael's condition.

Out, her mind screamed at her again. *Get out now!*

Sliding one arm beneath Michael's limp torso, Kat struggled to lift him. In vain, though; his dead weight was too much for her. She would need help. "Grace!"

Grace's screams had turned into whimpering sounds. Judging from the direction of them, she had not budged so much as an inch from where Kat had left her.

"Grace!" she cried out again. "Help me with Michael!"

She got no response.

"Grace, *now*!" she yelled.

Finally, her stepmother's face appeared at the second floor landing, pale and with her eyes bulging so far that she was almost unrecognizable. "Michael! Is—is he—?"

"He's alive. Help me with him!"

The older woman's legs shook visibly as she dragged herself down the stairs toward them, and for a moment Kat wondered if she was going to have to find a way to carry them both out somehow. But although Grace wasn't able to shoulder much of Michael's weight, it was enough help that Kat was able to drag the rest of him down one step at a time. She went first, trying not to bump his head against any of the steps and wincing at the sight of fresh blood on the bandage he'd gotten earlier in the ER.

A sconce light on the wall near them flickered as they shuffled past it, and the air grew cold again.

Kat froze in place.

"He's not moving," Grace wailed from a step or two above her. "Why isn't he *moving*?"

A picture frame detached itself from the wall across from them and hurled itself in their direction.

There wasn't time to blurt out a warning to her stepmother, but it didn't matter; it flew toward Kat, not Grace. It came too fast for her to get out of its way, not unless she dropped Michael. She barely had time to hunch herself into as much of a ball as she could before the frame struck her in the shoulder, and then she nearly dropped Michael anyway just from the sharpness of the pain. She gasped.

Grace cried out again, and her wild-eyed look was back. But maybe her fear for her son was stronger than her fear of anything else, because when Kat said her name, she redoubled her efforts to help carry Michael in spite of her shaking legs. They made it to the bottom of the staircase, half-stumbling and half-sliding.

Recovering her balance, Kat looked over toward the front door. The distance they had to cross was only a matter of feet, but the floor hummed with the same kind of energy that had been in the banister posts.

Coming. It's coming...

"Hurry," she choked out at Grace, trying not to look at where Alexis's body lay under a sheet that someone had draped over her. Heaving Michael up with a final burst of adrenaline—

So close. Just a few yards.

—she hauled him with Grace's help first one foot across the distance of the foyer, then another and another, struggling to stay upright as the floor shook beneath them.

A floorboard splintered with a snapping sound.

Kat cursed, narrowly avoiding being scraped by the edge of the now protruding board. "Watch it!" she cried out a moment too late, and her stepmother tripped over the same board to send all three of them tumbling to the ground.

Only three feet from the door now. Dragging herself forward, Kat reached up and seized the doorknob with a desperate lunge.

It turned, but the door refused to open.

Her heart stopped, then thudded faster. She twisted the knob harder.

"What are you doing?" Grace cried out, struggling to right herself and carry her son again at the same time. "Open it!"

"I'm trying!" She twisted again, pulled with all her might. The door remained closed, and she gave up on the knob to pound on the door futilely with her fists. "Damn it, come *on*!"

She might as well have huffed and puffed on it for all the good it did her. Abandoning the door, she dashed back and grabbed the fallen picture frame. Then she paused in front of the long window on the left side of the grand front entrance and swung.

It was a sturdy frame, solid wood and of good size. It cracked the window with the first blow, then smashed through it completely with the second. Using it to brush away the worst of the shards of glass, Kat then dropped it out of the way and picked up Michael under the shoulders again.

Cuts were unavoidable. That didn't make them hurt any less as Kat led the way through the makeshift exit and felt the first slice of glass shards on skin. She cried out but squeezed herself through the opening anyway because there was no help for it. Spots of red from similar cuts blossomed on Michael's shirt as they hoisted him through the broken window but if he felt the pain at all, he gave no sign. Grace slid through last, weeping openly as she did.

"No, don't—*don't,*" Kat insisted as her stepmother, looking on the verge of fainting started to set her son down on the porch. "Further, we have to get him further away!"
"Where?"

Kat didn't know—maybe no place was far enough—so she didn't even try to answer but only kept struggling beneath Michael's weight as she staggered down the porch steps and onto the grass until she simply couldn't move another step and finally collapsed with Michael in her arms, her chest heaving for breath.

Grace fell to her knees beside her and cradled Michael's head in her lap, sobbing. "What's happening? I don't understand what's going on!"

"Yes, you do. You just wish you didn't." Kat felt for Michael's pulse again, this time at his wrist, and while it was no weaker, it was no stronger either. They might have gotten him outside of the house, but he was still in its grip. And Emily…

Oh, God, what had it done with Emily?

The adrenaline that had gotten Kat this far was gone now, leaving her feeling weak and helpless as Grace sobbed next to her. Even Michael's hand in hers felt suddenly too heavy for her to continue holding it, so she lay it back down across his chest as gently as she could, wincing at the bleeding cuts on his skin. And caught sight of the gash he'd gotten on his arm the day he'd helped her in the attic.

She froze, staring at it.

The attic. It hadn't liked her poking around up there. When she'd found that door at the back—

Make it give up its secrets…

Kat turned her head to look upwards at the topmost floor of the house, the one where the windows were smallest and darkest. She'd been lucky to make it down one flight of stairs. Getting back up three of them seemed like an impossibility. And suicide.

But Emily...

"Stay here," she told Grace, shoving herself back to her feet and feeling fresh reminders all over her body of what she'd been through already. The sleeve of her shirt stuck to her skin at the bottom edge, and she wasn't sure if it was because of Michael's blood or her own.

"Where are you going?"

"I'll be right back—Just don't move!"

She took off at a run around the side of the house and to the back where the gardens were, and the garden shed. She'd not been in it since the day her father—since he'd had her help him get out the ladder, but she remembered it had lots of other things in it as well. Like shovels, and rakes, and—

Halting in front of it, she threw the door open.

And an axe.

In the absence of a key, it would have to do. She snatched it up as her eyes darted over the rest of the shed's contents. Nothing else she could see of use there. Pliers, hammer—useless to her right now.

Except for a small flashlight. It was so small that she nearly missed it, and had she not knocked over a shovel and sent it tumbling against a shelf of odds and ends when she grabbed the axe, she would have never seen it at all. But if the batteries were dead…

They were not. Weak, maybe, but not dead. She shoved the light into her pocket and stumbled back the way she had come, axe in hand.

In spite of Kat's instructions, Grace was in the process of hobbling to her feet. Had she not been so shaky on them, she might already have been halfway to the front door.

Kat grabbed her arm. "Grace, wait!"

Her stepmother tried to shake her off. "My baby. I have to find my baby!"

"You can't—it'll never let you. It's me it wants, not you. You have to stay here with Michael."

"I can't! I have to find her! I have to—"

"Grace, listen to me!" Kat pulled her around to face Michael's still form where it lay on the grass. "We can't leave him here alone. God knows what might happen to him."

"But he's outside now—"

"My mother died outside. So did Dad, remember?"

The other woman stared at her in shock. "But… but that was an accident. That… that…"

There was no time for this right now. "I have to go, Grace. I may be able to stop it, but I don't know. If I can't, you need to be with Michael and keep him safe. I swear to God I won't come out without her. Understand? I swear."

Their eyes locked, and Kat caught a glimpse of the struggle going on inside her stepmother. One daughter dead, and the other one missing while her only son lay catatonic. A hell of a way to be initiated into to the world of family hauntings. Finally, she nodded, crumpling, and with grief and fear all over her face. "Find her—please find her!"

Words seemed empty right now, so all Kat could offer by way of a promise was a curt nod. Tightening her grip on the axe, she retraced her steps to the porch and the broken window and hoped it was a promise she'd be able to keep.

◆ CHAPTER THIRTY-SIX ◆

WITHOUT THE WEIGHT OF Michael in her arms, Kat was able to step through the broken window without earning herself many fresh injuries. She was cautious anyway, her eyes darting around the entryway as she stepped into it again.

Bits of broken glass crunched beneath her shoes. The sound was abnormally loud in her ears. What did it matter, though? She could hardly sneak up on a ghost.

She shifted the axe in her hands, gripping it securely with both of them. Not that it could do much to protect her, but if anything else came flying off the walls at her, maybe she could knock it away.

As if on cue, a vase on a tiny entryway table began to tremble and teeter near the edge.

Kat tightened her grip. "That you, Charlotte?" she called out, anger mixing with her fear. "You still hiding?"

Movement in the parlor made her turn abruptly in that direction, movement that turned out to be the bottoms of the window curtains beginning to swirl as if a wind was passing through.

No, not hiding anymore.

The swirling increased. She half-expected to feel the force of a gust against her skin and in her hair. Instead she felt an icy cold finger touch her cheek Spinning around, she saw nothing. Playing. It was still playing with her. Her heart hammering inside her chest, she took a step toward the stairs and felt the floor vibrate beneath her feet. "So what is it? You lost your family, so you think the rest of us ought to lose ours also? Is that it?"

The vibrating increased, causing the sheet that was over Alexis's body to shift and reveal her left hand lying still and motionless.

There was no help for it. She was going to have to walk right past it in order to climb the stairs.

Choking back bile, Kat continued her advance on the staircase, every nerve in her body on edge as she waited for the next attack to come, whatever form it might take. Her eyes darted around in constant motion, and her ears listened for the faintest sound. There was little point in trying to find Emily on her own. *It* would reveal her when it was ready, and not a moment sooner.

And then what? a voice inside her head whispered. It would hardly let them just leave. Not unless she forced it to. *If* she could force it to.

The attic. It was all she had left now.

The sconce light that was mounted on the wall halfway up the stairs began to flicker again as it had before, just as Kat neared the base of the steps. Don't look, she told herself as she reached Alexis. Instead, she glanced up and around the room and called out, "I want my sister back, Charlotte!"

The house shook more violently than before. An intimidation tactic. An effective one, too, but Kat made her feet obey her anyway. She lifted her left one with the intention of stepping over Alexis's arm and on the bottom step.

That was when the floor gave way beneath her and sent her tumbling into darkness.

She screamed as she fell. It was an instinctual response that no one could have suppressed, not under those conditions. She didn't even try.

Her head struck something hard, and everything went truly black then.

◆◆◆

SOMETHING STICKY WAS IN her eyes. She blinked feebly in an effort to clear them, but it didn't work. Or had she even blinked at all? She couldn't really tell. The darkness was the same whether her eyes were open or not.

She was lying on her stomach on something hard and uneven. Jagged, even. Shifting in what she intended to be the beginning of rolling to her side, she winced at a sharp pain in her leg and an even sharper pain in her head, and all attempts to roll over were abandoned.

Instead, she moved one hand to wipe her eyes and felt it come away wet. And when she felt a little higher, a sudden stinging where her fingers touched her scalp told her she had a bleeding cut just beyond her hairline.

The floor. She'd fallen through it. To where, she wasn't sure. It must have been a cellar of some kind, but she had never known the house had one before. If her father had known about it, he had never shared its existence with her.

Maybe with good reason. The air was so thick with dust that it nearly choked her. Faint light trickled down, and now that she'd wiped her eyes clear, she could make out dim shapes in the darkness. Only in the area nearest to her, though. Beyond that, the darkness was impenetrable.

She had to get up, pain or no pain. And where was the axe? She'd lost it during the fall. It was a miracle she hadn't landed on it.

Rolling over in earnest now—and gritting her teeth against the pain—she felt something hard in her back pocket.

The flashlight.

Hoping against hope that it hadn't been damaged during the fall, she pulled it out and switched it on. A thin beam of light pierced the darkness, albeit not very far. She was surrounded by a shambles of splintered floorboards, including several that were underneath her. The dust in the air above them was in the process of settling—she couldn't have blacked out for very long then.

She glanced up, squinting as her vision swam. Getting out was going to be a lot harder than getting in. If she was going to climb out, she'd need to find something to prop up against the mouth of the gaping hole above her first. Unless there were stairs somewhere down here. Surely there had to be some somewhere. At one point, the cellar had to have been in use for something, even if it hadn't been for a very long time. She just had to find the exit.

She tried to shove herself to her feet with her free hand and wound up taking another spill as the broken bits of lumber beneath her slid out from under her. It sent her tumbling to a stop against something softer than wood. Pushing herself up, she brought the flashlight to bear on whatever it was and had to bite back a cry.

Alexis.

Her lifeless eyes stared back at Kat, who scrambled backward to get away from the tangle of sheet and limbs that was all that remained of her stepsister.

Breathe. She needed to breathe. Panicking got in the way of thinking, and she needed to think now, quickly, and before *it* reared up again.

The axe. She needed to find the axe, and then she needed to find stairs. Or at least a makeshift ladder. To do that, she would need to move and venture further into the cellar. Training the flashlight's thin beam of light before her, she swung it gently in an arc from left to right. It barely showed more than five feet in front of her.

But five feet was better than nothing. She pressed forward cautiously, limping on the leg that had been hurt in the fall and trying not to notice the deep, dark red stain on her jeans that seemed to be spreading.

Her head throbbed, and she felt a wave of dizziness. She stopped, waiting for it to pass, praying that it actually would. No more fainting. She'd be even easier prey than she already was if she did. But standing here made her an easy target, too, so she put one foot in front of the other again and continued her search for her missing axe.

Other than cobwebs, the cellar seemed mostly empty. The cobwebs were huge, though, and they stretched everywhere throughout the expanse. If she stopped to think about the spiders it had taken to spin them over the years, she would never get out of here, so she thrust that thought from her mind.

Something gleamed in the light. Drawing closer, she recognized the head of the axe and bent to pick it up. Thank God for small favors. Now to find a way out.

She crept on, turning her light this way and that as she moved. A makeshift ladder would not be an option after all. The cellar was too empty. An open doorway on one side revealed what might have been an old furnace, long out of use, and a couple of metal bins that were too large and cumbersome for her to even think of moving. No help there. She turned the other direction. Nothing but cobwebs and shadows, and there was no—

One of the shadows moved.

Kat jerked backward, nearly dropping the flashlight. A trick of the eye. *Oh, please let it be a trick of the eye…* She aimed the light toward it again.

The darkness before her rolled as though something twisted and turned in its midst. What it was, she couldn't tell; the light was too feeble for that. But something was definitely moving inside it.

A scream built up in her throat but died before it could get out. Her mouth was too dry to make any sound.

Something that looked like a tendril of black smoke curled out of the shadow before becoming part of it once more. Then another, and this one looked less like a tendril and more like…like…

Was that an arm?

It was trying to take shape. Somehow that was more terrifying than anything else, and the thought of seeing whatever that final shape might be filled Kat with something far too strong to simply be called dread. What final form would something that had been dead for over a century take?

An awful stench permeated the air around her, part sickly sweet lavender but part something else, something that was rotten and foul. Unable to help herself, Kat fell to her knees and started to retch.

Move, she screamed at herself inside her head. She had to move. Now.

Staggering back to her feet, she turned her back on the thing that was trying to form in the shadows behind her and ran as fast as her injured leg would let her toward the gaping hole through which she'd fallen. It was too high to reach, too high to jump—

She searched frantically on either side for something, anything, to use for a boost up but still found nothing. Like a trapped animal, she pressed blindly further into the darkness as her desperation grew, all the while wondering if the thing behind her was approaching, and then the feeble beam of light caught the edge of a banister.

Stairs.

Stumbling to them, she hauled herself up the rotted wood of the steps. Her foot broke through one of them, trapping her ankle for a moment, but so strong was her need to flee that she yanked it free without regard for the pain it sent shooting through her foot.

Go, go, *go*, she told herself, hearing her breath come out in shuddering gasps. Her hand found the knob, and she turned it.

It was locked.

She spat out a curse and dropped the flashlight so she could seize the axe in both hands and then swung it.

The wooden door was old. The axe was not. It bit deeply into the wood and splintered it immediately. Wrenching it free, Kat swung again.

Coming. It was coming…

She swung again, and then again, and then finally the door fragmented enough for her to pull a chunk of it off. Still too small for her to fit through, though. She hefted the axe again.

It could be at the bottom of the steps now. It could even be climbing them, and any second now she might feel one of those unearthly hands reach out and touch her.

Oh, God, please...

Two more blows, and the center of the door collapsed on itself with a groaning sound. Shielding her face with the arm that had the axe, Kat snatched the flashlight back up and leaped through the rough opening in a single motion while splintered edges caught at her shirt.

Or maybe those were fingers.

She tumbled into a small space by a washroom that was off of the kitchen, an area she had always assumed to be a kind of pantry. Her entrance was desperate and clumsy, and she would have fallen had she not grabbed the corner edge of the nearby wall. Dragging herself along the wall and away from the ruined door, she shot a frantic glance backward, fully expecting to see some awful apparition emerging close at her heels.

Nothing. The fragmented remains of the door looked like a misshapen mouth of jagged teeth, horrifying in its own way but empty of any sign of movement.

They have their limits...

Was that it? Was that why it didn't appear now? Had it overreached, or was it planning something else?

The vibrations she'd felt earlier had subsided after the fall through the floor, but as she ran through the kitchen and down the hallway, she felt the humming sensation begin again under her feet.

It spurred her on to run faster in spite of her injuries, and when she reached the yawning hole in the entryway floor, she grabbed hold of the banister and swung herself up and around the worst of it, feeling her feet land on one of the lower steps.

Her lips pressed into a thin line.

Go to hell, Charlotte.

She took the stairs two at a time.

◆ CHAPTER THIRTY-SEVEN ◆

CALLING FOR EMILY WOULD be useless.

Kat's gut told her that, but she tried doing it anyway as she reached the second floor. Only her own voice echoed back to her in a way that made her wonder if her ears were playing tricks on her—or if *it* was.

She paused on the landing. There were many places it could have stashed Emily on this floor. Many on the floor above it, too. She could search for a good thirty minutes or more and still not find anything, and with its endgame coming fast, she'd be lucky if she got five.

Wrenching herself away from the second floor, she continued running up the stairs. The railing trembled beneath her hands. The movement, slight as it was, repulsed her because she knew what caused it, but she didn't dare let go. The memory of Michael being knocked through the air was too strong for that. She expected to feel such an attack at any moment, and when it didn't happen, she could only wonder again if the old woman had been more right than she knew.

They have their limits, you know. The dead…

But by the time she reached the third floor and dashed down its hall toward the attic stairs, the shaking of the house had grown worse. Cracks appeared in the walls in places, and a window shattered when she passed it. Perhaps all *its* exertions so far hadn't fazed it after all, or at least hadn't done so for long.

"Emily!" she cried out again as she pulled herself up the attic staircase with one hand and tightened her grip on the axe with the other. Still no answer came. Her panic fed her dwindling strength, and she rammed her body against the attic door without even pausing.

It stuck, of course. Taking the axe in both hands, Kat attacked the door.

This one gave way sooner than the one at the entrance to the cellar, and as soon as it began to come apart, the invisible hold on it dissipated, and the door swung open.

Heart pounding, Kat wielded the axe before her as she crept into the room. The shadows weren't quite so thick up here as they'd been in the cellar. At least here there were windows, even if they were small and covered with grime. Some moonlight still managed to penetrate them and keep the room from being utterly dark.

She bumped into a chair whose silhouette didn't show up well in the darkened room, and the movement sent something behind it crashing to the floor. She didn't know what. Should she pull out the flashlight, or was it wiser to keep both hands on the axe for now? The axe, she decided, her eyes darting this way and that. She didn't dare lose it again.

The air turned icy, and goosebumps rose up on Kat's arms.

Frost appeared on the windows. If she'd held the axe any tighter in her hands—hands that trembled—it would have snapped in two. Time's up, she thought with a violent shiver, and she plunged into the depths of the attic to find the door that lay at the back. There. The door handle gleamed faintly in the dark. Reaching it, Kat raised the axe.

And had to fling herself aside as she caught a glimpse of motion out of the corner of her eye and turned her head just in time to see a tremendous vase hurl through the air toward her. It smashed against the door and shattered into dangerously jagged shards.

Gasping, Kat took aim again as her heart pounded and swung with as much speed and force as she could. She managed to get two more blows in before a brass candlestick hurtled at her head. With no time to duck, she barely got an arm up to block it at the last second.

Fresh stars of pain swam before her, and she lost her grip on the axe.

An unseen force immediately yanked it from her grasp and away out of sight before she could recover. Her fingers closed around empty air, and her stomach lurched.

No…

Desperation drove her to grab frantically at shapes in the darkness, searching for something that might be capable of battering the already splintered door. Most of what her hands touched was either too small or too soft. A quilt, a framed painting—

Her foot bumped against something that was too heavy to easily give way, and she nearly lost her balance. Reaching down, she felt for whatever it was and ran her fingers over it to identify it in the dark.

The figurine.

Seizing it with both hands, Kat braced her feet apart and rammed the statue against the damage the axe had made in the door.

More splintering, and a loud and satisfying crack.

Instinct more than anything else warned her to move, and she dropped to the ground a moment before the axe whistled through the air to bury itself in the wood of the door. Right where her head had been.

Panting, Kat scrambled up and pulled on the axe, but it was lodged much too deeply into the wood for her to work it free. The force that it must have taken to impale it—Her head could have been split in two.

The thought spurred her to move faster. The pain in her leg barely registered as she kicked the cracked center of the door again and again. Then she grabbed the largest fragment protruding from the damaged wood and pulled it free to make an opening halfway up the door. It wasn't quite big enough for her to climb through, so she retrieved her makeshift battering ram and attacked it again.

There. One more blow—

She heard a whispering kind of hiss behind her and froze. It had almost, but not quite, sounded human. She turned slowly and with a sense of dread.

And saw Emily standing not six feet away from her.

"Emily," she breathed in relief, dropping the figurine. "Are you—"

She was going to say *all right*, but the words died on her lips. There was an unnatural stillness to the little girl, an ominous sort of quiet.

Kat's voice dropped to a whisper. "Emily?"

Enough moonlight filtered through the frost and grime on the windows for the child's teeth to gleam as her lips parted in a smile. It was the same smile that had been on Alexis's face just before *it* hurled her over the banister to her death.

Kat's knees threatened to buckle, and she grabbed hold of the ruined door.

It was a trap. Surely it was a trap. Meant to draw Kat away from the door and whatever lay beyond it. What then? Would it throw Emily off the stairs, too? Or maybe throw both of them together. Why not simply toss Kat through the air right now as it had done to Michael? It glared at her through Emily's eyes as if it would like to, but maybe it couldn't, not while it was inside Emily. Maybe it had a different plan for Kat altogether.

And it was dangling Emily in front of her for a reason, bait of some kind. Effective, heart-wrenching bait.

Instead of taking it, Kat whirled back around to wrench another chunk of wood off the door.

She heard the hiss again and dared to glance over her shoulder even as her hands continued to rip away at loosened slivers.

One by one, objects in the attic rose up in the air and hovered as if taking aim, and the shards of broken vase at her feet started rattling.

No time for measuring. Hoping the hole was big enough, Kat pulled herself up and dove through it.

◆ CHAPTER THIRTY-EIGHT ◆

IT WASN'T QUITE BIG enough. Most of Kat made it through, but she lost a few layers of skin in places on her arms and hands and also reinjured her leg when she landed in a heap on the floor.

She bit back a cry of pain and scrambled away from the opening.

Barely in time. Most of the makeshift missiles smashed into the remains of the door, but one came right through it, dead center, and impaled itself into the opposite wall. A fire poker's silhouette, she realized, watching it quiver with the force used to embed it.

God only knew what would be next. Moments. She had only moments left. Yanking out the flashlight, Kat switched it on with fumbling fingers to see what her final hope looked like.

Not good. The room was small, little more than a large closet. There weren't even windows in this place. The only light came from Kat's flashlight—whose batteries seemed to be running low—and the faint thread of diluted moonlight that spilled in through the rough hole in the door. Both together were just barely bright enough to show that there was little in the room that looked promising. Several quilts and what looked like moth-eaten rags that had once been clothes, some much-worn and at least century-old children's toys, a turn-of-the-century bicycle that would have been better suited to a museum than to the attic of an old house…

Her flashlight flickered over a boxy shape.

A metal trunk. Crawling over to it, Kat grabbed at the latch. It would be locked, of course. Like everything else around here.

But it wasn't. It was slippery, though, because her fingers were bloody and raw by now, but she yanked it open and shined her light inside. More clothes. A woman's clothes from perhaps the very earliest years of the twentieth century or from the end of the one that came before it.

Charlotte's?

The door rattled behind her. Maybe the lock was too rusted even for *it* to get it open, but if it could burst through floorboards, one already half-destroyed door couldn't be too much of a problem for it. She had seconds left, a minute at best.

Hearing that awful hiss again, Kat looked up to see an eye watching her through a crack low in the door. Emily's eye. The girl was too short to see through anything else. That single eye gleamed in the fading light of the flashlight, and Kat couldn't help but shudder as she turned away and pawed ruthlessly through the rest of the trunk's contents.

Hurry, hurry...

More clothes, delicate things with handmade lace. Damn it, had Charlotte been nothing but a clotheshorse? There had to be something else in here. *It* had worked too hard to keep her out for there not to be. Had she secreted something damning in the folds of one of the quilts instead? Maybe sewn something into the lining? So close, and yet she felt as far away as ever.

Gloves, a lady's elegant fan…

The rattling grew louder.

A hairbrush with a few hairs still remaining…

Her throbbing fingers closed around something hard and smooth. A box. She pulled it out and held it up to the light.

A powerful burst of something unseen nearly knocked the box from her hand, but she dug her fingernails into it like claws and held on. "The hell you will," she snarled back at the eyeball that stared at her still, fairly glowing with malice as it watched her.

I can feel that it hates us, but I do not know why…

She reached to flip open the lid only to find that what little luck she'd had so far had given out. It was locked.

A sudden squealing sound made Kat look down. If she'd thought the number of rats from the other day was shocking, she was horrified by the steady stream of them she saw now, pouring out from a small hole in the back of the room. And they came straight at her as if driven on by fire or something even more persuasive.

Gasping, she slammed the lid of the trunk down and climbed on top just as the first one reached her. It managed to snag one claw in the hem of her jeans, but she knocked it away with her flashlight. The rest tried to climb the trunk but were unable to find any purchase in its smooth metal sides.

Yet.

And here Kat was with a locked box and no key, and no more options. To hell with it. She raised the box above her head before bringing it down hard against the trunk.

The box was more decorative than sturdy. It came halfway apart in her hand. Ripping what remained of the lid off, Kat looked inside.

A pair of books. Very small but thick books. No, no—more diaries.

The door's hinges shook so hard that in another moment or two they would give way. Maybe they would have done so already if *it* hadn't tried to stretch itself too thin already.

Her time was up.

If she was going to die, at least she wanted to know why. Flipping the topmost diary open, Kat shined the light on a name handwritten gracefully at the top.

And stared. Not Charlotte, but someone very close to her. The sister who had taken her place. The name came out in a whisper of surprise. "Miranda?"

The rattling of the door stopped.

A slip of folded paper fell from the diary in Kat's hand and fluttered to the floor. She raised her flashlight like a club, preparing to knock away more rats so she could retrieve the paper—

—and saw that they were gone. All of them. Vanished as quickly as they'd appeared. Had they been real, or illusion? Real, she decided, remembering the solid thunk her makeshift club had made against the one who'd attached itself to her leg. And their bites would have been real enough, too.

She grabbed up the piece of paper, opening it gingerly when she saw just how yellowed and brittle it was. It was a letter. Straining to make out the faded date, she finally read it: August 12, 1882.

The handwriting was familiar.

> *My dear Miranda. As our engagement is at an end, I am returning to you your correspondence from out courtship, and I trust you will do the same with mine.*

Kat glanced at the date again, thinking she had read it wrong, but she hadn't. Eighteen eighty-two.

> *Your sister and I are both humbled by your graciousness in the matter and your kind wishes for*

the happy future of our upcoming union. You are truly the very spirit of sweetest charity and decorum.

She read the signature at the bottom of the page. No wonder the handwriting looked familiar.

Richard.

Her sister. He'd left Miranda for her sister. Her prettier and younger sister. Then Miranda hadn't really taken Charlotte's place after all; Charlotte had taken hers.

She reread the date again. August of eighty-two. Tucking the letter back into the diary, she all but tore through its pages until she came to an entry from that year and month.

This handwriting was not quite so graceful as that of the word "Miranda" written just inside the cover, although it was undoubtedly done by the same person. This writing was messier, sharp and jagged, and the words matched the style.

I cannot help but wonder when it all started. When did he first begin looking at her instead of at me? How long did he pretend to court me while only seeking an excuse to be near to her instead? Can they really believe that I forgive them? Are they really such fools?

The word "fools" had been underlined, and that entire sentence was almost blurry with heavy ink, as though the writer had pressed harder with her pen. A blotch of more ink marred the end of the sentence as if to prove that point. But perhaps Miranda had paused to get her emotions under control again, because when the writing picked up again on the next page, the original elegance of the lettering had returned.

Cool and composed.

But I will smile and bide my time.

And then I will hurt them.

Kat stared at the words.

Hurt them…

She thought of the photograph she'd seen at the museum, the one with Miranda beside her new husband—and her dead sister's old one. The eyes had been mild, serene. Hers was the kind of face you could look at and not really notice, or at least forget soon after you'd seen it. The kind that it was easy to overlook. And people who went around unnoticed might be able to do all kinds of things without getting caught.

She flipped straight to the end, but this diary ended well before the year of Charlotte's death. Tucking it beneath her arm, she grabbed the other book and scanned it instead. Yes, this one picked up where the other left off, and she paused at an entry dated May 3, 1894.

I saw the first glimmer of doubt in Charlotte's eyes today as I was giving Frederick his "tonic."

Frederick. He'd been one of the children to fall ill, but had survived. Long enough to continue the family line, anyway. No wonder his illness had been so baffling to his doctors. It hadn't been an illness at all.

I dare not take the chance that she realizes what I am doing. I had hoped all her children would precede her to the grave, but the others will have to follow her now. I have enjoyed her tears, drawn out over so many years and in so many different ways. But now I will have to console myself with Richard's grief instead.

Something rattled around inside the damaged box. Kat looked in and saw a tiny glass bottle. Turning it, she saw the word Laudanum marked on it. No accidental overdose or suicide, then, but a very deliberate murder.

Something else lay in the box, pressed mostly flat from the weight of the two diaries for so many years. The second diary joined the first beneath Kat's arm, and she touched the last bit of Miranda's secret. It was soft, almost silky, and when she fingered it, she realized it was hair. Tiny locks of hair, each tied with its thin strand of ribbon and each lock a little different shade than the others.

Bile rose in her throat as she realized just from where they had come. Miranda's trophies.

There were five of them. Three had to belong to Charlotte's children; the boy who had fallen from his horse, the girl who had drowned, and the girl who had wasted away just as Frederick nearly had, poisoned by their aunt. A fourth lock that was thicker and coarser than the rest could only be from Charlotte. And the last...

She picked up the last and tiniest bit of hair. There was barely anything to it. It was sparse and incredibly fine, like that of a baby.

Kat dropped it as if it burned her.

Her own baby? Why—just to hurt Richard? God, how sick and twisted could one woman be? Sick enough to want to finish the job, surely. The remaining two boys had been sent away, Mrs. Davenport said, which had saved their lives. Along with the influenza that took Miranda.

How had no one discovered the diaries after Miranda's death? A last request, maybe? A final wish that the box remain locked and undisturbed? Or even simple luck. The grieving husband might have simply packed up her things without ever really seeing them, much like he'd done with Miranda.

Not anymore.

Kat suddenly became aware of the silence.

Emily. Where was Emily?

Her eyes darted toward the door, but the crack through which she'd seen the girl watching her was just an empty crack again. No one was looking through it now.

Shoving the diaries back into the broken box along with the rest of its ghastly contents, Kat scrambled off the trunk to look through the hole she'd made in the door. Cautiously, though. Too many things could come flying at her through it at any moment.

Nothing did, though. The frost on the windows seemed to be melting, and with the aid of the faint moonlight that came through them, her gaze travelled over the room.

If Emily was still in the room, she was hiding behind something. After coming after Kat so ferociously, hiding seemed like an odd tactic to take, but it did like to hide. Was it toying with her again?

"Emily?" she called out. She'd uncovered Miranda's secret— Had that been enough to shake the girl free from the ghost's hold? Could it really be so simple as that?

But there was no answer.

Kat kicked out more of the shattered door and squeezed through the enlarged hole to shine the flashlight around the room. Then, clutching Miranda's dirty little secret to her chest, she went to find whatever waited for her outside the attic.

◆ CHAPTER THIRTY-NINE ◆

THE STAIRS THAT LED to the third floor were empty.

She didn't know what she'd hoped to find. Emily, slumped over in a faint but released from Miranda's hold? And Miranda gone for good?

But she wasn't gone for good. As soon as Kat started down the steps with a scraped and bleeding hand on the railing for support, she felt the same vibrations running through it as before, if not quite as strong. The walls of the house at least had stopped shaking, which she would have thought would have been comforting—

Instead, the hairs on the back of her neck rose.

"Emily?' she cried out again as she stumbled down to the third floor as fast as her injured leg would let her. Throwing open the doors to the rooms as she passed them and shining the light inside them, she still saw no sign of Emily, and her anxiety increased. Was it toying with her again? If it was, she was out of options. She'd pinned all her hopes on the attic and what lay inside it. And if that wasn't enough—

There was movement up ahead in the dark, by the stairs.

The stairs.

Like Alexis.

Oh, God…

Dragging her leg as she hobbled forward, Kat trained the flashlight's beam in front of her. It still barely revealed anything more than five feet in front of her, but at least here there was a little more moonlight streaming in from the windows of the rooms whose doors she'd thrown open. And as she drew closer to the end of the hall, moonlight turned out to be enough.

Kat came to an abrupt halt a few feet from the third floor landing.

Emily stood on the banister, staring back at her. Her balance could not have been natural; she was as much in Miranda's control as ever. And the slightest move was all it would take to send the little girl tumbling three stories to her death.

Emily's mouth curved into a slow and spiteful smile.

"No, please—" Kat started forward.

The girl/ghost gave her a warning look, and Kat immediately halted again.

"She's just a baby. Please, she's just a little girl!" She realized as soon as she said the words that they would hardly sway the restless spirit of someone who had murdered four other young innocents for pleasure. And there could be little else of Miranda Delancey left except hate now anyway. Hate could not be reasoned with.

She could make a lunge for the girl.

She could try, a voice in the back of her head told her, but she would be too late.

As if to prove the level of its control, the thing inside of Kat's little sister began to walk along the banister towards where it curved downward.

Kat dared another step forward.

Emily spun abruptly in place to face her and held a finger up as if to chide her.

Kat froze. "Please." She had no other play to make. The thing had her, and it knew it. Begging was all that was left. Words tumbled out. "Please… Miranda. Please don't hurt her like you hurt the others. You got your revenge—it's enough. Charlotte's dead, her children are dead. But please don't take Emily, too, please—"

Emily lifted one foot up, slowly. Deliberately. And as if she intended to step off directly into empty space.

"No!" Lurching forward even though she knew she would be too late, Kat dropped the ruined wooden box and its contents and reached out her arms for the girl.

And watched as she tensed her muscles to leap off, her mouth curved in an awful grin—

—that froze on her face as the walls of the house began to tremble again.

Something hissed in the air around them.

Kat fell to the floor as the pain in her leg made it give out on her, close to the little girl but not close enough. She didn't dare move any nearer. Something was happening, or was about to happen. Damn it, it was *still* toying with her. After everything it had taken from her, and after all the people it had killed, it was still playing with people's lives for sport.

And yet…

The expression on Emily's face was one of shock, and her eyes seemed not to see Kat.

Kat blinked.

A trick. It had to be some kind of trick, even if the point of it was not yet clear. Still, Kat risked edging closer on her hands and knees. If she could just get close enough to grab the girl's wrist, or even the sleeve of her nightgown, maybe she could yank her back to the landing. Maybe even haul her into a room and block the door, for whatever good that would do. At least then it couldn't throw Emily off the stairs. Not without going through Kat.

The hiss came again, although hiss was perhaps not quite the right word to describe it. It was more like something in search of a voice, something not quite human.

And something, by the look on Emily's face, that was not Miranda.

…sssssssssterrrrrrrr…

It was almost but not quite a word. And when she heard it again and saw the look of shock on Emily's face change to one of horror, she realized what that word was.

Sister.

"Charlotte?" she said hoarsely into the air, and she thought maybe, just maybe, the house shook even more. Lights began to flicker on and off, and things on every side began to creak and moan. Hope flickered wildly inside, and Kat looked at Emily—or at the thing inside of her—with narrowed eyes and a surge of satisfaction. Something that was half-sob, half hysterical laughter spilled out of her. "Miranda—I think your sister wants a word with you." Her hysteria grew; she couldn't help it. "You *bitch*."

And a sliver of satisfaction slipped through her.

But her moment of triumph was short-lived. Something invisible knocked Kat off her knees and backward and then slammed into Emily, driving the little girl's body against the wall at the far end of the bannister.

Kat's vision blurred when her head struck the floor, and the walls spun around her. Blinking, she put a hand to her head to try and steady herself, then pulled it away when she touched the cut she'd all but forgotten was there. She rolled over and pushed herself up onto her hands and knees again.

Emily's small body was pinned against the wall still, her arms and legs kicking as she—no, as Miranda—struggled uselessly against the unseen force that attacked it. "Emily!"

Whatever had knocked Kat down before, whether it was one vengeful sister or the other, it slammed into her again; her interference was clearly not going to be tolerated. Biting back any more sounds, Kat stayed low and clawed her way across the landing toward the bannister again.

Something slid Emily up the wall, steady and inexorable, and if the thing inside Emily fought to free itself, it only seemed to slow things down, not stop them. She reached the wall and then slid onto the ceiling on her back, still kicking and waving violently to no avail.

It was like the world had shifted, like an hourglass suddenly flipped over. The ceiling should have been the floor, the way Emily's body remained there in defiance of gravity. But gravity couldn't be defied forever.

Kat's heart thudded wildly. Grabbing the nearest railing in case something should try to knock her away again, she edged closer toward the place where Emily hung suspended.

An unearthly shriek nearly made Kat lose her hold. Emily clawed at her neck as if something was choking her.

Alarm overwhelmed Kat, and she wasn't sure who she was pleading with now. "No, don't! Don't hurt her!"

Maybe she was beyond either spirit's notice, because nothing sent her flying this time as she lurched to her feet and tried in vain to reach her little sister. She was still too high, still pressed against the ceiling. Her features seemed to blur then in a way that made Kat shudder in revulsion, as if something was being pulled forcibly out of her, something that wasn't coming easily or willingly. She could only hope and pray that Emily hadn't felt that.

And then suddenly Emily's features were her own again. The eerie look that had been in her eyes before was gone, and they drifted closed as if the experience had been too much for her. Her body went limp.

Too limp. Whatever held her there before was gone.

She dropped.

Kat lunged for her just as Emily fell past the bannister. A shooting pain in her leg nearly stopped her, but the force of her momentum brought her to the railing just in time to snake out a hand. She caught her little sister around one arm, but only just barely.

Her other hand snatched blindly for the railing in a desperate attempt to keep them both from going over, and she managed to wrap her fingers around it a fraction of a second before she checked Emily's fall.

The girl's body jerked to an awkward stop, and Kat nearly lost her grip, both on the arm and the railing. Her fingernails of one hand dug into wood to brace them while the other hand—slick with perspiration—slipped down Emily's arm. She tightened her hold just as her hand reached the wrist bone, and the slipping stopped.

Gasping for breath and hanging halfway over the railing herself, Kat clung for dear life.

The shaking of the walls, the windows, and everything else in the house rattled violently now, and she thought she heard the sound of a window shattering somewhere. The railing in her hand trembled, the vibrations growing stronger with every passing second. At this rate, it couldn't hold up much longer.

Straining with every ounce of strength and energy she had left, Kat struggled to haul Emily upward. The girl still dangled limply. Alive or dead, it was impossible to tell.

A cracking sound split the air—

The railing was giving way.

Crying out—it might have been a curse or a prayer—Kat dug her heels in and pulled with a final burst of effort. She drew Emily up and over the railing and fell backwards with her as the section over which she'd been leaning split apart. The two of them tumbled back to land in a tangle of arms and legs, and Kat lay there, panting for breath while her heart raced.

Emily. Was she alive? Kat brushed the hair away from the girl's neck to feel for a pulse.

Before she could do so, a howl like nothing she'd ever heard before split the air. It was an unearthly noise, full of horror and terror and hate, and Kat nearly screamed herself when she heard it. She hugged her little sister tightly to her, expecting at any moment that the house would collapse in on itself, and on them.

The howl rose to a deafening crescendo, echoing throughout the house and inside Kat's head.

She squeezed her eyes shut.

But then the howl ended abruptly, as if cut off in a sudden and violent manner. It's echo reverberated a moment longer, but even that died away. Slowly. Everywhere except inside of Kat's head.

The house grew still.

Nothing rattled, nothing vibrated. The hum that had been in the air and in her nerves lessened and then ceased altogether. Everything was quiet.

Kat didn't move. When it sank in that she was still alive and in one piece, she finally pushed herself up with Emily on her lap, wincing at the pain that every little movement sent through her. "Emily…" Her voice sounded raw and foreign, even to her own ears. She cleared her throat and tried again, brushing the hair from the little girl's face and feeling again for a pulse. "Emily, can you hear me?"

She felt nothing. Then a faint beat started up a rhythm beneath her fingers.

Emily stirred, lifting her head slowly as if it was a struggle for her. Her eyes fluttered open, then closed again. "K-Kat?"

That one word said aloud, albeit in a feeble voice, sent a torrent of relief through Kat. Her cheeks were wet, and it took her a moment to realize it was from tears, not blood from new injuries. She who never cried. "Yes, it's me, Em. It's Kat. I'm here. We're all right."

"W-what happened?"

"It's okay, it's over now. You're okay."

"Something… there was something…" Emily trailed off as if too exhausted to speak and rested her head on Kat's shoulder, her small arms wrapping around Kat's neck.

"Shh, it's gone now." Closing her eyes and listening to the sound of approaching sirens in the distance, Kat hugged Emily tighter. "It's gone. It's over."

And then her tears really started to flow.

◆ CHAPTER FORTY ◆

THE ATTENDANCE AT THE memorial service for Alexis was low. Friends of hers mostly, and not many at that, although a few of the ones that were there did look genuinely somber. Maybe they had seen a kinder side of Kat's stepsister than Kat ever had. But if she wasn't able to actually weep over Alexis's death, that didn't mean that she felt nothing. Especially when she saw a large arrangement of flowers whose card bore the signature of Alexis's father, and she realized that he'd sent them in lieu of actually attending himself. Even in death Alexis couldn't seem to win his attention. And if that wasn't enough to make Kat love her stepsister, it did at least help her to understand her better, and maybe pity her a little more.

Hardly anyone got up to speak, maybe because they weren't sure what to say about Alexis or the nature of her death. Bizarre seismic activity, that was what authorities had finally decided. A localized event that seemed to be the most logical explanation for all the damage done to Delancey Manor. The cracks in the walls, several shattered windows, the gaping hole in the first floor... and Alexis. A tragic fall during the quake for a girl who'd had the misfortune of being caught on the stairs when it happened.

And although Grace wept afresh at the mention of her eldest daughter's name when she was first questioned and also held her youngest closer, none of that night's survivors chose to dissuade people about that assumption. Why would they? It would only earn them strange looks at best and far more unpleasant things at worst, to which Kat could attest.

No, some secrets were best kept secret.

◆◆◆

KAT HALF EXPECTED MICHAEL to say no when she asked him to drive her to the manor, and she wouldn't have blamed him if he refused her. Although he had no memory of any of that night's events after his mother burst into Kat's room looking for Emily, he had heard plenty about it from Grace since then. Enough, at least, to leave him paler than before and quiet. Still, maybe he said yes to Kat's request out of a need of his own to see things for himself, even if there wasn't much left *to* see.

The manor looked different now. And not just because the sun was out, shining brightly down on Michael's car as it pulled up to the house as if nothing out of the ordinary had happened here only weeks ago. The sun had lit up the stonework countless times before just like this, but somehow it never seemed to warm it. Today the grey stone walls looked like just that: ordinary stone walls. Harmless.

But Michael still parked the car several yards back from the house, and Kat could understand why. She didn't object.

They both peered out through the windshield at the manor. Boards stretched across shattered windows like bandages that were meant to hide scars, and there were cracks visible now in the once immaculate stone exterior. Not irreparable damage, but significant nevertheless. The hole in the floorboards inside had to be much worse, but Kat was not curious enough about them to find out for herself. Let others go inside and take stock of those things if they wanted to. She never would again.

"You going in?" Michael's voice was subdued. Small wonder. The way Grace told it, he'd blinked and come out of his catatonic state the moment the house finally quieted down and stopped shaking. Whatever it was that had really happened to him while under Miranda's hold, he claimed he had no memory of it, much the way Emily did. Hopefully that was true. But while a weight seemed to have lifted from Emily's small shoulders now that she and her mother were staying at Michael's apartment, a different kind of gravity had settled over Michael.

"No, I'm not going in." *Hell no* might have been a more apt answer even though the house itself no longer held any dread for Kat.

"So why come here?"

"To say goodbye," she said finally, and she opened the car door to step outside.

A wrecking ball might have been the most appropriate way to deal with the place now. Either that or a cleansing fire like the one she suspected Thomas had tried to set years ago. In the end, though, she had decided on a different option. One that she thought her father would have appreciated.

She heard the driver's side door of the car open behind her and then the crunch of gravel beneath Michael's feet as he came to stand beside her. He cleared his throat. "So you're really going to do this?"

She nodded without taking her eyes off of the house.

"You sure you want to? Even in its current condition it's worth a fair bit." But there was an undercurrent of distaste in his voice as if he couldn't imagine anyone wanting it.

"I'm absolutely sure. It's either that or torch it."

"You'll get a much bigger tax write-off without the arson."

It was the first attempt at anything remotely light he'd made since that night. *The* night. And although she saw lines of tension in his face when she looked at him, it still seemed like an encouraging sign. "I'm sure the historical society will take much better care of it than I would. And I think Dad would be okay with it."

"Probably, yes."

And—if she was totally honest with herself—maybe it was her way of getting back at Miranda. Opening all of her dirty little secrets up to the public. The diaries had been Kat's very first gift to the historical society, and Mrs. Davenport had been speechless with joy.

Kat felt well rid of them. She'd read through them once, just once, curled up in the safety and warmth of Michael's apartment, and afterwards she was almost sorry that she had. That one woman could hate that much... "Her own baby," she murmured, not realizing that she was speaking aloud until the words slipped from her mouth. "How could anybody do something like that?" Her whole life, she would never be able to forget that tiny little lock of hair.

"A sick woman."

"No, she was *evil.*"

Michael didn't disagree.

They stood in silence for a while, and Kat studied the manor, reliving moments in her mind from both that last night here and others long before it. Thinking about everything it had cost her, had cost her parents... Wondering if she would be more or less likely to sleep at night, knowing what she now knew. And wondering how much to tell her grandparents.

"What really happened in there?" Michael asked from beside her, and his voice took on a hoarse edge.

"I think..." Kat started, then stopped. Speaking so freely to another person about these things felt foreign to her, and she had as many unanswered questions about it all as the rest of them did. Had there been more than one "other" lurking in the walls of the manor all along, or had it been the discovery of the diary that had summoned Charlotte back, the discovery of the truth? And if not that, then what?

Maybe she would never know. Not in this lifetime anyway, she amended to herself. Maybe some questions were best answered in the next.

Well... She could wait.

"I think that maybe Charlotte died not knowing what her sister did," she said finally. "That was why she didn't get her revenge until then, not until I found those diaries. And then Charlotte finally knew what happened." Kat glanced up at the third floor windows, the ones nearest to where she and Emily had been when those other two sisters, so long estranged, finally had an overdue reunion. "I think Charlotte got mad. And then I think she got even. Does the rest really matter? My parents can rest easy now at least, along with a lot of other Delanceys." Her gaze drifted toward the hill on which the family plot lay.

"Does that include you?"

"Maybe." Eventually. Nights and the darkness that came with them would probably still be hard for a very long time. And that God-awful howl still echoed faintly in her head at times.

She felt his eyes on her. "Are you all right, Kat?"

"Not yet. But I will be." The way he asked it made her wonder about him, though. "Are you?"

He didn't answer right away. "I don't know," he said finally, a hoarse edge to his voice. She didn't push him to say more.

After a moment, she felt his hand curl around hers, and because of the way he continued to stare at the house, she wasn't even sure he was aware of what he'd just done. It could have been a simple reaction to being near the house again, an instinctive need for comfort and reassurance that had no other particular meaning behind it. She could certainly understand that.

But whether it was that or something else altogether, she didn't feel as stiff and awkward as she usually did with such things. She let her fingers curl around his in return, and no, the warmth of them wasn't a bad thing at all, especially here in this place.

He drew a deep breath, his eyes averted from the house. "So, are we done here?"

She was, yes. She'd wanted to see if the house still had its old familiar hold on her, and she was fairly sure she had her answer now.

Sure enough that she felt ready to leave it behind anyway. "We're done, yes."

They turned as one to go back to the car. Michael paused beside the driver's side door to look back at the house one last time. "I guess it finally happened."

"What happened?"

"Miranda finally met a Delancey she couldn't beat."

"Emerson."

Michael looked at Kat in surprise. "What?"

"Emerson," she repeated, firm and decisive. Except for Emily, she was done with Delanceys. "I'm taking my mother's maiden name."

The End

AUTHOR'S NOTE

Thank you for reading The Bloodline! I hope you enjoyed the story. Now that you've read it, I hope you'll consider leaving a review because reviews are a great way for readers to discover new books. I would sincerely appreciate it!

ABOUT THE AUTHOR

C. S. Feldman writes both novels and feature-length screenplays, and she has placed in screenwriting competitions on both coasts. She lives in the Pacific Northwest with her ballroom-dancing husband and their beagle. Visit her on Facebook at https://www.facebook.com/AuthorCSFeldman or follow her on Twitter at https://twitter.com/FeldmanCS.

Also by C. S. Feldman:

Fey

Heroes for Hire: Discount Prices

Heroes for Hire: First Contact

CPSIA information can be obtained
at www.ICGtesting.com
Printed in the USA
BVHW040411250420
578470BV00014B/1559

9 781542 716727